ASHLEY MACK

The Taste of You

to Paige.
You never gave up on me writing a book,
and even though you'd feel awkward as heck about the spicy stuff,
I know you'd be proud.
I miss you every day. Always.

Everyone is a moon, and has a dark side
which he never shows to anybody.

- MARK TWAIN

Contents

Preface

This is the second book in a series.

This is the last one that can be read as a standalone. If you want to continue with the Sorrelle sisters you've got to be all in after this. Things are complicated and intertwined, and even though each couple will get their own story and ending, the overarching story of the series picks up from here.

This is also significantly darker than the first book, or the rest of the books in the series. Aster has a very singular sense of justice, and a very specific way in which she carries it out. I warned you in the first book that she's the scary sister. That was not a misconception on the part of others. If situations involving violence, torture, and vengeance are too much for you, I do not recommend this book.

1

Freelancer

Aster Sorrelle started as a contract.

I have a pretty fucked up job - at least compared to any person you could pull off the street.

You want a hitman? I'm an annihilator. You want a bodyguard? I'll be a fucking stalker. I have no hesitation to kill, maim, and sabotage for the job. My conscience is clean because I know my boundaries and they're minimal.

When Don Sorrelle got in touch with me through my usual broker, I was surprised. He had his own well-trained coterie of able bodies that protected him and his family, but it ended up he needed the variety of skills that I possess to resolve the issues he was experiencing. I think he also wanted someone she wouldn't suspect of being a plant during the day, even if she picked up on the extra eyes at night.

The job was twofold - help find the worm that was trying to hack Designation Technologies and steal their base codes. To be an effective stalker in the modern age, or an effective hitman, now that I think about it, you need at least a minimum of hacking skills. I have more than the minimum. He needed my daylight persona to work for him as a programmer, and help catch the hacker or group of hackers that was trying to undermine them.

The second part was that I needed to protect Aster from the shadows when we weren't at Designation. Along with the attempted hacks were threats against Aster - bloody, violent threats that talked of torture and destruction. They wanted to kidnap her, use her to get the codes, and then kill her. Based on what I knew, there was no way Aster would give in to torture, but Don was by all appearances a loving father and would give them up if someone took her. That's where the stalking came in. My nighttime persona made her an extracurricular activity.

Turns out, I enjoyed it.

Aster Sorrelle was not what people thought.

They were afraid her, and they had a right to be, but they had her all wrong. Was she capable of killing men twice her size? Yes. It was the idea that she did it without emotion that they were wrong about. Aster felt things deeply - but it was no one else's business that she did. The only other person I knew of who kept their feelings and emotions as locked down as Aster - was me.

I knew Aster as well as she knew herself by now, and better than her sisters knew her or ever would know her. When I closed my eyes, I saw her. Sometimes I even dreamed of her, and I hadn't had dreams since I was kid. When it came to her, it was beyond doing the job well. It was obsession like I've never known. Knowing everything about her became vital to my survival.

I've followed Aster's tiny ass all over the city, the suburbs, and wherever else she wanted to go. I knew what she did in the dark when no one else did. I knew what she liked and didn't, her secrets, her fears, and the deepest impulses that lived inside her skin.

My daylight persona was already part of her life.

Soon, the people we were in the dark would meet, and she'd never escape me.

2

Aster

The first time I killed a man, I was 7 years old.

My mother had died, and my home was shattered. No one was paying attention to me, or to each other. Each of us was an island of our own pain, distant from one another as we wallowed in what we had lost and let ourselves drown in memories. For every time that I thought about her and every tear that I shed, I promised myself I'd never let this happen to me again. I'd never cry over another person for the rest of my life.

My sisters thought I was fine because when I did cry, it wasn't in front of them. I was the youngest, the baby, and I wanted them to worry about themselves instead of worrying about me.

Except it became so suffocating in that house. My normally happy father was a shell of himself, always exhausted and quiet. We couldn't escape the memories of her when she'd been well and we were terrorized by the memories of her being sick. It was overwhelming.

Even at that young of an age I understood what it felt like to want to climb out of my skin. I thought about hurting myself to feel something, anything else. I'd scratch at my wrists and the tops of my thighs, desperate for a strong enough sensation to overpower the need to claw and scream at my own face, my own throat, anything that would make this feeling go away.

When I thought no one was paying attention, I left the house. I started to run. We lived in a secure area in the middle of nowhere. There was no reason for me to believe that I was anything but safe.

I ran down the side of the road as fast as my little legs would carry me, feet thumping the pavement and arms pumping, pushing myself faster and faster until my lungs started to burn. It was the burn in my lungs that finally set me free - it hurt, but it was also a sign that I was alive. A sign that my body was fighting to keep me that way. I ran until I couldn't run, until the muscles in my legs were shaking.

In the end, I wasn't that far from my house, having run in a big circle.

When I couldn't take another step, I sat down in the grass on the side of the road. I picked up a stick and started stripping off the bark. Once I had my feet under me again I'd go home, and then when I thought I could I'd run again.

A car pulled over a few yards from me. No one got out for a moment, but it ruined my peace and I didn't like that.

Then a man got out of the car. He looked familiar, but I couldn't place him. He was wearing a suit, had too much gel in his hair, and his eyes were flat. When he stepped closer he smiled at me but I knew it was fake, so I didn't smile back. Lots of adults smiled at kids that way.

"What are you doing out here, Aster?"

So he knew my name. "I went for a run."

"Does anyone know you're out here?"

Even little me knew that question was suspicious, but I hadn't learned how to lie to adults when they asked me a direct question yet. Instead, I shrugged.

Something dropped over his face then, like the mask he'd been wearing to speak with me was removed. Before I could even try to get up he was on me, grabbing my ankles and dragging me along the ground toward his car. I tried to kick him but my muscles were too exhausted.

When we got to the car he bent down to pick me up to throw me in the trunk.

I still had the stick in my hand, and without thinking too much about it, I raised it, and with all the power in my little body I stabbed it into his throat.

It went in, and it went in deep. The sensation of pushing through his flesh was one I never forgot. The sound he made as his hands clenched around my arms from the invasion of the stick echoes in my dreams sometimes. This man was trying to do something bad to me and his punishment had been swiftly dealt by my own hand. He dropped to his knees and let go of me.

I tumbled back onto the grass and watched him reach up to pull out the stick. That was a mistake because blood gushed out of the wound. I stared, still and without reaction, as he gargled and groaned. I was there until he died.

I was there after he died too, for almost an hour. I'd worn out my little body so thoroughly that I couldn't move. It would've been longer but by then someone had noticed I was missing and one of our guards found me.

No one ever asked if I left the house. They assumed I'd been lured or taken and figured out how to save myself. Dad tried to send me to therapy but how do you explain to them that your daughter killed a man and didn't seem affected? At 7 years old I killed a man and learned that I liked it. There were bad people in this world who deserved what was coming to them.

The man who'd tried to take me was an employee at Designation. High up, too. With the way my father was falling apart he thought that he could attack during a moment of vulnerability and take over, or get more than his fair share. I don't know what he planned to do with me, or what his plan had been when he headed to our house. I just knew that I stopped it before it could happen.

I spent the rest of my life chasing that truth.

Some people deserved what was coming to them, and I was an instrument of justice.

3

Freelancer

The first time I followed Aster on one of her secret endeavors, I had no idea what I was in for. That night, I learned Aster's true dark side.

It was a Friday night and she snuck out a side door of the Sorrelle house. No one would know she was gone since I got the impression she spent most of her time in her room. None of them would have the guts to check on her and potentially interrupt her. I watched her walk off the property, and followed her to the road where a cab was waiting. After a few moments, I took my bike from the bushes and followed it.

After a long drive, we were deep in the party district of the city. The cab pulled to a stop outside a seedy, neon-lit club. I could see the driver asking Aster if she was sure this was where she wanted to be, but she waved him off. If I hadn't seen exactly what she was capable of, I wouldn't have left her here either.

Especially not when she's wearing a skintight dress the color of ripe berries. It has long sleeves but she might as well be wearing nothing for how closely it clings to her small, high breasts and nice round ass. She's got thick thighs for a small girl, and I know it's from all the running and squats she does.

THE TASTE OF YOU

I've never seen anyone run as obsessively as Aster.

Her outfit amuses me though because even in a sexy ass club dress, she's still wearing Converse. Tonight it's black low tops.

Once she's inside, I find my way in and stay out of sight because I can't let her see me.

I watch her, and I would even if she wasn't a job because there's something magnetic about her. Not to other people, just to me. No one else really seems to be paying attention to her. She's just another girl out on the dance floor, moving her body. As the night goes on she gets sloppier, which I don't understand because I haven't even seen her drink. It's possible she took a drug in the cab and it's hitting her over time, but from all my studying of her that doesn't seem like her style.

I'd think I would've found if Aster liked to do drugs.

From what I could tell, Aster hates substances, and barely tolerated the fact that she needed caffeine to function. Any altered state of mind made her anxious.

Now people were paying attention.

As it got closer to bar close, I watched Aster stumble her way out of the bar. I made a move to follow her, and noticed that I wasn't the only one.

Even though I was hired to protect her, I couldn't reveal myself unless it was life or death. This wasn't - yet - and I also knew that even drunk, Aster was still dangerous and capable of protecting herself.

I watched with confusion as she turned into an alley, walking off into the dark and isolated space between buildings.

I watched a man follow her into that space.

I followed too.

I watched from the mouth of the alley as the man walked quietly behind her, and went to reach for her.

Then he was clutching at his throat and dropping to his knees.

8

It happened so fast that I didn't understand what was going on at first.

Aster, totally sober, stood above the man with a small knife that was dripping blood. Even from this distance I could tell it was a Boker Subcom because it's the only knife sharp enough to kill someone but tiny enough for her to hide under that fucking dress.

As I watched her watch him die, something stirred inside me. I'd already found her fascinating, but now I wanted inside her head. I wanted to know every thought that ever went through her mind.

The man collapsed to the ground, still, his blood steaming in the cold air.

Then, shocking me further, Aster leaned back onto the brick wall of the alley, pulled up her dress, and slid her hand into her panties. The knife was still gripped in her right hand as she worked herself with the left. From the other end of the alley I could hear her panting, ragged breaths as she played with her own body over the man she had killed.

When she came she bit her lip to try and stifle the sounds of her pleasure, but it didn't stop my cock from getting rock hard.

I won't lie and deny that sometimes taking a life gets me hard. That there's not sexual arousal in the hunt, the take down, and the destruction. Living on the edge between life and death can cause a very specific kind of euphoria, nearly orgasmic, and watching someone's life drain away makes you very aware of your own. It heightens your senses.

The image of me, fucking the hell out of Aster next to a victim we shared is irresistible. I needed to have her after that night. I will have her. I just have to figure out how to keep her once I capture her. She isn't just a job anymore. She's my life.

Later, I look up the man she killed.

He'd been arrested and imprisoned for sexual assault in the past, and gotten away with a few as well. It was his pattern to follow the

THE TASTE OF YOU

drunkest girl out of the bar and rape her, hoping that she wouldn't remember. There's no doubt Aster knew this, and had set him up to take him out. The scariest Sorrelle was a motherfucking vigilante.

That was the moment I think I fell in love with her.

4

Aster

When 5am hits, I can call it a night on trying to get any more sleep. I try all the tricks and advice, but I can't fall asleep like normal people, and even when I do sleep it's in fits and starts over the course of hours. Most of the time I do end up well-rested, it just takes a long time.

It's Monday. I can justify being up and starting the week with gusto. Not that anyone would accuse me of having gusto, but that's okay. The treadmill is calling.

There's a part of me that has never ever stopped running - metaphorically speaking. I am still that little girl running down the road with all her might. After that day, when my legs recovered, running became one of the constant releases in my life. We had a treadmill in our gym at home, and I used it every day for years. Then made dad get a better one, and a better one, and then wore another one out. I don't keep track of how far I run although I did do a lot of research on how to run without hurting myself. Every morning I get on and I go until I don't want to go anymore. Until the restless feeling dims.

It's never gone entirely. Some days I run 3 miles and some days I run 13.

Today is going to be a short run. Despite a frustrating night from a sleep perspective, I'm looking forward to work today.

After a brisk walk to warm up my muscles, I increase the speed on the treadmill and start to run. After only a few moments, my mind empties. I can't think about anything at all when I'm running. It's like I disappear into a place inside myself that is nothing but complete focus on my breathing and my pace. The feeling of my lungs expanding and contracting, the way my feet land with each step, even paying attention to the feeling of the loose curls that dampen and stick to the back of my neck.

I know I've had enough when the tightness in my chest relaxes, and my hands no longer clench. The tension has been released.

Then I can turn off the treadmill. I went 5 miles today. Short and sweet.

Everyone in the house is still sleeping or in their rooms, so I try not to make too much noise as I head back to my room to get ready for work. Most 22 year olds are about to finish college and barely out of their partying phase. I've got my master's degree in computer science and I'm already leading my own team at Designation. I know I've got an in with the bosses but I also know I'm fucking smart.

The kind of smart that kept me isolated from forming friendships. I never had the chance to form a friend group of people my own age because I was never in school with people that were the same age as me. Technically, I didn't even take all the grades because I kept testing out of them, higher and higher until I graduated high school at 16. If I'd had a mind to, it could have been even earlier.

Working at Designation feels like the first time I've been with my own people. Not that I'm friendly or have friends, but I do feel like we're all speaking the same language when I'm in my pod with our team.

After a quick shower and a very long hair care routine because my curls won't manage themselves, I pull on a random assortment of clothes because no one cares what you wear when you spend all day behind a computer. It ends up being a huge, old Metallica t-shirt, fishnets, and a pair of cutoff shorts. I round that out with my black high top Converse.

By the time I get downstairs, there's signs of life from the rest of the household.

Dad and Owen are at the dining room table, talking quietly and eating their very normal, healthy breakfasts. I don't say anything when I enter the room. I pour my coffee and put peanut butter on an english muffin without saying a word. This is how breakfast usually goes. Dad probably wants to talk but Owen and I are the silent types.

It's not that I don't like interacting with other people, or that I don't know that I'm being weird and awkward. It's this persistent fear inside of me that if I start talking I might never shut up. If I start talking about my feelings, I will go and go until they are all gone and I will be unable to get them back. Everything needs to be held inside, that's the only way that I survive.

Owen breaks into my zone out time.

"Are you riding with me today?"

I nod. I ride with him nearly every day, but he still asks every day.

I can drive but I don't like to - I'm destructive enough without adding a two-ton vehicle into the mix. The therapist I saw when I started college said things like that are "intrusive thoughts." It is intrusive that every time I'm driving I think about wrenching the wheel and crashing. That I imagine in detail the sensation of hitting the concrete underside of a bridge, or how it would feel to drive off the side of a road with a steep incline. If I have the option to be driven, I take it.

There are lots of things in my life where intrusive thoughts find their way in, and I deal with some of them better than others. I know there's nothing more dangerous than my own mind, and there are some impulses I give in to and some that I don't. The ones that are aimed outward are probably more dangerous, but also tightly controlled.

The itch is under my skin right now that I need to find release. Tonight is a bad night to hunt - no one worth finding goes out on a Monday. I'll run myself to exhaustion and hope that I can make it to Friday. That's when my prey is most likely to be out and think that they're on the hunt when they're about to be the hunted.

My fingers twitch at the thought, sloshing coffee out of my cup and onto my plate.

Dad looks at me and frowns, trying to read something from my affect but he'll get nothing. Few people can read me because I work hard to make them believe there's nothing to read. I am a blank slate, a smooth, empty wall. Nothing to see here.

I sip the rest of my coffee slowly, gazing into the middle distance, until Owen gets my attention that it's time to leave. My bag is waiting in the small closet by the door and I grab my favorite black pea coat. It's about three sizes too big for my 5'1" frame and that's what I like about it. The weight of the coat on my body is comforting. Like armor. It's May and probably a little too warm for it, but I don't care.

Owen walks to the Escalade today, and I get in the back. His guard, Alonzo, rides in the passenger seat. It's a weird arrangement but Owen likes to be in control and Alonzo keeps an eye out. Our rides are always silent. The first few times Owen drove me to work Alonzo tried to talk to me but I would stare him down until he looked away.

I've found that size is irrelevant to intimidation if you know how to make people feel uncomfortable. I know how to kill a man with a few effective slices of a knife. I've tortured people who threatened my family without blinking an eye. I've looked in their eyes while they screamed in pain and didn't flinch. In some cases, I smiled.

Alonzo knew all of that when he tried to talk to me, and it all came to mind when I gave him the same dead-eyed stare that he'd seen me give my victims.

14

My reputation as the scariest Sorrelle sister is earned.

What's funny is none of them know the extent of what I've really done.

Owen and I don't say goodbye as we part ways to our different areas of the Designation Technologies campus. He's headed up the 7th floor, the executive suite. Dad will mosey on in a few hours from now, a figurehead more than the actual CEO these days. He's working hard to make it clear that Owen has his blessing to take over, but hasn't been able to commit to retiring yet. I've heard him tell Anora he doesn't know what he'll do with himself if he doesn't have to go to work every day.

My phone buzzes with a text. It's to the group chat with my sisters, and it's from Alina.

I have to shop for dresses today. Barf.

She's been in Seattle for a month now, and I miss her. I miss having someone to spar with that isn't afraid to hit me or hurt me, that gives even less of a crap than I do about the girly stuff that Anora and Aro love, and who is as paranoid as I am about safety when we leave the house.

Anora is too fucking trusting and Aro would never leave the library if we didn't make her on some days and is so inside her own head she doesn't always notice what's around her. I feel like I'm watching out for them all on my own now, except I can't let them know I'm watching out for them, because they'll immediately be all up in my business and put expectations on me that I cannot meet. Caring, loving even, doesn't mean that I want to engage with them. It doesn't even mean that I'm capable of it.

I take the stairs to the second floor where the programming pods are setup.

Because my team deals with extremely confidential internal shit, we get a room rather than a grouping of cubicles. It has a door with a lock that only we and the head of security have a code for. When dad hired me to work at Designation, doing this is exactly what he hired me for.

No one is as motivated to protect our work like someone who was raised hearing about it. I'm not sure I believe in the importance of legacies, but I am against anyone stealing what doesn't belong to them, or destroying the work of others. Designation's security software was groundbreaking, and I'll be damned if I let anyone take away what my family has made.

I tap in the code, and I'm surprised to find that I am not the first one there.

Isaac, Dominic, and Tella are already at their computers. Tella has her headset on and she's talking to someone as she types notes into her computer. She's the only one of us that has social skills in addition to being a great programmer, so she also handles all of the administrative work for our pod. Even though I'm the team leader, I don't want to talk to anyone, so Tella talks to them for me.

Dominic was at Designation for awhile before I stole him for my team, and Isaac has been with us for about six weeks. As much as I can trust people, I trust them. They are mirror opposites in most ways except their badass programming and hacking skills. Both are around 6'2", but Dominic is all dark and Isaac is light. Where Dominic has thick, black hair, scruff on his face, and eyes so brown they are black, Isaac has light reddish brown hair, well-maintained facial hair, and bright green eyes that can be a little bit disconcerting behind metal-lined glasses. Dominic dresses like I do - ripped jeans, old t-shirts, destroyed hoodies, while Isaac wears button-up shirts and dress pants. He even keeps the sleeves buttoned at the wrists instead of rolling them up. The psycho.

They became friends the moment they met, so it's not surprising to me that if one is here, so is the other.

16

What surprises me is that they're here early.

I let my bag thump to the floor next to my desk. "What the fuck is going on?"

Dominic's head lifts from his screen. "Sup, boss."

After a moment, Isaac looks up too. "There was another attempted hack."

"Why didn't anybody call me?" I snarl, and move so that I'm standing behind Isaac's chair and looking over his shoulder. The design of the bug that attempted to infiltrate our system is similar to the ones that have tried before - it's the same person, their fingerprints are all over it. The design itself is inelegant, using brute force to try and break our firewalls and get into the servers where the base codes are.

If someone got the base codes - the core of our security software - it would give them what they need to find a way into any system that uses our software for protection. Not quite a master or skeleton key, more like the foundation to build a virus upon that would get them in where they wanted. They aren't getting anywhere close, luckily, but the more annoying part is that we can't trace these bugs back to the source.

They bounce around, protected by a solid VPN that must be self-made, because despite our patience and willingness to follow the signal through thousands of nodes, we've gotten nowhere.

We need to find a way to trap this bitch, then I will find them, and I will destroy them. No one fucks with what is mine, and Designation is mine.

Isaac is working on picking the bug apart, looking for any details or strings of code that might tell us something or prove useful. Sometimes their own work can be used against them to keep them out or track them down.

"Send me anything unique, I'll see if I can find their signature in known attacks."

Isaac nods, still caught up in what he's doing.

I sit at my desk and start looking through all of the data we analyzed from the previous attempts. Sometimes when I sit with information, new insight or ideas come to me. I get inspired by my anger at anyone who would try and ruin us.

An idea starts to form, but I'm not sure how I could make it work. I spend the rest of the day making notes and diagrams, hoping that this might be the way we catch this asshole.

5

Aster

Somehow I make it to Friday. There's an itch under my skin but if I try and scratch it I'll only end up hurting myself. I don't like it when people touch me. Sometimes I don't even like it when I touch me. It's too much input and too much to think about. Other people don't understand what it's like to overthink something as simple as a hug from your sister, but I do. When I'm going into a situation where affection is expected, I visualize before it even happens so that I'm prepared.

When Alina left, I'd spent an entire day visualizing hugging her goodbye. My brain went through every motion, every possibility, and then thought about the emotions that I might encounter when saying goodbye to her. I had to think about not wanting to disappoint her when I didn't cry - I should've known better on that one, it didn't bother Alina at all. Instead, because she knew me well, all that she cared about was that I was there and I was willing to try.

After dinner, I go to my room like I always do. I lock the door like I always do.

Then I go to the farthest, most hidden layer of my closet and pull out my secret stash of dresses. I mostly order them online for cheap since I don't care if they get ruined in the course of events.

Tonight's victim is a tricky one. He's the kind of douchebag that calls himself Ricky Fiasco and thinks he's some kind of big time thug when he's actually just a shitty drug dealer that amuses the actually dangerous men, and he likes to hit women. His real name is Ricky Finley and he grew up a middle class white boy that graduated in the top 5% of his high school class.

Two months ago, he accidentally killed a woman, and covered it up. It didn't take a lot of work for his heavy to give him up and spill all Ricky's idiocy. A lot of shots of vodka and Big Dog told me all of Ricky's secrets.

The problem is that when he goes out, he goes to the same place every time: Lacy Ladies. It's a mid-range strip club with solid drink specials and hot girls. Ricky thinks he's a favorite but it's that he gets drunk enough to give the girls a lot of money without realizing it. The problem is, sometimes he convinces a girl who doesn't know better to come home with him. He attempts to get dirty but because the asshole has a tendency toward whiskey dick, it doesn't go well. Then he gets angry.

I've seen the photos of what happens when Ricky loses his temper because he can't perform. The broken eye sockets and black eyes, the broken wrist, the solid purple abdomen of one poor girl. They all get treatment but they never report him because he threatens to kill them if they do, and they believe him.

Since the one he murdered, he's managed to hold himself in check and even drinks less.

I plan to change that tonight.

Because I'm not an idiot, I have a safety plan in place. I text Dinah who I'm going after and where I'm going. She's the source of a lot of my information, especially anything regarding police records. While I could hack my way in to a lot of it, that could leave a trail. When you are the daughter of one of the most powerful men in the Irish mob, certain cops are happy to give you anything you want.

Most human beings are happy to give her anything she wants. Dinah Riley is everyone's friend and she makes them feel it. The closest I've ever come to actually having a committed romantic relationship with anyone was with her; we were some kind of exclusive for almost a year even if no one knew that but us. Not only was she hot and fun, Dinah came from the darker side of things just like I did. We never had to explain to each other the things we did for our families. I learned a lot from her about drawing people in, especially the kind I like to hunt.

The hunting is what broke us up, or really, the inspiration for the hunt. Dinah understood my pain but not my need for revenge. It doesn't stop her from believing in my cause and helping me out - getting me information, adding to my target list, and she's my emergency exit if things go really south. I haven't needed her yet.

My dress is a little longer tonight, black, with two high slits up each side. It reveals a lot while covering a lot at the same time. I wear a knife sheath that I used hot glue to cover in black lace so it looks like I'm wearing a garter. My favorite little subcom is tucked into it, ready to be put to work when I'm ready. Even though I'm supposed to be sexy, I wear Doc Martens that go up to mid-calf. I'll need some weight tonight.

The rest of the house is quiet when I leave my room, lock my door, and head down to the garage. There's a door to the yard there that no one thinks to check and isn't armed with the same security as the main doors.

I'm not wearing a jacket and the air is cold now that night has fallen. Hopefully my cab is waiting already so I don't have to freeze.

There's a sound behind me, but I ignore it. I know he's there, like usual. Maybe tonight he'll show himself.

My dad thinks he's cagey and sneaky but he isn't. He thinks he can keep secrets from me but forgets that I'm the one who sets everything up for him, and that I have or can get access to just about anything. I know about the threats against Designation and specifically against me. I know that he hired Freelancer.

I overhead him on the phone talking to Clive Branson. Clive is a well-known broker, connecting people with certain kinds of skills to the people that need them. I saw the fund transfers and I read the communications between them. Dad hired Freelancer to keep an eye on me.

It wasn't easy to pick up on it at first. Freelancer is every bit as skilled as his reputation indicates. It was almost two weeks before I realized he was tailing me, and even then it was what I would hear and feel more than anything that I could see.

It had been almost two months and I'd never seen more than the shadow of him.

He also kept my secrets, and that intrigued me. If my estimation of how long he'd been following me was accurate, this is the third of my outings that he'd be tailing me through. Yet, he never told dad what I was up to. After the first killing he watched, I was sure that the next day I'd be read the riot act.

There was nothing.

It was that night I'd realized I was being followed, and put together that it was Freelancer. I was more embarrassed that he'd seen me pretend to be a sloppy drunk than that he'd watched me masturbate over a fresh kill, and I'm not sure what that says about me. Or what it revealed to me about him.

Hunting and taking down bad men is exhilarating. It turns me on to get vengeance and revenge for the people, especially the women, that they've hurt. The victims aren't always strong enough to take what they deserve from the people who hurt them, so I will be strong enough for them. It's fucked up thinking, I know that. I know that it's not healthy, and I should really contemplate the compulsion to kill that I feel flood my veins sometimes. I should be afraid of the way my anxiety stills for weeks, sometimes months, after taking the life of a monster pretending to be a man.

I've never denied that I'm a monster too.

I'm just a monster with a mission.

6

Aster

Getting to Ricky's table at Lacy Ladies was easy, and I should have expected that. He thought I worked there - one of the girls who would go from table to table, join groups and flirt with them, get them to order drinks and lap dances.

I'm sitting right next to him and he has his arm around me, completely ignoring me while also keeping a possessive hold on my waist. Ricky is talking to the other people at his table, including Big Dog, trying to brag about some bullshit that he got away with. Big Dog keeps looking at me with confusion, and I know that he knows I look familiar but can't quite place me.

The night wears on, and I put my hand on Ricky's thigh as I pass him another shot. He doesn't notice that I don't drink one. That I haven't had anything to drink the entire time I've been sitting with him.

"Wanna come with me, sweetheart?" Ricky breathes into my ear, the scent of alcohol wafting into my nostrils. "Come home with me."

I squeeze his thigh and fake a squirm. "I can't wait that long. Come outside with me," I whisper in his ear, then bite the lobe. The scent of his cologne is so fucking strong I can't breathe, and getting him out back will not only get him alone, but I'd also rather take a breath of the trashy cold alley air than his cologne again.

The funny thing is, he's going to turn up dead in that alley and all the guys sitting at his table won't even give a shit. They won't tell the cops about the woman he left with, who they'll say works at the club except the club will say that I don't. They'll scratch it up to an asshole who ran his mouth too much getting taken out, and move on to the next person they can leech off. It's so easy to read the dynamic of this group.

They follow Ricky because he's loud and flashy and is willing to pay for their friendship. Once the cash flow stops so does the care.

Ricky follows me down the hall to the bathrooms, and then out the back door into the alley. I tease him a little bit, walking backward to the far wall. It's actually a delay tactic, giving Freelancer enough time to catch up. I want him to watch me work.

Sure enough, I see his shadow come into the alley when he thinks I'm not looking. Ricky is kissing and biting at my neck, gripping my hips and squeezing my ass. I free one of my legs from the slit in the dress and start to slide down like I'm going to get on my knees for him - but then I spring up, driving my knee into his balls.

Ricky goes down quick.

"You fucking bitch!" he screams at me. "I'm going to fucking kill you for that."

I reach into my dress, pull out the Boker, and flip it open.

I grin down at him. "Not if I kill you first, Ricky."

Then I kick him in the face, smashing his nose. Ricky has to look like he was taken out. Like many people beat the shit out of him. It will make anyone even less likely to suspect the tiny girl in the club took him out. Maybe they'll believe I was bait, but that makes me even less relevant.

I keep kicking and stomping on him, putting him through everything he put those women through. I want him to feel every contact the way that they felt it. Women who thought they were going to get fucked, not fucked over. They were blamed for his lackluster dick, and his insecurity pushed him to hurt them.

When he's good and broken, I straddle him and pull him up by his hair to face me.

"Taste of your own medicine, asshole. Now, go away."

When I move my knife down toward the apex of his legs he starts begging me to stop. The idiot thinks I'm going to cut off his dick.

No, I go lower, slicing the knife precisely across his thigh to sever his femoral artery. I hunch over him as he bleeds out, watching the life drain out of him and form a dark pool on the dark concrete.

Then I stand and wipe the blade on my dress before tucking it back in to the sheath in my inner thigh.

I turn toward the mouth of the alley.

"I know you're there." I call out. I don't need to be too loud, I know he'll hear me. I know he's paying attention.

From a dark corner, a shadow moves, and then he's standing in the alley with me, only a few yards away. I'm surprised when he walks closer, but then I see why he's not afraid to do that.

Freelancer is in jeans and a black hoodie, and under the hoodie he's wearing a mask. It's some kind of mesh that I can't see through, and reminds me of the helmets that fencers wear. He tilts his head and looks at me.

"How long have you known?" His voice is low and gravelly.

"Awhile."

I step closer to him and feel all of my senses light up. I'm already on edge and worked up from taking down that stupid bastard, but being fully in this man's presence is doing something to me. It should be an overload but it's not. The arousal already thrumming inside me heightens, becoming a desperate shake in my skin, and making my breath come faster.

"Do you like to watch?" I ask, stepping close enough that we're not touching but I can feel the heat radiating from him.

"Yes."

"All of it?" He knows what I'm talking about.

"Yes," he nearly growls.

I move to the other side of him, leaning against the wall there, and his body follows my movement. Right now I'm hidden by the size of him, barely visible and outside of the reach of the light above the back door of the strip club. Then I put my hand inside the slit of my dress and touch myself. My panties are soaked, and even the slightest brush of my hand causes me to hiss from the sensitivity and immediate satisfaction. My nipples get tight and I know it won't take much for me to explode. Not just because of the satisfaction of beating the shit out of Ricky, but knowing Freelancer is up close and personal, watching me get off.

I moan as my fantasies become reality as I watch him watch me.

"May I?" he asks. I nod and move my hand away.

His hand is big, with defined knuckles and visible veins on the back. I'm mesmerized as he trails his fingers up my thigh, then under my dress. When he presses against my mound, I gasp and grab onto his hoodie. Freelancer crowds me against the wall, masked face tilted down toward me as he moves his hand beneath my panties. The touch of his skin against my bare pussy is decadent and wonderful.

Immediately I start to grind down on his hand, and he moves it deeper between my legs until two of his fingers are teasing my wet hole.

"Want to fuck my hand, baby?"

"Yes," I moan, and that turns to a cry when his fingers slide inside me, filling me up.

"Move your hips. Fuck yourself."

I nod and do as he says, bouncing up and down on my toes and rocking my hips. The heel of his palm presses hard against my clit and the wet sounds of me fucking myself with his fingers are so loud that anyone who leaves the club door will hear them. That turns me on even more. I had no idea I had it in me to want someone to catch me, watch me, being pleasured. Not until him.

I throw my head back as I orgasm, clenching around his fingers, pussy fluttering with delight as I gush all over his hand.

He pulls out slowly, gently, and then sticks his fingers in my mouth. I suck at them ravenously, eager to taste him beneath the taste of me. It isn't enough. I need more.

My hands slide under the edge of his hoodie and I start unbuckling his jeans.

He doesn't stop me, but asks, "What are you doing?"

"I want to taste you."

The masked face tilts down even further when I get on my knees and free his cock. It's pale, so I know he's a white boy, and thick and veiny. Precum already leaks from the tip and I quickly suck on the head, savoring the salty flavor. My lips wrap around him and I slide down his cock, groaning at the full, musky flavor of his velvety skin.

When I look up he's still looking down at me. I keep my eyes on the mask as I work my mouth up and down his cock, lavishing him with sweeps of my tongue along the underside of his head. He lets me play with him, taking him as deep as I can and then increasing the speed.

"How badly do you want to taste me?" his voice is raspy and aroused.

"So bad," I murmur, only stopping for seconds before resuming trying to get him as far down my throat as I can.

"Are you going to swallow my come, baby?"

Never in my life have I enjoyed being called baby, but I'm pretty sure I'd let Freelancer call me anything he wanted. If he wanted to call me his little whore, I'd let him. Right now I want to know that I drive him as crazy as he drives me.

I don't stop sucking, but I look up at him and nod as his head hits the back of my throat, causing saliva to flood my mouth.

His hips start to thrust slightly, and I pick up speed, sliding up and down on his smooth, wet skin. One of his hands slides into my hair and grips it tight, and with no warning he pushes me down on him. Not so far that I gag, but far enough that when he comes, the thick, salty fluid fills the back of my mouth and slides right down my throat. I swallow and swallow until it's gone, then jerk his cock with my hand a few times to make sure I got every fucking drop.

Like a gentleman, he helps me to my feet before putting his cock away. Freelancer runs his thumb down my bottom lip, the move soft and possessive.

"Get home safe, little monster. I'll be watching."

Then he steps back and walks away, leaving me in the alley. I don't watch which way he goes and I don't try to follow him. He isn't going far.

I take a moment to gather myself, then head the same way he went, out to the main street. Cabs are running up and down the road, so it doesn't take long to flag one. The driver is a little perturbed at how far he has to go, but I hand him a hefty tip to make it worth his while.

Then I close my eyes but don't sleep, replaying the last 20 minutes in my mind.

Fuck, I'm going to have to masturbate like 10 times when I get home if I'm going to get any sleep at all.

7

Freelancer

Aster calms after our encounter in the alley. I can see the lack of tension in her body, even if she still frowns as she makes her way through life. I barely see my own bed because I'm watching her - she fascinates me.

I like the way she pretends like she's not paying attention when everyone talks at meals. She plays a game on her phone but her body knows the game so well that her mind doesn't need to focus. It's like she's afraid for them to know that she's absorbing what her family is saying and how they're feeling. As if she thinks she'll scare them if she focuses on them. It might be true. I haven't quite grasped her dynamic with any of them except Aro yet. She adores Aro.

Based on her text messages and calls, she trusts Alina. That's her go to person for making decisions, for sharing concerns, and she's got a lot of programs and traps running for information on Alina's husband's company, Venture. Their marriage merged Venture and Designation and they've got their own problems. Aster is keeping an eye out for her, and I'm not sure Alina is aware how closely.

She has almost no relationship with Anora, and I think her oldest sister makes her actively uncomfortable. I'll dig into that some other time. Anora is aware of it, and tries hard to be nice and open to Aster. Even if I don't understand someone who goes through the world the way Anora does, I respect her for trying to step up and be there for Aster in the absence of Alina.

It's been interesting, and hazardous to my health, to watch Aster when she's alone now that she knows I'm watching. Some things are her being herself and going about her life, which I love knowing that she lets me in. But some things are her driving me insane on purpose now that we both know I'm watching. She leaves the curtains open and treats me to her naked body and getting herself off.

The night I nearly broke my way into the house to fuck her stupid was when she recorded a video of her playing with herself. I don't know if she knew I mirrored her phone or assumed that I'd have access to her cloud, but I've watched it what feels like a hundred times. Her throaty moans and the sounds of her arousal drive me fucking crazy. If I didn't have any self-control I'd probably be dealing with massive chafing from constantly jerking myself off. I'm as much of a pervert as the next guy, but the attraction and reaction I have to Aster is off the charts.

During the day job, we're working desperately hard to figure out who the hacker is. It's been frustrating because everything indicates they have more money and opportunity than they do skill. Not that they are unskilled - someone who can do what they are would be hired at Designation in a second - but there's something chaotic about the approach that you don't see in a lot of corporate hackers.

We've ruled out corporate espionage. Through the usual we're-friends-with-other-programmers channels it's been made clear that none of our competitors are trying to fuck with one another. It's happened before but we usually give each other a bit of a heads up. To make it a real challenge for one another.

This is brute force, smashing away like Grond on the door of Helm's

Deep. It's effective, and there's only so much we can throw in front of it to stop them. Aster and I have been making the case to the leadership of our division as well as to security that we need to do more protection internally. We have to be prepared to fail, and it's hard to say that you're doing good work while also talking about how that might not be enough.

With every meeting we go to that we don't win, with every document and PowerPoint we create with Tella that isn't enough, Aster gets more defeated. I know that she's going to want to kill again to take back control soon, and I'll be there when she does. Not because I think anything is going to happen between us, but because she needs me. Even when Aster isn't alone, she's lonely.

She's isolated by her brain and the way she was socialized because of it - never being able to integrate with people her own age and at her same stage of social-emotional development. She always had to play older and more mature to survive with her classmates who were actually older and more mature. It made her draw even further inside herself. Not to mention her homicidal urges and the way she can flatten her emotions down to nothing. People feel it. They feel the otherness of her and step away from the unknown.

I feel the otherness of her and it makes my body resonate like I've found home. My instincts tell me that for the first time I've found my own kind. I'm not alone in the universe, and I think she feels the same.

So I do my job. I'm content to watch her and know her, and every move we make now is up to her. I don't want to invade her life until she invites me to - I'm happy to let her dominate mine.

I'm watching Aster run on the treadmill at 5 in the morning, her headphones in, and I have one bud in my ear so I can listen with her. She's got hilariously eclectic taste in music, but especially when she runs. Today she's listening to the Phantom of the Opera soundtrack, but specifically the title song over and over, with occasional appearances from "Masquerade" and "the Point of No Return."

My phone rings and interrupts my watching. Clive is calling.

"Sir." As soon as I say it he barks out a laugh.

"The job going well?"

"No attempts on Aster yet outside of the hacking, but it feels like something is brewing. None of this makes any sense."

"It doesn't. I've been looking into it as well."

"Anything?"

"Someone has a vendetta against the Sorrelle family. There are rumors going around that this hit on Aster and the Designation hacks are 'just the beginning' but no one is willing to say who has it out for them. I have reason to believe it's tied up with Don's son-in-law as well."

"Derick Clayton? How?"

"His problems might be exacerbated by his marriage to Alina Sorrelle. It's put a bigger target on his back."

"That's marriage for you."

Clive snorts again, but sobers quickly. "We're blinder than ever in this case. Be careful, Freelancer."

It means a lot that he genuinely cares. I'm not just an asset to him - honestly, when it comes to some of my skills I'm replaceable. There's always someone else to take and train, who's desperate to feel safe and strong in this world. Like I used to feel until Clive found me. Except I know I'm not another number or asset to him - none of us are. Most of us never experienced a hint of belonging until he found us.

"I've got eyes on."

"Are you sleeping?"

"When I need to." My answer is cagey and incomplete, and I know that he'll see through my bullshit right away. The silence stretches between us over the line, and I watch Aster mouth the words to the song, probably not even realizing she's doing it. I love how little she gives a shit about anything. The way she makes sure she's herself all the time.

"Is there something I need to know?"

"Not right now." It's not quite a lie, but enough to keep him off my back and not push too hard. He knows that if I need to talk I will, and that I'll back off and shut down if he doesn't let me come around in my own time. I don't know what the future holds for my feelings for Aster, or after this job.

I want to find a way to be with her. I can't be her full time stalker and not have some sort of work or income. I'd waste away, and I think she feels that this is something special too. I could keep the day job. I've been useful, I don't think they'd stop me if I asked. It's about what Aster wants.

If she wants me and understands, I'll give up the contract work for her. Then I don't have to leave her for long periods of time and isolate myself from her for both our safety. Unless she wants to become a hit squad duo, which I also don't love the idea of, leaving the life is the only option.

She's the life I want, and as soon as I know she's safe, I'll make sure we build it together.

8

Aster

There are no run-ins with Freelancer for almost a month. I haven't felt the need to go out and I don't want to turn this weird dynamic into something that it isn't. It's not like some hitman-bodyguard who is hiding his face from me is going to be my boyfriend.

It almost bothers me that I can't talk to my sisters about it because I want to talk to someone. The thing is, I know that I'm a fucked up weirdo pervert and I don't want them to know that. They already think something is off about me, I don't want to give them even more reasons to believe it.

Anora and Aro would be scandalized, and even though Alina would hear me out, she'd be mad at me for putting myself in danger. Because I can't explain what happened with Freelancer without also explaining how we got ourselves into the situation in the alley. Alina would be livid if she knew about my hobby.

I also once heard Anora tell Alina that she thinks I'm a virgin.

Under the right circumstances, when the need takes over my body, I don't mind people touching me in a sexual way. Sex is different than affection. Affection is where I struggle. It drove Dinah crazy. We really were kind of terrible together.

The reason they don't know about any of the people I've had sex with is because when I told my hookup partners that I would kill them, slowly, painfully, and with full eye contact if they ever told anyone that we fucked, they believed me. Fear is an excellent motivator to get people to keep shit to themselves.

Still, my existence is lonely. I don't even know what he looks like but I know Freelancer takes that feeling away. Knowing he's watching me has given me a feeling I can't name and don't understand. I feel lit up, a new aspect of my dark side that wants to perform just for him.

He's seen me the way that no one else ever has. When he touched me, I wanted us to crawl inside each other's bodies to live and feel there because it was the first time in my life there was more than just a physical response. There was something inside me, an abstract thing in my mind, that came alive when we engaged with one another.

Without it, I'm feeling emptier than I did before. I didn't know what I was missing and now I do. Now I want more. It tempts me to do stupid things, and I am not a stupid person. A stupid person would find an excuse to go out in the world and put herself in danger so that he'd have to save her, and they'd get to interact again.

Instead of doing that, I leave my room and go down the hall to Aro's room.

As usual, it's empty. Her bed doesn't even look slept in and I feel a brief flare of concern for her spine because that means she's been sleeping in chairs again.

Aro worries me in general. Not that I'll ever tell her that. Even though she's trained well and she can fight, the wariness and alertness that Alina and I have is non-existent in her. When we're in the gym and training, she's great - strong and fast, confident in her movements and her body. Outside the gym it's as if she's wandering in the mist, only paying attention when it suits her.

When she puts her skills to work and focuses, she's amazing. There's something she picks up on that the rest of us don't - body language, movements and gestures, posture - all these things that communicate without words are what she sees.

When she's paying attention.

I swear if anyone ever considers kidnapping Aro, it's going to be too damn easy. She won't even see they're coming until it's way too late to do anything about it.

That's why I shut down conversation about her getting out of the house as subtly as I can. Aro isn't safe. She finished her degree and hasn't done anything since then. Most days she reads and does research, trains because Alina set an alarm to remind her to do it, then goes to bed, rinse and repeat. It's better for her to be in the house. I like knowing where she is and that she's safe. Especially now that Alina's gone.

I find Aro where I knew she'd be - in the library that's also dad's office. Right near the window is an old green velvet chair that is so well-used it's shaped to her body. Currently, she's sitting in it sideways, legs dangling over one arm while her head rests against the other.

She's reading a non-fiction book about hosting a Viking funeral. I'm almost intrigued but don't have the patience or the imagination for reading.

Aro reinforces my concern by not even noticing I'm there until I slap the back of the book so it bumps into her face. When she puts the book down she glances up at me owlishly, and blinks a lot as if she hasn't looked away from the page for a few hours. She probably hasn't.

I sit down on the couch in the seating area. Aro isn't reading but she isn't talking either. The silence stretches on.

If she asks me what's the matter, my instinct will be to deny that there's anything, and I'll shut up out of pure piggish spite. If she waits me out, it will eventually burst out of me. I came down here to talk to her, she knows that, and she knows me so well that I know she'll wait me out. I did get lucky in the sister department.

At least 5 minutes go by without either of us saying anything.

"Dad's having me followed."

Aro's eyes go wide but she doesn't say anything.

"I kind of like him."

Now her mouth drops open. "What." It's not a question, it's a declaration.

"We - interacted." That's the safest way to explain that we made each other orgasm in an alley after I killed a guy.

"He's not very good then," Aro frowns and leans forward, focused now.

"No, he is - but I think he wanted me to see him. To know that I was being followed."

"Okay, so stalking turns you on, got it." She fights a grin but loses it when I flip her off.

"Am I crazy?"

Aro deadpans. "We already knew that. But are you crazy for being interested in this guy, no." While that does make me feel better, I don't think she'd say that if she knew the whole story. Then again, Aro knows parts of me like we're twins, and never judges me for anything. Maybe she'd understand. Maybe she'd see that this makes sense for me, even if it would be unthinkable to anybody else.

"So what do I do? Do I try and…date him? Kidnap him?"

"Both," Aro says before rearranging herself in the chair again to resume reading. "I recommend kidnapping."

"I'm not ruling it out." I get up to leave, but she stops me with a soft, "hey."

"I like the idea that you found someone that intrigues you. Even if it's unconventional, I don't think we expected anything less."

"Thanks."

It's not like she said anything I didn't already know, but once and awhile I need someone to reassure me that not all my thoughts are intrusive. I am unconventional in a lot of ways, it's why I'm always questioning myself about what I'm doing or why I'm doing it.

I don't have a death wish or anything, but sometimes my brain puts the most dangerous pictures in my vision and I'm tempted to follow through on them. I have to babysit my own impulses carefully.

There's no doubt that he's out there somewhere, and I want to know if I can find him.

First, I go upstairs and change my clothes because dammit, I'm still a woman. I want him to think that I look good. As myself, not as the personas that I dress up as when I go hunting. It's June and still kind of cold at night because it's Illinois and the Midwest likes to pretend we don't go straight from winter to summer with only a few days of spring.

I put on a pair of black cotton shorts and an oversize hoodie that goes down almost to my knees. Sometimes there are advantages to being tiny. I put my hair up and a tiny bit of makeup on - mascara on my lashes and a swipe of deep pink lipstick.

Then I make my way out of the house the normal way, through the back door and down to the gazebo. In the dark you can't see much in here from the house, and if he shows up I don't want anyone to see. The entire property is fenced and censored so I know that I'm safe back here.

It still doesn't make sense to me that I'm the one being threatened. I know that if someone could bring down or make Designation vulnerable that would be a big deal, but there has to be a more efficient way to destroy us.

That thought triggers something in my brain and bounces around so furiously I almost miss the movement of him coming. It's like when a deer freezes at the smallest sound. I'm on alert because another predator is present, and he's hunting me.

I watch him stand in the shadows beneath a tree, looking around for minutes before he crosses the open, moonlit stretch of lawn to where I sit on the steps of the gazebo. Freelancer sits down next to me, drawing my attention to his long, rangy build. I want to climb him like a tree.

"How many have their been?" he rumbles.

"Eleven."

He makes a sound but I can't tell what he means by it. "Eleven men?"

"No," I shake my head and don't look at him, instead focusing on the night sky. "Nine men and two women."

"What did the women do? I got the theme with the men." He sounds amused.

"One of them hurt children, the other facilitated women being assaulted. That was a twofer, I got her and her partner that night."

"It's dangerous."

"Yeah," I shrug. "But somebody's gotta do it."

We don't say anything for awhile. "Did you like watching me?" I ask.

"Yes," his voice is low. "I like seeing how deadly you are, Aster. I like the way they don't see it coming and they can't imagine that you are the bigger monster."

"Are you a monster?"

"Yes."

I put my hand on his thigh, and slide it higher. I still haven't looked over at him - I can't. If I see him, that stupid sexy mask, I will fucking combust. The energy coming from him slides right between my skin and into my bloodstream. Sitting next to him is giving me a contact high. I feel my blood rushing through my veins and pulsing in my clit from arousal. The desire to rip off his clothes, rip into his skin, while we fuck under the moonlight is putting me on edge.

"What would you do to anyone who hurt me?" My voice is barely a whisper. I want to know his violence the way he knows mine. I want to know that it turns him on like it does me.

Freelancer pulls away from me to stand and I'm afraid I've asked the wrong question or upset him. Then he moves behind me and sits, placing me between his legs so my back is to his front. He wraps his arms around me possessively, his hands going into the pocket of my hoodie. This is the kind of thing that I shouldn't like, but I'm not having any of my usual reactions to casual touching.

I'm pulled tight against him and I can feel the cold mesh of the mask on my cheek. I have to look up if a mask kink is a thing because if so, I have it. I want to fuck him when he's wearing nothing but the mask.

"Oh baby," he rumbles. "I'd start by removing their eyes to punish them for looking at you, let alone thinking they could touch you. I'd pull off their fingernails one by one until they were begging to apologize to you, and apologizing for existing at all. Then I'd cut out their heart and present it to you to do whatever you wish."

Shivers race along my skin and my nipples get hard. I lean against him and squirm.

"No one will hurt you as long as I'm watching."

"No one but you?" I prompt, my voice breathy.

"Only if you ask really nicely." I gasp when his hand dives under my hoodie and his hot, rough hand splays across my stomach. "I don't think you really want pain, Aster. You want to feel the extremes, and there are other ways to get that. The things I could show you, baby." Freelancer groans into my ear and my pussy floods with arousal. He's driving me insane as he traces shapes on my stomach, draws circles around my belly button, and sets off tingles on my sensitive skin. "I don't have to hurt you to get you to the edge."

When he slides his hand into my shorts to touch my bare pussy, I have to slap my hand over my mouth to muffle the moan I let out. Freelancer slides his finger through my slit, taking some of my moisture and

41

dragging it up to tease my clit.

"I'm going to play with you now. Try not to scream."

I can only nod.

His finger circles faster and with more pressure, and I rock my hips against his hand, my inhibitions non-existent when he's touching me. When I'm about to go over the precipice, he pulls his hand away, reducing the pressure.

I whimper, and he laughs in my ear. "Again, Aster."

This time he slides further into my shorts until his fingers can slide inside me. He takes short, firm strokes that drive me crazy. I grip onto his legs on either side of me as my own start to shake.

Then he pulls back again.

It feels good and terrible at the same time. I can feel everything happening around me, every sense is on alert, my body is practically vibrating with desire. I gasp into the night air, body moving around nothing.

Freelancer takes his hand from my shorts and presents me with the two fingers he had inside me. Dutifully I put them in my mouth. As I'm concentrating on that, he puts his left hand in my shorts and gets back to work. He's fucking my mouth and my pussy at the same pace with his fingers and it's absolute overload. I'm moaning hard, sucking and writhing as he brings me back to the edge. I try and hold off, hoping he'll touch me and play with me just a little bit longer.

I cry out when he pulls out of me.

"Do you want to come?" he asks, and again I can only nod, so overwhelmed with sensations that words escape me.

"I need to hear it."

"Please." I beg, sounding desperate. I am desperate. "Make me come."

"If I left you like this, would you go to your room and play with that little pussy?" He slides his fingers down to play with my clit again, and I love the sound of his voice even changed by the mask. "Would you fuck your fingers and wish it was me?"

"Yes," I moan, rocking hard against his hand.

"Would you think about sucking my cock, and the way I tasted when you make yourself come?"

"Yes." I'm almost there and knowing that he's not going to stop this time makes me rabid.

"You've thought about it already, haven't you? Gotten yourself off just thinking about the way I taste."

"Yes," I answer again.

"Good girl," he says, then presses down hard on my clit, and pulls me back into his body so I can barely move. When the orgasm hits, my body shakes and I bite my lip to stop myself from screaming at the intensity of the pleasure. It gets worse when he puts his free hand over my mouth to muffle the sound. I can smell his skin and my pussy and it's incredible.

After, I can barely move, and I rest against him. He holds me, and in the back of my mind the fact that I'm so comfortable with him like this registers. I don't cuddle. This is as close to cuddling as I've ever been in my life. I have no interest in moving, and let myself have this moment without overthinking. I'll do that later.

Freelancer was right that extreme doesn't mean painful. Although being denied my orgasm is it's own exquisite kind of torture, the build up was...like nothing I ever knew existed before.

"Will you text me?" I ask. "I'm sure you have the number."

"I do," he agrees, "and I will."

"Good." I extricate myself from him and turn to face him. Through the mask I see nothing and yet I feel like I know him anyway. Before I can think too hard about it, I lean forward and press a kiss to the mask, over where I approximate his lips are.

Panic rushes up, and I give him a nod before turning and rushing toward the house.

It's not that I kissed the mask, it's that I had the desire to kiss him at all. I don't kiss outside of fucking. Kissing is too intimate, too affectionate, too much.

Yet I wanted to kiss him. To touch my lips to his because I could.

Fuck.

9

Freelancer

Consumed would be an understatement. The Aster that I got to see when I was in the mask, when I was the truest version of myself, was easy to obsess over. The Aster that I knew in the day, the one who didn't know I was Freelancer, was so different. It was like she diminished the spark inside her on purpose because she'd been taught that it scared people. People found Aster intimidating and they had no idea how much more terrified they should be. I loved it.

Fire was in my veins whenever I touched her, and I couldn't control myself when she was close. She offered herself in invitation and there was no way in hell I'd ever say no. There was so much we could do together, and I was going to take advantage of that.

After she was safely closed up in her room, I went around the house to the front door. I entered the house and made my way to the library. Everyone was already inside, so I closed and locked the door, then removed my mask.

The people in this room are the only ones on this job who know my face. We'd all agreed that I needed to be with Aster as much as possible, and that my computer skills would be valuable. Most jobs didn't ask for my daylight persona and didn't need it. This one did.

The mask wasn't new, but with this job it was more essential.

Don sits at his desk and Owen stands behind him like a good second in command. His guard Alonzo is standing by the back window. Don's new head of security, Gailen, leans against the front of the desk, the usual frown on his face. The guard that is occasionally assigned to Aster, Nino, sits in a chair, looking very much like he doesn't want to be present.

Gailen needs to get over his shit. He'd been firmly against Don hiring me, even going so far as to calling my broker, Clive, to convince him to reject the job. Gailen felt that they could keep Aster safe and that an outsider was unnecessary.

Considering the alarming rate at which Aster snuck off the property, they were fucking wrong. I wasn't going to betray Aster's secrets, but they should be kissing my feet for the fact that I've been with her every step of the way for the last 3 months. Aster can handle herself, but when someone is out to get you, backup isn't a bad idea. By now I thought of us as a team. Wherever she went, she knew I was there, and I'd noticed the way she modified her movements as if giving me time to always keep up with her.

Don smiles at me, because he's probably the most pleasant human being I've ever met. He means it too. When they first hired me and I had a meeting with Don, he'd actually asked about my life and what could be done to make the job easier. It was more than wanting to protect his daughter, he wanted to know me. I didn't give him much but felt oddly touched that he asked. It had been a long time since anyone had cared about anything outside my skills and usefulness.

"How are things?" Vague question, but I know what he's getting at.

"No one's been following or monitoring her and her devices are still clean. The direct threat to her seems less of an urgent matter than the repeated attempts on Designation. We're doing what we can but this hacker, or outfit, are good. As good as we are."

Gailen snorts and I work hard to keep my face from scowling at him in return. Asshole probably barely knows how to turn on his phone let alone write code. I'd bet money he needs help to turn a word doc into a pdf.

"Any progress on who this might be?" I ask, staring expectantly at Gailen. That's been his job - go through their potential enemies and rivals and try to find out who's got a vendetta.

The problem is that even with ties to crime and shady as fuck people, everyone likes Don Sorrelle. He's fair and honest and so goddamn nice - even criminals like him. They also know they need what he's got, and he's nice about it. Cuts them a fair deal. Which is a far cry from his deceased partner, Roman Carver. From my research, it's not surprising Owen's father got released from his contract, permanently. Anyone who wants to come at Don would do it more directly.

This reeks of something personal, but that's just as confusing. Don doesn't have personal entanglements, and when he does they're discreet and both parties know what's really going on. The closest they ever came to an issue was when Anora was supposed to get engaged and the guy fucked off with Alina instead.

Who could be so goddamn mad at the Sorrelles? And why was that anger focused on Aster?

There was a lot of drama going on with Alina's husband as well. Broderick Clayton was upstanding on the surface, but the underworld he was connected to and the parts he ran were blowing up in his face. They were trying to keep things quiet but if there was anything the Sorrelle family was good at, it was getting information. They'd decided to stay out of it unless Alina or her husband asked for help.

They'd also decided not to tell Alina about anything that was going on here.

That was probably a good thing - she had a tendency to get overprotective.

I listen to them all talk and theorize but there's nothing concrete.

The thing is, the issues with the hack and the threat against Aster might be separate things. The hacks started months ago, and Owen put Aster in charge of a special team meant to defend Designation and try and trace the culprit.

Shortly after that, Don had been sent an email with a photo of Aster leaving Designation and a brief message: *I will rip her away from you.*

It was specific language but the motivation for it was still unknown.

After a circular conversation that doesn't get anywhere, Don calls the meeting to a close. Nino hightails it out of there like his ass is on fire, followed more slowly by Owen and Alonzo.

"Would you stay for a moment?" Don directs toward me. I nod in response. When Gailen doesn't move, Don turns to him and waves that he can leave the room.

"Is that really a good idea, sir?"

I can't tell if Gailen really doesn't trust me or he is that butthurt about being dismissed from the conversation. Security staff know a lot, but they don't know everything.

"Gailen," there's a warning in Don's voice. The man nods and leaves the room, but not before he shoots a glare at me. When the door shuts behind him, Don sighs and looks at me.

"How is Aster?"

"What do you mean?"

"I mean - is the threat getting to her, is work going well, is she... fitting in? Does she have a social life I don't know about?"

It takes everything I have to hold back a grin. "The threat isn't getting to her. I think it annoys her more than anything - to feel restricted."

Don nods in agreement. "And at work, with your team? Friends?"

I choose my words carefully, not wanting to offend while also being honest. "Aster doesn't have friends in the way other people do. Most people don't understand her and don't want to - but the team is close.

I would say we're friends, we do things together. Everyone likes her, even if she doesn't realize it." I make zero mention of her connection to Dinah Riley. Don would have a stroke.

"Good," Don nods, very solemn. "I know she's different, and it makes me worry. She experiences so much and processing it all overwhelms her to the point she just...shuts off."

I'm surprised by how well he understands her, and that he's never tried to - for lack of a better term - fix her. Most parents would be shoving every form of therapy down their child's throat trying to get them to be "normal." I had life experience with that one. Don seemed to accept Aster for exactly who she is, even if he didn't understand.

"Do you know the last time I hugged my daughter?"

Weird question, but I went with it - I shook my head.

"After her mother died, we were - I was - lost." The pain of his grief is on his face like he lost her only yesterday. "Aster went out and someone tried to kidnap her - an employee, one of my VPs. A man I thought I trusted. She killed him."

Hell yeah she did. She was probably 7 or 8 at the time but it still didn't surprise me.

"When we found her, that was the last time she let me hold or comfort her, and I think it was only because she was too tired to fight me. Fucking Benjamin Forrester. I was warned, but he charmed me. All the Forresters are the same - a festering rot of a family, spread across the country and killing it from the inside."

I'm intrigued. This was the meanest I'd ever seen Don be about or toward anyone. This wasn't just about the man who tried to take his daughter - it went beyond that. There was more to this story.

"Why have I never heard about this?"

"We made him disappear. God knows what he would've done to Aster to get to me, and I didn't want her to have to deal with the questions, and the treatment she'd get, for protecting herself. Not even Aster's sisters know. As far as I know she's never told them."

"Why tell me?"

Don thinks for a long time. "After, I obviously got her into therapy, and she went and she talked, but they were all concerned by her reactions. She wasn't scared, guilty, ashamed - it was an act of pure, almost innocent, survival to her. I took her out of therapy, but I think she became convinced she was deficient somehow. I have nothing against therapy - I go regularly, as does Aro, but it wasn't right for Aster then. It might've done more harm than good."

I still don't understand, and he can tell.

"Aster will kill herself if it means she's doing something good or right. She thinks she needs to redeem herself because she thinks she's missing something fundamental inside. I hired you because I know the lengths she will go to in order to protect Designation, or to make sure nothing happens to any of us. She'll take the blow. You can't let that happen."

Struck by the truth of his words, I speak before I think. "I would never let anything happen to her." There's more emotion in my voice than I'd like, and Don gives me a piercing look before his face relaxes into the usual soft smile.

"Then we understand each other. I'll see you next week."

I nod and prepare to leave the room. The mask goes back on, and I slide out into the dim hallway. Gailen and Alonzo are talking by the front door, and instinct tells me he's waiting for a chance to confront me without Don to call him off. I won't give that fucker the satisfaction, and want to remind him that I'm better than him for oh so many reasons.

The shadows hide me as I move down the hall, behind the stairs, and out the back door into the yard. I've learned a lot from watching Aster sneak around, and it doesn't take long for me to get off the property without tripping any sensors. My bike is waiting, and I get on to head to the hotel room I'm renting for a few hours of sleep before I'm back to wait and watch for Aster.

When I park, I pull off the mask and look at it. There's a hint of pink where Aster's lips pressed against it. The kiss had surprised me, but I also felt pleased. She wanted to kiss me. Before I could think better of it, I lifted the mask to my lips. There was still a hint of the taste of the lipstick, and I was oddly satisfied knowing that we had kissed the same place even if we hadn't kissed each other. Yet.

10

Aster

Work is a much-needed distraction at the moment, but I'm frustrated that we aren't making much progress in tracking down the hacker. On the upside, we've developed some new watchdog tools that have caught hacks and and leaks, and after implementing them to protect our system, we turned the concepts over to the development teams to potentially become new products.

At least I'm contributing, I guess.

Tella is dealing with all of that, so she's not in our pod very often the last few weeks. Our newest team member, Thor, is the quiet type but he's taken over some of her duties when she's out. Despite his Norse name, his hair is a natural deep black, which makes his bright eyes all the more striking. From what I managed to get out of him, his mother is Italian and his father is from the Netherlands. If he wasn't such a crabby bitch he'd be rolling in pussy because he also has an accent. I never thought I'd meet someone pricklier than me.

We let him hang out in his corner by himself, and he primarily communicates through email even when we're in the same room. It endears him to me, along with his programming skills.

Isaac sits down next to me and I pull up his screen on my own monitor.

"These lines here," he points, leaning close to me. "I know I've seen that code before - outside of the other hacks. I can't find it but it's really specific - some kind of tracking."

I read through the string of code that would look like nonsense to anyone outside of this room. "It doesn't look familiar to me, but I'll see if I can figure out how they're using it."

"Right." Isaac drops his hand, and his fingers graze the back of mine where it rests on my mouse. I've known since his first day that he had a crush on me, and I have no idea what to do about it.

He's good looking, in a sharp, nerdy kind of way. He has hair that's somehow red and brown at the same time, clever green eyes behind metal-framed glasses, and close cut facial hair that makes him look put together. I like his hands. Objectively, I find him attractive. Except he's so…nice. Isaac is always considerate of me, even outside of the fact that I'm his boss. I don't know what to do with someone who is sweet or soft.

I pull my hand away to tuck a stray curl behind my ear.

"Let me know if you find anything else," I gently dismiss him. I can feel him looking at me, so I stay focused on the screen as if I'm intent on nothing but playing around with this line of code. He leaves, and I let myself breathe again.

The day wears on, and I make a point of telling the rest of the team to leave at the close of business. Isaac and Dominic both offer to stay behind, multiple times, but I practically push them out the door.

"I need some alone time with the hacker codes."

"Kinky," Dominic winks at me, and drags Isaac away before he can protest again.

I make sure the door is closed and locked, crack my knuckles, stretch my neck, and settle in to work my ass off and hope something comes to me. I've been building a false version of our system - complex enough to hopefully fool the hacker but at the end of the day it's a trap. The trap part is the problem. I'm sure I can lure them in, but then it's deciding if I try and lock them down, or trace them back.

The other option is to try and mimic our base codes enough to be convincing, and creating a version of it that contains a virus or a backdoor to follow the tether to their system or their location. I don't know if I want to be able to get into their system or trace their location more. The location seems more important overall, but my own personal vendetta wants to play around in their house.

Once I give up on looking at their code, I go back to fleshing out the fake base codes. We have plenty of server room, especially with the expansion we got from Venture. I knew Alina's husband would come in handy.

Which reminded me that I needed to run some checks on their systems in the next week or so. Derick had given me the contact information for his secret right hand, Kade Reynolds, and sometimes I sent him things that I picked up on. He got kind of sassy with me in return and it amused me. In my book, that made us friends.

Finally my back and ass were sore enough that I had to call it a day. It was almost midnight, and aside from some security staff I'd bet the entire campus was empty. I'd driven myself today because I'd planned to stay late and wasn't parked too far from the building. Plus, Freelancer was probably out there somewhere. Watching. Waiting.

A shiver of anticipation ran through me, better than a hit of espresso at waking me up. Not that anything was going to happen, but even the idea of his eyes on me lit my body up. Could someone orgasm from being stared at, without even being touched?

I make my way through the darkened building, appreciating the muffled silence of the empty carpeted halls, and then the echoing taps of my boots in the grand glass entry. The building is big and sprawling, and I feel safe and comfortable here, hidden inside these glass walls and even further hidden behind my screens.

My Tahoe is the only car left in this parking lot, and I feel confident as I make my way over to it. I'm swinging my bag off my shoulder when a man comes around the back - he'd been hiding behind it waiting for me. I drop the bag with a thump, and quickly assess the situation. I've got a little folding knife in my back pocket that I reach for while feigning shock.

He's bigger than me, but everyone is bigger than me, and he doesn't appear overly muscled. The man is holding a knife and looks comfortable with it, but it's not how I'd be holding it if I was going to do damage. This isn't a hit, it's a kidnapping. He'll only hurt me enough to subdue me, and that's the difference between us. While it would be helpful to keep him alive, it's not a necessity.

He charges at me, and I think he expects me to turn and run, confident that he can take me down and subdue me in a chase. It takes everything I have not to smile as adrenaline races through me for the fight. I can almost taste it in my mouth.

Instead of running, I charge back. In a panic, he swipes at me and manages to cut across my stomach, but it gives me the time to bring up my heavily booted foot and nail him in the balls. There are no rules in the game of survival.

When he cringes in pain, I grab a fist full of his hair and bring his head down as I bring my knee up. The crunch of his skull is incredibly satisfying, especially since he cut one of my favorite shirts and now there's blood all over it. I'll never get it out, and you can't repair a t-shirt without it looking like shit. I let his hair go and he tumbles to the ground, unconscious. I pocket my knife and wait for a few moments to make sure he's really out.

Just as I bend over to pick up his knife, footsteps behind me have me turning, blade held in my hand for attack. When I see who it is, I immediately relax. It's Freelancer.

"What the fuck?" He sounds pissed as hell. "He must've been there for hours waiting for you. I would've seen him." No one is perfect, and this was the energy explosion that I needed to get my mind working. By the time I crash from the adrenaline, I might even be able to sleep.

"Whatever," I shrug, and walk to the back of the Tahoe and open it up. I grab a duffle bag and toss it at him. "Tie him up."

Now, most people would look at the contents of that bag and think it was some kind of kidnapping and murder kit. They'd be especially concerned to know that it's the standard kit I keep in my car. In my life you never know when you're going to need to tie up someone who tried to kill you and transport them for interrogation.

When I'm done laying out the plastic in the back, I come back to where Freelancer and my would-be kidnapper should be. The kidnapper is still unconscious and he's been tightly hog-tied, his back arching so his wrists are nearly touching his feet.

"Nice," I grin. "Throw him in the back." At least I'm not stuck doing the heavy lifting by myself. Freelancer hefts the dead weight and dumps him on the plastic, and then closes the hatch. He turns to me, and I can feel the frustration even if I can't see it on his face.

"You're bleeding." He comes close and lifts my mangled shirt, examining the cut across my bare stomach. His eyes on my naked skin sends heat through me, and I know it's weird to have an injury examined and get a little turned on. I look down at the cut.

"It's not that bad - won't even scar, doesn't need stitches. I need to get back to the house. I have an idiot to question." I can't keep the grin off my face and I don't bother to try. This is my favorite game. Answer my questions and I won't make you scream. Based on his lack of finesse, I think this one is going to give it all up way too easily, but who knows, maybe this time I'll be surprised.

"I'll ride with you."

"Actually…would you drive?" I'm too keyed up and know that I won't have complete control over my impulses. The adrenaline rush overpowers everything else, and I'll be shaking at the wheel. "Can you see well enough to drive in that?"

It's weird to me how quickly the mask became completely normal to me. Sometimes I almost don't notice it because it's so much more about the way his presence feels. His looks are irrelevant to me.

"If I can ride a motorcycle, I can drive your car," he snarks, and takes the keys from my outstretched hand. He doesn't ask why I want him to drive. Without hesitation, he gets in the driver's seat and I climb in the passenger side. The adrenaline crash is coming, and until then I will hold myself as still as I can, holding everything inside until it collapses and dissipates.

Then I'll be ready to bring out the monster, and play with my new toy.

11

Aster

The man is tied to a chair in our basement. It's got to be more comfortable than how Freelancer had him all bound up. The chair is anchored to the floor, his ankles are tied to the legs at the bottom, and his arms are stretched behind his back so his wrists are tied to the back legs at the top. It's very efficient.

When we came in the front door with Freelancer in full mask carrying a body, chaos erupted. Gailen absolutely lost his shit, demanding to know what happened and blaming Freelancer. Alonzo had it more together than that, and took the initiative of leading Freelancer down to the basement where they could get my toy set up to play.

Gailen ranted at dad for a bit - how Freelancer had failed at his job, that I'd been hurt, that we needed to pull me from work and fire "the outsider" and a bunch of other dumb shit. I'm not sure what got such a huge bug up his ass, but this feels less about my safety and more about him having an issue with Freelancer. His distrust isn't going to keep any of us safer.

"Shut. The. Fuck. Up."

When I finally snapped, both dad and Gailen stilled. I only had eyes for Gailen.

"He's kept me safe for months." Gailen blanched. "Yes, I've known the whole fucking time. He makes me feel secure. This was well planned but terribly executed, and in a way, it's a gift that fell right into our laps. Freelancer stays, Gailen, or you'll fucking go."

"Aster," was all he could reply, appalled. Gailen was the same age as Aro. We'd known him since they were both freshman in high school. He was loyal as they come, but I think because we'd pulled him into our orbit so young, he forgot who taught him everything he knew. He forgot who he answered to at the end of the day.

"This is my life, and I'm choosing how to protect it. Now, if you'll excuse me." I shoot them both a sarcastic wink that is entirely out of character for normal me but seems about right for the me that's about to become unhinged.

My prisoner, my toy, my source of information, grunts as he comes back to consciousness.

I'm standing in front of him to make sure that I'm the first thing he sees. Whole, unharmed, and armed. Freelancer is standing in the back corner, leaning casually against the wall as if he was waiting for a friend to arrive. I'm excited to have him see this - to have him know yet another side of me.

"Hello," I smile at my toy. "What's your name?"

"Fuck you."

My smile gets bigger. "Hi Fuck You, I'm Aster." Behind me, Freelancer snorts. Dad jokes for the win.

"Did they send you in here to poke me?" The toy taunts. "I tried to take you so they'll let you get your closure before they send the real bad guy in?"

Freelancer laughs darkly and I'm immediately aroused. Not only the sound, but what it means. His confidence in me is so sexy.

"Either you didn't do your research, or they sent you in grossly under prepared, Fuck You."

He glowers at me. "Noah."

"Noah what?"

"Hunt."

"Hi Noah Hunt, I'm Aster Sorrelle. So tell me," I remove the thin, razor sharp blade I prefer to begin with. "What was your assignment?"

"To kidnap you from Designation." He isn't holding back - interesting. I step forward, in his personal space, and use my blade to cut off his shirt, exposing the bare skin of his flat, smooth chest to me. He isn't muscular but he isn't fat. They sent someone who was barely a threat to me - and I think they knew it. This was a test, and a warning.

They wanted to draw out my protection, and they also wanted to make sure that I knew they were coming after me hard too - not only Designation.

Message received.

"What did they tell you about me?"

Noah looks at me, confused. In his mind, there was nothing special to tell. They didn't warn him at all. If I wasn't ramping up to have fun I'd almost feel bad for him. He was utterly disposable and didn't even know it.

"I got a picture, a location to find you, and somewhere to meet up to drop you."

"Where?"

Silence. The grin on my face, pure Cheshire cat insane delight. I bring the point of the blade to the hollow at his throat, and press down with enough force to split open his skin but not go in too deep. I drag the knife down the center of his chest, over his sternum, and down to his belly button. Noah hisses. The cut is meant to sting.

"Every time you don't answer a question, I'll trace that line again until your gut is open before me. It's going to hurt worse with every stroke."

"Fuck you."

Ah, we're back to that. So typical.

"Where were you supposed to take me?"

I ask three more times and he starts sweating and shaking, his body trying to jolt away from the knife as I press deeper with each pass. His stomach goes concave as he tries to move away from me, but there's no room for him to get away. On the last pass, I move very, very slowly. I can hear him trying to keep a whimper of pain inside. Finally, he screams out a warehouse just outside the city limits.

"Good boy," I pat Noah on the head. "Now, who hired you?"

He thinks he knows my game now, and remains silent, convinced he can take another slice down the center of his body. I'm done with that now, and instead walk over to a table by the wall and clean off my knife. With each shift of my approach, I like to start fresh.

I walk back to Noah and kneel in front of the chair. His leg has been tied very specifically and I know it was Alonzo who made this happen because he's seen me work before. There's enough room for me to remove Noah's shoes and then his socks. Most people don't know that the arch of the foot is as sensitive to being tickled as it is to pain.

Noah does not look impressed. "Going to tickle it out of me?"

The blade fits easily in the small space between the floor and the arch of his foot. I tilt the blade up and the point starts to push into the sole of his foot, the center of the arch, and he breaks almost immediately. Noah screams, trying to move his foot away but every time he tries it opens the wound further and wider.

I remove the blade and smile when he takes a deep breath, thinking he has a reprieve. I don't bother asking the question again because he knows what I want to know. Instead, I go right to the other foot, making repeated pokes and stabs as a small pool of blood forms beneath it. He's screaming and squirming, trying to escape the chair or move away from me and my persistent blade, but it won't do him any good.

Even if he managed to escape the chair somehow, Freelancer would shut him down in a minute. There are goosebumps all over my body and my nipples are hard. The excitement of this, especially when the threat was against me, makes the fire inside me turn into an inferno.

When his voice starts to become raw and hoarse, I pull back. Noah is drenched in sweat and shaking. This man started his day thinking he was a tough guy. Thinking that he could kidnap a woman with nothing but a knife, and dump her at a random warehouse. When he woke up in this room he thought he could withstand whatever we throw at him even though it's clear he's untrained. Everyone thinks they know how to withstand torture until they feel true physical pain for the first time.

This guy is some random thug that was hired to get me, who was given no context about who I was or why they wanted me, and didn't bother to do even a Google search. I've seen the message boards about me. They're very entertaining. I got on the radar after being seen with Dinah, and the speculation was a good time.

I stand before him in silence, waiting to see what his next move will be.

"Some guy who called himself Mr. Romeo," Noah finally breathes out. "I don't know how he found me, but he was going to pay me $100,000. I got half when I took the job."

I'm almost insulted at the amount but I also know that this wasn't supposed to work. Whoever hired him wasn't worried about a measly $50k - they needed it to be enticing to someone who wasn't smart enough to know better or do even the bare minimum to learn about their target. It was almost laughable.

"Did they tell you I had any protection?"

"No. They said there was nothing."

Now I was pissed and he was going to die. The insult has been heard.

"Thank you, Noah."

Whoever was running this show had made it inevitable for us to fall into the trap. They had suspected there was someone watching me and now they knew for sure. Even if I was the one that caught him, someone had been watching and knew that Freelancer was on me now.

They had taken away my feelings of safety at Designation. I never imagined someone would be brazen enough to try to interfere with me there. Fighting in the digital realm was one thing. This was something else.

Time passed as I stared down at Noah, who couldn't even meet my eyes anymore. He'd told me everything there was to tell, and I'd get no satisfaction from killing him. He wasn't the mastermind, and he didn't even know what situation he'd sunk himself into. I felt Freelancer come up behind me. He wrapped an arm across my chest and pulled me back into his body. My breathing immediately slowed and some of the fear that was building inside of me diminished.

"Let's be done with this. We got all he knows."

My body slumps against Freelancer, shaking and full of the crash of adrenaline from any questioning session. I'm adrift, torn between celebrating getting information that I wanted and knowing that it wasn't enough. We know things but nothing useful. I'm vibrating with anger and I'm going to head off a cliff into exhaustion soon. I had to do this, I had to find out what he knew, even though this was more personal than it had ever been before. This was about me, and I'll leave him to the men to decide how to end him.

I pick up a bar from the table of toys, and before I can think too much, I smack Noah in the head with it. He's out. He's out until someone else decides to play.

Bad people needed to pay for doing bad things. He paid.

I'm still shaking and I can't stop. Even when Freelancer holds me tighter. He tries to talk to me but it's like I'm hearing him from the end of a long tunnel, only catching his tone, not his words. I'm on a ride I can't get off of - I don't know how to come down. I've never had to pull myself out of torture-mode without Alina.

Freelancer takes my shoulders and shakes me slightly until I'm forced to look at him. I drown in the pattern of the mask. I need something. I need something to break the anger.

"Do you trust me?" Freelancer asks.

"Yes." I do. I trust him so much it should make me hesitate because I don't know him. I could maybe pick him out of a line up based on his body, but I wouldn't know a picture of him if I saw it. I wouldn't know it was him if I walked past him on the street.

"Go put your hands on the wall. Spread your legs. Close your eyes."

I shiver and do exactly what he says. The wall is cold and my body is so hot. It jolts me, grabbing onto a heightened awareness. There's no surveillance in this room because it isn't worth the risk. It's us, alone. I need the rest of this energy to go away, and I think I'm about to get what I need.

Freelancer comes up behind me and runs his hands up and down my body, from the sides of my breasts down to the middle of my thighs. It feels good and the tension that I've been holding since the start of the attack starts to dissipate. Being attacked did get to me. No one had ever come after me directly.

If Freelancer hadn't been there today, I would've been fine, but there's a good chance I would've been hurt much worse. By the time I'd gotten the guy tied up or even in the Tahoe, he could've woken up. It would've been a fight over and over again. Not to mention the drive back home...my mind would've been spinning out of control like it is now.

Freelancer kneels behind me and pushes my skirt up over my ass. He grabs my tights at the apex of my thighs and tugs, ripping them open all the way across my butt and down my thighs. Then he pulls down my panties, exposing me to him. He pushes on my back so that I bend down a little further, opening myself for him.

I shudder and moan the moment his rough fingers trail over my pussy lips, enjoying the tease as he barely grazes my clit. It won't take much for me to come and the way he's making my body and heart race is slowing down my racing thoughts.

"Face forward, eyes closed, or I stop."

"Okay," I promise in a voice that's very nearly whiny. I squeeze my eyes shut and press my forehead to the wall.

There's a shuffling noise and before I can ask what he's doing, I feel the swipe of his soft, warm tongue along my slit. I also feel the soft texture of facial hair. I think Freelancer has a beard. My sensitive body immediately overreacts.

"Holy shit." I moan, and I moan loud. It's all I can do to keep myself still as Freelancer starts to devour my pussy, building me up to an orgasm that will let out the rest of this insane energy. I cry out louder and harder when he sinks two fingers inside me, scissoring them and driving me up further.

His tongue and teeth attack my clit, and the hand holding on to my ass is gripping me so hard it's going to bruise. I can't wait to see those bruises days from now, and think about this moment again and again. Because it's all I'll be able to think about from tonight - not what I did, not what happened to me - I'll think about feeling him dive into my pussy for the first time and how it felt.

"Baby, you taste so fucking good," he growls from behind me. "Come on my tongue like a good girl, like my dirty little monster."

My nails dig into the wall as he licks and sucks, his fingers pressing hard into my center and massaging my favorite spot. I rock onto him, chasing the release he's giving me. I almost don't want to come because I don't want him to stop. I want this to keep going. I'm afraid it won't be enough to take me down.

He draws away from me and moves his fingers in and out with firm, slow strokes that nearly drive me up the wall. I'm so close. The edge is near and I'm going to crash over it.

"Do you like it when I call you my little monster? Do you like that watching you unleash yourself gets me hard as fuck?"

"Yes," I moan.

"Is this pussy mine, little monster?"

"Please," I whimper. I want him to move faster, but he keeps his steady, punishing pace.

"Please what, baby?"

"Make me come."

With that, he dives back into me, sucking my clit into his mouth and biting gently with his teeth. As he does this, he moves his fingers faster and it's the sensory attack I need to explode.

I scream, grinding into his face and onto his fingers as the world around me disappears. There's nothing but the feeling, the pleasure, and it goes on for a long time. When my pussy relaxes, he slides his fingers out of me but continues to lick from my clit to my asshole, lapping up my release. It's soothing after the insanity of the last few hours and that orgasm.

When he stops, I hear him put his mask back on. His hands are warm when they pull my skirt back down to cover me, and then he's pulling me back until my knees bend and I fall into his lap. His big arms wrap around me, and I disappear inside the cradle of his body. First, he gave me my release, and now he's giving me recovery. It's something I never experienced before and didn't realize that I needed.

It grounds me and pulls me back the rest of the way into my body from the place I disappear to deep inside my mind. The anger is fading, the shaking is slowing, and I can breathe deep again. I'm safe. I'm okay. Right now, nothing can touch me.

"It smells like pussy in here." I can hear the humor in his voice.

"Good."

We stay like that a little longer before I extricate myself from him and stand. He's still sitting on the floor. I take his masked face in my hands, and he stiffens until he realizes I'm not trying to remove the mask.

"Are you ever going to let me see you?" I didn't mean to ask the question, but my walls are down right now and I'm vulnerable.

"Yes."

"Okay." I nod, and then leave the room without looking back. I need to crash. As I get to other side of the basement, the part where we have a game room and we use it like normal people might use their basement, Gailen stands up and approaches me.

He puts a hand on my arm, cupping my elbow and pulling me close. "Are you alright? Do you need anything?" I'd have thought his first questions would be about what information I gathered, but Gailen is completely focused on me. His thumb is running back and forth over my arm and it's too much. I slide out of his hold and step back.

I shake my head, unable to speak yet, letting the release flood through me. Today was too much. I need to be alone. Without a word, I flee the basement. It's not the first time I've behaved like this after an interrogation. It won't be the last. I have to get away.

12

Freelancer

After eating Aster's pussy and seeing that she was safely in her room, someone else had a date with my knife. I left the would-be kidnapper to the devices of the Sorrelle guards. I'm sure he's already dead.

It didn't take long to get to the warehouse on the outside of the city, and the place was all lit up and waiting for my arrival.

There was a man there, waiting. It took me seconds to subdue him, and the warehouse was already set up for a captive. Except the captive was supposed to have been Aster. The chances of the kidnapping attempt working were low, but it didn't appear that the man at the warehouse was aware of that.

He had it all set for torturing my woman. There was a table for him to strap her down, tools on another table next to that, and a fucking dog kennel where he was going to keep her, or potentially for later transport. I strap him down to the table. I have to make some adjustments since they were set to Aster's tiny specifications when he set them up.

When he comes to, I'm not wearing my mask. I want to feel this motherfucker's blood on my skin as I peel off his while he gives me fucking answers.

Skin rips. Easier than you think.

All it takes is the right cut in the right place and you can begin the painful and informative process of skinning a man alive. I would do worse for Aster. I would do worse to keep her safe, to solve this problem, so that I can be with her without barriers. So I can pursue her in the way that she deserves and the way that she needs.

I don't bother asking his name because it's irrelevant. It doesn't take much to get him to start spilling everything. Aster likes to play with her toys. I like to break mine, and they break quickly. They will tell me anything I want once they are resigned to their deaths because death will be a release from what I put them through. The pain is exquisite.

I find out he was hired by Mr. Romeo as well, but he knew a little more. He was given more specific instructions. He'd never tortured anyone before but he wanted to try - he was in a forum on the dark web talking about this specific, sick fantasy, and that was how Mr. Romeo found him. He could do whatever he wanted to Aster, as long as she was still alive at the end of it for Mr. Romeo to come and get her. He was also banned from doing any damage to her hands, as she would need them. He had been given 48 hours to have his fun before she was going to be collected.

This sick fucker had all sorts of shit on that table, but I guarantee she would have been able to withstand it all. He didn't have the skills, the patience, or the true motivation. Torture for fun is a fantasy that gets pathetic men off, but they rarely have the true lust for that kind of thing. He sure as shit didn't.

I do. He dies slowly, screaming and struggling to breathe through the pain. I can see his exposed muscles twitching, and I watch the light leave his eyes. Then I take off all my clothes, clean the blood from my skin, and burn it and him. I sure hope there's no one to miss him because they had no idea what kind of creature was in their midst.

Two days later, I go back. No one comes. They know she's safe.

Aster avoids me as if it's something she can do. As if I'm not already invisibly entwined in her life. I'm at her house before she wakes up in the morning, I'm at work all day with her, and then I follow her home or wherever she chooses to go.

When she thinks she's retreating to the safety of her room - it's temporary. When the lights go out I stand in the dark of her space, listening to her breathe, listening to her moan when she gets restless and masturbates. I've heard her talk and whimper in her sleep. Sometimes I sit next to her on the bed - she settles when I touch her, the nightmares slipping away and her body going deeper into sleep. Someday soon I'll wake her in the darkness.

I've cloned her phone so I see every message she sends and receives, every song she listens to and video she watches, every random google search, and what she does with every app she has. I know what kind of porn she likes to watch and read. I know her comfort shows and favorite episodes, the podcasts she listens to, every random thought in her notes app. Sometimes when she's bored she uses a coloring book app and I find it relaxing to watch the colors appear and fill in on the picture. Imagining her dainty fingers poking at the screen, the soft tap of her nails on the surface, makes my brain tingle.

I know she feels the same energy that I do, and I know she'll come back to me when she's ready. This kind of thing is overwhelming to me, I can't imagine how it feels for her. I'll be here, waiting. We have time, even if it doesn't seem like it.

The kidnapping attempt bothered her, even if she had fun with the interrogation at first. Aster is young, and hardly the one someone would use for leverage. They'd take Anora for that. She's always been fighting from the shadows and this thrust her into light and attention she wasn't ready for.

I've watched the guards follow her more closely than before, and the way she gets tense in their presence. Gailen does it personally most of the time, and I watch as they get in a fight. He keeps trying to touch her and she keeps pulling away, and I want to cut off his fucking hands. She says something that makes him angry. After that, she's with Nino all the time, and I find out that she agreed to have a guard with her when she's outside of her room as long as it's him.

Nino seems like he doesn't give a shit in meetings, but he's not like that with Aster. It takes me a little bit of observation to realize that he doesn't want to talk, he wants to act. When he's with Aster he's alert but gives her space. They do talk, and their friendship seems genuine. I'm glad she at least has someone she trusts if I can't be by her side.

It makes me miss her.

How can I miss her? I've done a lot of fucked up things in my life - even beyond killing, when you're in the underworld, you get pulled into some weird shit from time to time. Somehow, the thing that feels the strangest is falling for a woman who doesn't know she's seen my face, looked into my eyes, laughed at my jokes. A woman who wants the me behind the mask, rabidly, dangerously, who I would let claw through my skin, literally.

She's the most dangerous person I've ever encountered.

13

Aster

Things are good. We finally made progress against the hacker.

Thor and Isaac worked together to develop a new firewall specific to their method of attack, and Dominic logged every attempt and it gave me data to start picking apart. The way a hacker attacks helps me create a profile. Yes, I've watched a lot of *Criminal Minds*, and that got me to read a lot of books, which helps me realize that a hack is like any other serial crime. It can be profiled, and the way someone attacks is incredibly personal.

This hacker follows a pattern, and I think we've been so successful at keeping them out that they are starting to get lazy and bored. It's the same attempts, in the same order, through different access points into our system. They could also be inexperienced and unaware of the need to vary their approaches. The next time they try, if they do this again, that will give me even more information.

It's not enough to find out who they are, but it might help us to form an offense rather than constant defense. Defense is making me itchy. Defense is making me feel the crawl in my skin that tells me I need to hunt.

At the office, since the attack, I haven't engaged much with everyone else. Tella runs interference without me having to ask and I appreciate her for that. My desk is abandoned for a dark corner of the room. None of us use the overhead fluorescents and instead we've got all these soft, yellow desk lamps and some LEDs because we're actually cave people who like to work in the dark.

Things got intense after my interrogation and I've been avoiding Freelancer. He makes me feel too much and I let him touch me too easily. None of my reactions around him are normal for me. I relax, I can be touched, and I want to touch him. I don't touch people. Even when I let them hug me I don't hug back. Freelancer makes things blurry for my boundaries and I need to decide how I feel about that, and what I need to hold on to in order to survive.

It's changing my view of myself and I'm reeling a little.

My sister Alina was always focused toward the future. She trained to be a soldier and protect our family and always be someone who faded into the background - an invisible protector. The extent of her sense of self was duty to family, duty to us. No marriage, no kids, no obligations outside of protecting my dad, Owen, and her sisters.

Then she had a one night stand with the guy who ended up being in a business arrangement with dad to marry Anora. Suddenly, Alina was getting married instead, leaving us in a matter of days, and life got fucking weird. The interrogation the other night was the first time she wasn't there to take care of me and make sure I didn't lose myself. Freelancer had helped, but I was used to Alina coming into my room and laying down next to me until I told her it was okay to go.

That night I laid in the dark, staring at nothing. I didn't sleep.

So I've pulled back.

I've been running at least 10 miles every morning, unable to control the restlessness. Unable to control my heart racing for reasons it's never been affected by before. There is something wrong with me. I'm on the edge of obsession.

It's not that our unconventional relationship bothers me, it's that it can't be all I have or I'll spiral into something else. Right now, I can't rely on him for other things that I need to keep my head above water rather than sink into the feral murder beast that takes over when my emotions aren't kept in check. I need someone to be there to make sure I'm pulled all the way back into my rational self. I don't know if he'd pull me back, or if we'd dive into monstrosity together.

He's texted a few times but I haven't responded, and I haven't let myself be alone for him to find me. Every day when I go home I retreat to the darkness of my room, put on whatever music seems to work that day, and stare into the nothing until I fall asleep. There's plenty of thoughts - intrusive and otherwise - but there's no motivation to get out of my bed and do anything. So I think about dying, and how to die, but instead I breathe and do nothing.

It's Friday, and I can see Dominic and Tella whispering to each other. Tella is texting on her phone, and guarding the door, which means they're up to something. Isaac's and Thor's phones buzz at their work stations, and they both move simultaneously to check the notification.

"No," Thor says from his corner.

"Yes," Tella challenges him. "It's team bonding."

Oh, for fuck's sake.

Thor turns to me. "Boss?"

I'm not sure how to answer him. Tella and Dominic clearly have a plan, they told Isaac and Thor before approaching me because they're going for the peer pressure approach. It's true that team leads like myself are encouraged by our supervisor, Marie, to do team activities outside of the office to increase our team connection. This was apparently Owen's idea, who is one of the least teamy people I know after myself, and I keep forgetting to corner him and ask what the hell.

"We are expected to do team activities outside of work." It's as close as I'll get to agreement. Damn it.

74

"Fine." Thor turns back to his computer.

Tella smiles at me in an overly cheery way that tells me whatever this is, I'm going to hate the absolute fuck out of it.

"We're going to Baile. Manuel is meeting us there - time to dance!" She does a little step and the skirt of her dress swings around her tan, shapely legs. I know the club she's talking about - it's mostly Latin music and some modern stuff, it's less grindy than the usual club and more actual dancing.

When the day ends, Tella has already organized everything. I drove with Owen, so she's going to drive me and Thor, then Dominic and Isaac will drive together. Tonight is going to be very hard unless I do something very stupid. Maybe I'm due for some stupid.

Tella drags us all inside. The club is nice inside - all warm colors and wood, very classy. Manuel has already claimed a table for all of us, and moments after sitting down the server is already bringing us a pitcher of margaritas. That's a good start, but it's not enough, and I ask for shots of tequila.

Everyone stares at me, shocked. They have reason to be - we've gone out plenty of times and I've never had anything other than water, maybe a soda. Well, they are about to see a whole new Aster Sorrelle.

I don't wait for the rest of the table to take their shot, and I don't use salt or lime. It isn't bad tequila, but not great either. With a weird look on his face, Thor slides his shot over to me and I take his too.

Like a break in reality, everyone starts talking to each other at once so they don't have to talk about what just happened with me. I think all of them except Thor know me well enough to know that if they ask me anything, I'm not going to tell them. They talk around me as I drink, waiting for the tequila to hit, and for everything inside me to relax.

Isaac's hand brushes the outside of my thigh. "You good?" I like his voice when he whispers like that. Working in the dark all the time has a tendency to make you speak quietly as well, and I'm used to him talking in a low voice. But drunk me really likes his voice. I get a little tingle at the base of my skull.

"I'm great," I give him a sarcastic smile, no teeth. Then I laugh.

"She just wants to have a good time," Dominic leans over on my other side, and I'm smooshed between them, and I find that hilarious. When I let out a giggle, they both look at me with something close to horror.

"I want to go numb. We should dance." I wiggle in my seat.

The music winds it's way through my barriers and into my ears, and I can feel the rhythm of it in my chest. The dance floor is decently full with both people who are moving to move, and people who actually know how to dance to this music. I am the former, and I go to an open space and start moving my body. Isaac and Dominic follow and stand guard, giving a look to any guy who starts to come close to me.

Manuel is moving Tella around the dance floor, an elegant pair that are obviously, wildly in love with each other. I almost feel jealousy watching as their hips move together, and he possessively puts his hand on the curve of her ass. Tella blushes. Because she's fucking precious. I want to squish her cheeks. The ones on her face.

I walk back to our table. Really, I stomp back, because I'm just over the line into drunk and when I stomp I feel steadier on my feet. I fill up my glass and then gulp it down, enjoying the sour of the lime and the tang of the tequila. I really like tequila.

My phone buzzes and I pull it out of my pocket.

What are you doing?

I give my phone the finger, and put it back in my pocket without responding. Even if he's here and watching from somewhere, he has no say in what I do. I have to go about my life as if nothing is affecting me. I can't let anything affect me. I am a stone and inside I am a calm pond. I cannot be a wildfire, and I cannot be a rushing river.

My thoughts move quickly, and I pour more margarita.

"Dance with me." Dominic demands and then pulls me onto the floor without waiting for me to answer or letting me drink my drink. The club is playing more modern music, and I'm moving to the rhythm of "Smooth" by Santana and Rob Thomas, mouthing the words. Dominic watches my mouth move and raises his eyebrows in surprise.

"What?" I challenge him, holding on to his t-shirt to keep myself steady.

"Wouldn't have thought this was your jam."

I whip my arm up and almost hit him in the face, then point accusingly. "Everything is my goddamn jam. I like everything. Everything!" I shout, throwing my arms out. I roll my hips and move my body to the music.

After a moment, hands rest on my hips, and I know that it's Isaac. I don't know how I know - do I smell him? Did I see him coming up behind me in my periphery? Or is it because I know that Dominic would never let any dude who isn't with us get that close to me? It can't be that I know Isaac.

He leans down next to me, his beard brushing my cheek, the edge of his glasses grazing my temple, and I have a flashback to Freelancer doing the same thing, his mask rubbing my skin as he edged me to a brilliant orgasm. I shiver and my nipples get tight and hard, my panties starting to get damp.

I forgot that when I get drunk I also get horny.

"Do you want to go?" he asks me. Then he pulls away, respecting my usual need for distance.

I tip my head back, still holding on to Dominic's shirt although he isn't touching me. The move presses my hips into his. The top of my head rests on Isaac's chest. I am sandwiched between the two of them and my body is so very aware of that. They are both quite pretty and although I've never been in to group work, the flash of the three of us naked and sweaty and both of them focused on me is not unappealing.

"Not yet," I say, my voice high and a little slurred.

I put one hand on Dominic's neck to help me keep my balance as I lift my head upright again. Then I bring my other hand behind me and dive into Isaac's hair and keep him close to me too. The men share a look but I'm too drunk to understand it. Dominic lets me hold onto him, and then Isaac presses into me from behind. There is very little space between the three of us. All of my senses are awake and I can feel so much.

The warmth of Dominic's skin beneath my touch. The silky glide of Isaac's hair on my fingertips. Dominic's stomach pressing against mine when he breathes deep, and the same press of Isaac into my back. We're all breathing deep and hard, caught up in my drunken mess of a moment.

We aren't grinding hard or doing anything obnoxious, just touching each other and kind of swaying to the music, moving softly. It's relaxing more than anything, even though I am astronomically horny. I know they are too because I can feel Dominic against my leg, and Isaac against my ass. I shimmy a little and even drunk I catch the barely suppressed groan from Isaac.

At some point, I'm not sure how much later, the signal to stop all of this gets through from my brain to my body. I turn and place a hand on each of their chests, pushing them away from me. Neither stops or resists, going with the flow and I think very aware of exactly how intoxicated I am.

It goes to show how much I trust them both that not once in that entire interaction did I get bad vibes from them, or even consider that they would take advantage of me. Not only because they were under the watchful eye of Manuel and Tella either. It's not in their nature. Even if both of them are attracted to me in some way - Isaac I knew but Dominic's response was kind of a surprise - they would never do anything without me being fully present. Both of them know that I get weird about touching sometimes, and even my blurry recollections are of the two of them letting me take the lead.

I know good people. Good people exist in this world. I need to remind myself of that sometimes - I need to go out and see it and live it. Good people need protecting, and that's why I have to take down the bad ones.

I stomp away, still using my tried and true method for walking strong while drunk. They call after me and I wave my arms hoping they understand that I'm headed to the bathroom. My phone vibrates in my pocket, going off again and again, buzzing from text message after text message. I'm so sexually on edge that even that gets me more turned on.

The bathroom is empty, and I make my way into a stall and break the seal. Part of me doesn't want to check my messages because I have a feeling I know who they are from. I've been avoiding him, he's tracking my every move, and he probably watched me get all up close and grindy with my coworkers while drunk.

I haven't been drunk in 2 years.

The last time I was drunk was the first and only time someone tried to take advantage of me without that being part of the plan. I let some friends from my graduate program talk me into going out with them to a club. We were a bunch of computer nerds trying to find a good time. They were good and safe people, my instincts were right about that, but I'm fucking small and got separated from them after a few too many shots in honor of Ada Lovelace.

Some guy had grabbed my wrist and started dragging me away, down the hall and out into the back alley. I could've gotten him off of me the second he grabbed me, even drunk, but with all my barriers lowered I was curious, and I was spoiling for a fight if I wasn't going to fuck. He thought he'd hit the jackpot - tiny, drunk, defenseless.

What he got instead was a knife to the testicle, and then my blade through the soft skin of the underside of his chin, one hard tug slicing open his windpipe. I'm still not entirely sure how I got away with it, but later one of the people in my cohort told us all about a murder the night we went out, and that the guy was a serial rapist with warrants out for his arrest. The police thought the murder might have been revenge for one of his victims.

I hope they felt avenged. The women he'd harmed. I hope they felt peace knowing he wasn't rotting in a cell but cremated and stored in a cabinet because there was no one to claim his remains. I thought about doing it and spreading them at a sewage plant or something, but if anyone had been looking for his killer, a completely random and unconnected woman claiming his ashes would look pretty suspicious.

That's what gave me the idea of vigilantism to get the itch out from under my skin, and the pain that was still burrowed inside me so deep. I wanted to kill, so why not kill bad guys?

Taking a deep, cleansing breath that wasn't going to do shit, I open up my messages. They were all from Freelancer.

I know you think you can avoid me but it's my job to stalk your ass. I know and see everything you do, baby.

I could smell your pussy even before you let those two assholes get on you.

They're lucky they were respectful or they'd both be missing their dicks by now.

You're fucking mine, little monster. There's nothing you can do to break the connection between us.

Next time we're alone I'm going to pound that pussy into submission, until you can't think of ever being with any man except me.

You need something in that tiny fine ass of yours while I fuck you? That's what toys are for. That pussy is mine, that ass is mine, that perfect mouth is fucking mine. I will never share you.

Another message comes in as I sit there.

If you don't hurry up I'm coming in there, and you won't like the results.

I believe him. I put myself back together, wash my hands, and stomp back to the table where my team has reassembled. Part of me is burning with curiosity about what Freelancer would have done, but despite his factual statements about him being my hired stalker, I am still not ready to be in his presence. I don't look around the bar to see if I can figure out which person is him because I'm not ready to know.

I'm scared as fuck because my emotions are hard enough to handle without throwing this kind of attraction in there. Having feelings for Freelancer is committing arson against all of the barriers and boundaries I have within myself. It's freeing all of my darkness, all of my impulses, and seeing what happens when they come out to play.

Before him, even drunk, I never would've let myself be between Dominic and Isaac like that. That was too much touching, too much drama. On the other hand, some of the walls that Freelancer has crushed gave me a new perspective on our hacker problem.

I might be getting orgasms out of it all, but I haven't decided yet if he's going to be my downfall, or my salvation.

14

Aster

Things are weird with Dominic and Isaac for a little while after the night at Baile. They both keep finding reasons to touch me or be around me. They both know I hate that shit but can't seem to stop themselves. I don't react and they eventually stop with the touching.

I can't go anywhere in Designation without one of them clinging to me like a barnacle. Usually Isaac, which I mind less. Dominic can be a bit too much for me sometimes. It's like I'm in the middle of a tug of war and we're pretending I don't know I'm the rope.

Things have been tense between them. They don't talk as much and stopped sitting next to each other. I feel like an asshole but I also blame Tella and Freelancer. Tella for making us go out together and Freelancer for making me emotionally unbalanced which led to stupid decisions.

I can't handle the tension so try my best to sneak out of our workroom without anyone noticing. When no one follows me, I make my way to the staircase and head to the roof of the campus. It's not a high building but it's wide. Someone put chairs up there years ago and I like to get some air sometimes.

The sky is heavy and dark with thunderheads. We're due for a summer storm today and I'm looking forward to it. As soon as the rain starts I might skip out early to enjoy it. It reminds me that I need to pick a time to visit Alina. She thinks I'd like Seattle and I agree.

When I get to the chairs, one of them is already occupied. By Isaac. I didn't even notice him leave let alone realize that he wasn't there when I left the room. It goes to show how off my game I am.

That's a huge problem considering someone is trying to kidnap me.

"Hey." Isaac pulls me from my thoughts and my eyes from the cloudy sky. In this light he looks tired, and I hate that I haven't noticed that either. He's always so put together - a dress shirt, a tie, and his sleeves are always buttoned at the wrists. It makes me wonder if it's a mask he wears for whatever is going on inside him. That if he dresses the part it'll change him somehow.

I sit down in the chair next to him and watch the heavy clouds move in on the wind. It should feel ominous but for me it feels peaceful. People who are shitty planners are deterred easily, and a thunderstorm is a good deterrent.

"How did you end up here?" I ask.

"When a man and a woman fuck sometimes they don't use protection…"

"Shut up." I laugh. Isaac is one of the only people who ever makes me laugh. "I mean coding, Designation- why here? Who are you?" Despite the fact that I read his resume and agreed with his hiring, I don't know much of anything about him.

Isaac stares for a moment, and I contemplate how deep of a question I'd asked. I wasn't expecting a deep answer, but I'd listen if he was willing to give it to me.

"I have an older brother - he's not a good person. I'm not perfect, but he's evil."

"Do you believe in evil?"

He looks over at me. "Don't you?"

I don't answer him because it's a word that's been applied to me before.

"My parents knew he was different, even when he was young. They got pregnant with me on accident and maybe they thought they'd get a do over with me. Except he took up all of their energy, all of their time, and it meant I grew up alone. Occasionally shoved into therapy. Computers were there when people weren't, and I understood how they worked. Coding follows rules. Other things happened that got me here, but it also got me away. I haven't spoken to my parents or my brother since I turned 18."

"What happened to him?"

"He joined the military. As far as I know, he's still serving."

I sit with that information and let it sink in to my brain and mesh with what I know of the Isaac that I interact with every day. He does strike me as lonely, even when he and Dominic spend time together. Dominic is gregarious and friendly - being his friend isn't a choice. He chooses you, and you are friends. End of.

Isaac probably needed someone like that in his life. It also explains why he's always understanding of me and all my weird anti-social ticks.

"Did he ever hurt you?" My voice is timid and Isaac has no idea how much this question matters. I know I have dark, terrible impulses. I know I'm capable of turning off my feelings and doing unspeakable things in the name of vengeance or to protect my family. I would never, ever hurt my sisters or dad though.

"Surprisingly, no. I know he hurt my parents, and other people, but he was oddly protective of me. I think it's why I can't hate him, even when it would've made my life easier."

Silence falls between us again, and it's comfortable.

"I'm glad you're here," I say quietly.

Isaac doesn't answer. This is the most at peace I've felt in weeks.

Even though he's been kind of annoying after the whole club thing, this is what I needed. I needed to feel like I wasn't alone in a simple way. I needed something to feel easy, normal, and natural. Sitting on a roof, watching a storm come in, beside a person who likes the version of me they see. The awkward programmer, the insecure woman, the stressed out team lead. All of those aspects of myself and I never get anything but acceptance from Isaac.

"We're going to catch this asshole," he says out of nowhere. "We are smarter than they are - there's something we're not seeing."

"I know. I know there's something we're missing."

At that moment, both of our phones buzz. When I look at the screen and the message there, my heart crashes down into my stomach. Isaac and I are running to the door to the stairs without another word.

15

Aster

When we get onto our floor, it's complete fucking chaos. People are running all over, the doors to the server room are wide open, and the internal data teams, of which we are one, are pooled together in the hall trying to communicate with each other.

A harsh whistle sounds out next to me, and silence descends. Isaac got everyone's attention, and they all turn to me. I might be another lead programmer in title, but I'm a Sorrelle in name. I take a deep breath, and feel warmth spread through me when Isaac puts a reassuring hand on my lower back. That's not a gesture I'd think would comfort me, but it does.

"Marie," I address our boss. "Brief Owen." She nods, and leaves immediately.

I turn to Dave, one of the other leads. "It's the internal server?" He nods in confirmation. "You and Kelly's team get it back up and running, or get a backup working. Trent, start working on rebuilding security. My team will start working on the hack. Jan, you need to be tracking security on the external servers."

Everyone nods and when it's clear I'm not going to say anything else, they head off in the direction they're needed. Isaac and I go back into our work room, and I know it's bad because the overhead lights are on. We are in full shit show mode.

"Tella!" I shout a little to get her to focus on me. She's the kind of person who needs a little bit of a jolt to get her out of a panic spiral. "Take a breath, get to work." She nods at me, and calms down enough to do what I ask.

Thor, Isaac, and Dominic are already circled up, tearing through the code. It will be on me to go through the server and see what got accessed and modified or damaged. The internal server, this particular one, is a weird thing to hack. The base codes we were sure they were after isn't even on this server. The server basically holds a lot of our internal functions and documents, it's the basic stuff we all access every day.

Maybe that's the real point.

This time they weren't trying to take or access anything, it was to create chaos. We'd be breached, we'd scramble to fix it and protect ourselves, and we'd lose time and focus trying to protect low level information because any hack is bad.

That makes us vulnerable. This is misdirection somehow.

"Isaac," I call. He comes over to me and I step back, out of everyone else's earshot.

"Something is off about this."

He frowns. "What do you mean?"

"That server isn't important. It's not anything they've tried for in the past."

Isaac thinks for a minute. "You think this is a cover for something else?"

"Yes. But what?" I start to chew on my thumb and Isaac reaches out and pulls it away. He has nice hands, and his skin is surprisingly rough on the thin skin of my wrist. It's also warm, and a little shock travels up my arm that is not unpleasant. We both look at his hand and then he drops it.

"Let's go talk to Owen." I take a few steps back and he follows me. Everyone on the team is doing their things so they won't miss us. Isaac stays a few steps behind me as we cross the floor to the elevators. The silence on the ride is awkward.

We make our way up to the 7th floor, and to what I refer to as the Tower. Designation is a big flat building, but the front pinnacle has three extra floors where the executives do their evil overlording. Two of those overlords live in my house and eat breakfast with me every day, but I can't fight the fuck the man streak that comes with the work that I do.

Owen's door is open when I walk over to his suite, and his admin doesn't bother trying to stop me but gives me the nod that he's not doing anything I'll get in trouble for interrupting.

He's clicking away angrily at his computer. If he does it any harder he's going to break his mouse. There's something about his expression that reminds me of my dad when he's in work mode, and I take it as further evidence of the way people who spend time together mirror one another. He looks nothing like our family - we're all tan and dark - while he's got golden hair and pink skin - and yet, he looks like us in expression and mannerisms because he's with us all the time.

I don't know how Owen feels about us, or if he thinks of us as family. At the end of the day, I think of him as someone that I trust. Trust is given sparingly by me, and Owen knows it. He doesn't underestimate the value of my trust, and it's why he lets me run a little wild at Designation. It's definitely nepotism but it works out to their benefit.

"Aster," he grumbles at me.

I flop into the chair across from his desk. Isaac is paused inside the office door, looking from Owen, to me, to the other empty chair. Isaac and Owen make eye contact, and then Isaac slowly makes his way to the other chair. I'm not actually sure why I brought him up here with me, but it felt like the right thing to do. Maybe because he went with my thought process and didn't question it as paranoid or improbable.

"I think the hack is misdirection for something else."

"For what?" Owen rests his forearms on his desk and knits his hands together.

"I don't know - I came to you because I know my little island well but I think this needs a bigger picture look."

"Talk me through it," he says. There it is. Owen's trust in me. If I had a brother, I'd like him to be pretty close to like Owen. Scary, aloof, but smart as fuck.

"The server they got into doesn't have anything useful - I suspect it was crashed as a distraction and a disruption; it only interrupts internal work and functions. Any breach makes us go crazy though, so currently all our focus is on the internal systems and protecting it from outside intrusion. What protocols go into effect that might leave something else vulnerable?"

Owen thinks for a moment, and in the silence I let my brain wander. When it goes off on it's own, sometimes it leads me interesting places as it fits different pieces of information together. Most days I don't feel like I'm in charge of my own brain, I'm just strapped in for the ride.

"What happens with physical security?" Isaac asks.

"Additional staff is called in, even in a cyber breach."

"Where does the security come from?" I ask, and lean forward in my seat, my brain tickling at the edge of something.

"Founders Security; it's who we always use when additional staff are needed."

"Hm." I whip out my phone and get to work, ripping through their protections and getting into all the nitty gritty. Founders is owned by a shell company, and it's name is not unfamiliar to me. I don't even have to dig deeper. This is not good.

"Who's idea was it to use Founders? How long have we used them?"

"We entered into a contract with them two years ago, after that attack on the farm." Two years ago someone had tried to break into one of our data storage farms. We had to add physical security for awhile until we could hire full time staff to guard it.

"They're owned by the Forresters."

Owen freezes. "What?"

"The shell company that owns Founders Security is the Forresters."

"Who are the Forresters?" Isaac asks. He and Owen share another weird look that I can't interpret.

"Dickheads," I answer when Owen doesn't. "Old money assholes with their fingers in all the fucking pies."

There's a long moment of silent tension. "Where did extra security get assigned?" Isaac asks.

Owen pulls up a document on his computer. "Four men to the farms offsite, and three additional men to internal areas here."

"Where?"

When Owen swallows and takes a moment before answering me, I already know we're fucked. "Unit 3."

"Fuck."

Without waiting for any further conversation, I leave the office. Isaac doesn't follow and I can barely hear the murmurs of the two of them talking, but I don't have time to think about that too much right now.

Unit 3 is basically an internal digital safe. Things have to be physically taken down to the server there and uploaded. It's not connected to any kind of internet and the only way to hack into is it to be onsite. It's why we haven't been in panic mode about someone trying to get the base codes for our security software. They'd only get bits and pieces that are actively used - the full code itself is in the server in Unit 3.

I don't bother with the elevator and run down the stairs. Unit 3 is, of course, in the basement. Nothing is down there but the facilities maintenance storage and then Unit 3. There are only 4 people who have access to that room during regular times, but in a crisis the security would be modified. That makes perfect sense.

That means they might have let someone inside the room in addition to outside security. Or that someone would have the uninterrupted time to break into the room itself.

My worst fears are proven when I run down the hall and turn the corner. The Unit 3 door is open, and the body of one of the guards is on the ground, dead or unconscious. My brain and body automatically slip into vengeance mode.

I slow my steps, I steady my breathing, and I sneak up on the door to look inside. There are two men in guard uniforms - one of them has a small laptop hooked into the server, and I'm pleased to see he looks frustrated. The other man is standing with a gun at his side, not as vigilant as he should be.

The guard on the ground isn't armed, and I'm annoyed. He is breathing, however.

I take off his shoe, and throw it down the hall way. The sound echoes, and I can almost feel the men in the room go stiff at the sound. I hear footsteps, and then the armed one comes out of the room, gun aimed forward, looking for the source of the sound.

He's no match for my Subcom, and he doesn't see me standing in the corner next to the door, where the shadows obscure me.

When he's far enough in front of me, I step smoothly behind him and jam my foot into his knee. Instantly, he bends and goes down, gun flailing wildly. Honestly, who the fuck is training these losers?

My hand grips his hair and I yank his head back, exposing his throat. Before he can say a word or fight back, the Subcom leaves a bloody smile behind with a quick slash of my arm. I let him go and he slumps forward, a pool of blood rapidly spreading out from his body.

The man in the room is still typing, unaware that he's in danger. When I step into the room, his partner's blood dripping from my knife, he doesn't even look up.

"What was it?" he asks.

When I don't answer, he finally looks up. There's fear on his face, and then he steps back, taking his hands off his keyboard and putting them up in the air.

"It was just a job," he stutters out.

"How far did you get?"

"Nowhere. I got nowhere."

"You better hope that's true." I tilt my ahead and assess him. Physically, he'll be easy peasy. The real question is, do I need to keep him alive for information purposes? Since I'll have his computer I'll be able to find out a lot about him, but he's working directly for a company that setup this infiltration. He might know more.

I could get him to tell me more.

I run at him and in terror he stumbles back, slamming into the wall. When I jump on him, we fall down to the floor in a wild tumble, but I've got a good grip on him. My hands are wrapped around his skull, and I slam it to the floor until the fight goes out of him. Just in case, I check his pulse.

Good. I didn't kill him.

I sit on his chest and take out my phone. "I've got them. One dead, one unconscious. One guard hurt."

"Stay there until extraction arrives."

I hang up the phone on Owen and then get up to look at the laptop hooked into the vault. He was running a series of programs that were meant to confuse the security - they were trying to overload the program by having too many different kinds of attacks at once. It's not a bad idea, and I'll have to take that into consideration when we're building and strengthening our other systems.

From what I can tell, the method wasn't working. I start shutting down different programs, reading over the code quickly and trying to see if there's anything that I recognize. I can figure out if the man who I gave a hell of a headache and maybe a concussion to, is also our hacker. Nothing matches from a quick scan, but the team and I will spend all our free time now ripping apart everything on here and finding ways to fight it.

I hear footsteps and turn, on alert, knife out.

Alonzo and Gailen come around the corner. They rush to the bodies on the floor, stepping around the blood. Alonzo takes care of the guard, and Gailen comes straight to me. Without a word, he hands me zip ties and I wrap the present that's still unconscious on the ground.

"You good?" he asks.

"Yeah. We made it in time."

"That's not what I asked," Gailen says. He waits.

"I'm fucking angry, but I'll be fine. Can this wait until I get home?" I gesture at the hacker. It's barely past lunch time and I still have a lot of shit to get done, especially given this turn of events.

"Do we need to wait for you?"

"Can you ask him about his coding and programming?"

Gailen grimaces. "No."

I smirk at him, and he punches me in the shoulder. "Be good."

"Never," I reply, as I walk past him and into the hallway. I don't look back, and I don't have any regrets.

By the time I make it upstairs with the laptop, Isaac is back as well. Everyone stops and looks at me, and I look down at myself making sure that I didn't get any blood on me so I won't have anything to explain. I have no idea what Isaac told them. As far as I know, he doesn't know what Unit 3 is and I doubt that Owen would've told him. Few people knew about it, and the only ones with access were Owen, dad, me, and Marco, our head of security for Designation.

"Someone tried a hard hack. This is their laptop." Isaac reaches out for it but I move past him to Dominic. "Get everything on here mirrored and onto our server. He's not the hacker we've been dealing with but I want to know everything he was running, and anything else that might be useful on here."

"You got it, boss," Dominic answers.

16

Aster

The rest of the day flew by in a mess of code until my eyes started to hurt. We called it a day at our regular time because at least we knew everything was secure, and we also knew not much would get done if we didn't recover and get some rest. Despite computer nerd reputations for existing at all hours on energy drinks, professionals like us knew better. I tried to take care of my team even though they would've stayed all night with me if I had asked.

Plus, I had other things to do.

The interrogation of the thief was a complete bust. He didn't know much outside of the method he was contacted and that he'd be working with Founders Security for awhile to create a solid cover until they were given word that they would be infiltrating Designation under the guise of extra security. He hadn't met his partner before that day and didn't even know his name.

We lived in a world where it was easier to remain anonymous than you'd think, and our attacker was still very good at hiding in the shadows. Mr. Romeo came up again but that was a dumb alias that leads nowhere.

I was on edge. I couldn't settle down, couldn't take a deep breath. I hadn't even finished off the hacker and turned things over to Gailen because I needed to get out of that room. Looking at our captive was like a visual reminder of my failure. The proof of it was tied to a goddamn chair. I hadn't done enough. I wasn't good enough.

My skin is crawling and my stomach is a black hole.

I need something I can control. I need to hunt.

Tonight, I go after my white fucking whale - Ryan Volkov.

This one is a little bit personal. It's why it's the perfect time. I need redemption, and I want to get vengeance for one of his victims in particular. It's her that's on my mind as I get ready tonight. I text Dinah for his location.

She replies quickly: *Are you sure?*

I tell her that I am, and that there's no reason to put it off anymore. In a way, I've been hiding from this. Not anymore. She sends me his location and it's exactly where I expected him to be. I'm ready for this.

I wear a soft blue dress with a skirt that lands at mid-thigh, but swishes gently when I walk. I'm wearing pale pink low tops, and I keep my makeup light and demure. In the mirror, I practice looking innocent and vulnerable. A lot of people make that assumption because of my size, but this needs to go deeper. If I'm going to reel him in, I have to play the part.

Owen and dad stayed at the office, I have no idea where Anora is, and Aro is in the library. It's easy to sneak out, and I ignore the reality of Freelancer's existence. I need this, and he isn't going to stop me. No one is paying attention today, and that's what I'm counting on.

The cab is waiting in my usual spot, and I make myself get into character right away. I sound hesitant and gentle, using a higher pitch to my voice than where I'm naturally comfortable. The cab driver is a woman, and she keeps giving me worried looks as we drive into the city and to the club.

It's owned by Ryan's dad, because everything he does is with daddy's money, including cover up a rape. This club has become his playground. Although since his last monstrous act, he's kept things quiet and behaved himself. I'm sure his dad warned him he can only pay off so many women before Ryan will get cut off. Especially when he has no ambition to get a job or be anything remotely productive.

Inside, the club is all in purple, white, and blue, and is so filled with blue light it almost hurts your eyes. I let myself react to it, looking nervous to be there.

I've been here before. I've sat a table from open until close, on more than one night, so I know how the club functions and I know how Ryan Volkov operates when he's here. Even though he hasn't hurt anyone, he does take advantage of his VIP booth and classic good looks.

When you really look at that pretty face, it's easy to see the malice that lights up his eyes.

Ryan has very specific tastes. He likes them innocent, virginal is preferable, and he likes to break them. By the time he's done with their bodies, he's also shattered their minds. He wants women so innocent they don't know to fight back until it's too late. The power is too intoxicating for him to ever stop.

I get near his booth, and then put myself in the path of a drunk idiot. He spills his drink on me, and I call out in shock. Not much lands on my dress but enough that I can fake a look of upset. There are tears forced into my eyes as I look around as if trying to make the situation go away. When I turn toward Ryan, he's watching.

Like a wolf wearing the armor of a shining knight, he comes down from the castle of his VIP booth to help little old me.

"Are you alright?"

I look up at him and gasp, as if caught off guard by his smile. "Y-yes. It was cold," I shiver a little and cross my arms, which presses up my cleavage to the neckline of my dress. Ryan's eyes drop, and then graze

THE TASTE OF YOU

down the rest of my body.

"What's your name?"

"Alice," I smile softly at him, letting that vulnerability I practiced show in my face.

"Come with me to Wonderland." He smiles again and holds out a hand. I slip mine into his and let him lead me to his booth, where he pulls me down next to him and under the shelter of his arm.

I make a show of looking nervous and unsure as he drinks with his friends, as I fake my way through having some drinks as well. As I fake more, I let myself lean harder onto his body as if I'm under the influence. Tentatively, I rest my hand on his thigh, just above his knee. Ryan stops talking and looks at me, and I try and look full of lust as well as innocence, my eyes dropping to his lips and then back up.

Ryan holds me closer, possessive and unfortunately, getting aroused. All my soft, unsure touches are the things that tell him he has all the power, all the knowledge, and I'm another one of his unsuspecting, innocent play things.

When he leans in and kisses me, I still, both because of my own very real disgust and as an act of hesitation. His lips part mine and his tongue is wet and sloppy, shoving into my mouth as if he wants to taste my tonsils. I cling onto the lapels of his jacket and lean away, but he follows.

I'm closing my eyes and thinking of murder.

He pulls back and I bat my eyes, faking surprise.

"Want to go to my place?" he asks, trying to make his voice sound low and husky but actually sounding like he's pretending to be Batman.

I nod eagerly. He shares a look with his friends, and I make a note of them. They know who he is and they know what he does, and while they are not as guilty as him, they are guilty. They watch him take women out of this club and into the darkness, and know that most of them never walk out of it the same ever again.

We slide out of the booth and he keeps my hand trapped in his sweaty one, pulling me through the back to where his car is waiting. Before getting into the back, I look to the end of the alley. Freelancer is there, resting over his bike, ready to follow me. I'm thrilled and I'm angry. I subtly give him the finger before sliding in.

It's only a 2 block drive to his apartment but Ryan is too entitled and lazy to walk from the club to his own door. Instead, he keeps a death grip on my thigh that will leave a bruise until his driver stops at the door.

I give a little "oh!" of surprise in response to the opulence of the building entrance and lobby. Ryan smirks at me and pulls me across the marble floor and under the grand golden chandelier to the elevator, where he has to slide a card to get to his top floor apartment. On the ride up he pulls me against him, grinding his erection into my stomach and gripping my ass.

I giggle and pull away, pretending to be embarrassed by his attention.

When we step out of the elevator and into his apartment, he puts his hand around the back of my neck, holding on just a little too tight. Ryan yanks me back to his body and his breath smells of liquor as he whispers in my ear.

"Gonna fuck you, baby."

When he calls me baby, it makes me think of Freelancer. No one ever called me baby, ever in my life, until him. It gives me another reason to punish Ryan.

"O-okay," I respond, hesitation clear in my voice.

Ryan presses his body against mine, pushing me further and further into his living room until my knees hit the couch and I fall down, my dress flipping up above my hips. He stares down at my exposed panties with hunger in his eyes, and palms his cock over his pants.

I watch with forced trepidation as he undoes his belt and then his pants, removing himself. It's disappointing that he has a decent dick for such a piece of shit. I stare at it, fearful, and then back up at him.

"Give it a kiss, baby," he croons at me.

With a shaky hand, I reach out to wrap my fingers around him.

Except I don't do what he asks.

I twist my wrist hard, stretching the sensitive skin of his dick. It catches him off guard and he screams, knees bending automatically. It's enough for me to also use my grip on him to yank him forward now that's he's off balance, and my fist flies at his face. I get a good crack in, right over his right eye. There was enough give when I hit him that I think I might have broken his eye socket.

I let him go and Ryan falls to the ground, rapidly deflating dick flopping out of his pants and he starts to move into the fetal position. With the toe of my shoe I kick him over onto his back and then step down on his crotch, my heel pressing into his precious penis. Ryan freezes, terror on his face.

When he starts to move to sit up and push me off, the knife comes out. It was hidden in a pocket I built into this dress - it was all ruched on top so easy to hide the slight bulge of the knife. There was a good chance he'd see too much of my legs for me to wear my usual sheath. He stills, but I can feel and see the tension in his body.

For good measure, I press my foot down hard and fast. He squeals and curls in on himself.

I step off of him and move to the ottoman he has next to the couch. When I open it, everything I need is inside. Everything he uses to hurt and abuse the women who come up to this apartment, some of them willing and some of them not. I start with the rope.

Still trying to recover from the blow to his junk, it doesn't take much of a fight to get him on his stomach and tie his hands behind his back. Ryan has never been trained to fight and while he's not fat, he's also not fit. No gym bro time for him. It doesn't even take much for me to drag him up and flop his body on the couch.

"What the fuck is this you bitch?" He's breathing heavy, his chest heaving.

"Vengeance, sweetheart," I smile at him and slide out of my shoes so I can maneuver better. I walk back over to the ottoman and look at his assortment of toys. On their own and in the right contexts, there's nothing wrong with having these things. People can consensually engage in pain and punishment, with communication and safe words. That's not what Ryan is into.

I grab some nipple clamps with long chains hanging off them. Then I straddle Ryan and he relaxes slightly.

"Did Eddie buy you for me?" he grins up at me. "A little too much pain for my taste, but I'll play." It takes everything I have not to roll my eyes. While looking straight into his eyes, I rip open his dress shirt. He's getting hard again and I can feel it underneath me, so I attach the first clamp. He hisses but tries to hold back the grimace of pain, and then I attach the other clamp.

I stand back up, taking the chain with me, and give it a testing yank.

"No one bought me. No one knows who I am or that I'm here with you."

"What do you want?" Ryan finally displays a teeny bit of anxiety.

"Tamara Fielding was my friend."

It takes him a minute to figure out why he knows that name, and it makes my vision get hazy. His face falls and he pales slightly. I watch as his mouth opens and closes like a fish out of water, but nothing comes out.

Tamara decided in high school that I was her friend. I was a 16 year old senior, and had never stayed with any one class long enough to make friends, or let any of them get to know me outside of my reputation as being smart and creepy. She was new, coming to our fancy prep school her senior year. She was tall, blonde, willowy, and her resting face was a slight smile - the exact opposite of me.

She was also quiet. It's how we found each other. On the second day of school, she found me in the library and sat at the table next to mine. The week after, she moved to the same table as me. Tamara wasn't afraid of my intensity - all she wanted was someone who cared about school, and didn't mind the quiet.

After the second week, we exchanged phone numbers. We texted about whatever. We would tell each other shows to watch and would send our reactions back and forth. At school our communication was minimal, and we never hung out because I was a loner and she had a lot of family obligations, but she was without a doubt, my best friend. The few times she did get me to socialize were private, discreet gatherings. It's how I met Dinah Riley, and the other children of the underworld that dad tried so hard to keep us away from. Alina would have shit a literal brick. It was nice to have a life, even if it was a secret.

Tamara went to the University of Chicago, and we stayed in touch but didn't get to see each other often. She was trying really hard to break out of her shell and do more now that she was living in the dorms and had a little bit of freedom from family expectations. Tamara was innocent by her family's design, to be pure and virginal for her eventual arranged marriage to the son of one of her father's business partners.

A few weeks after her 21st birthday, Tamara's friends took her out. I was still only 19, and while I thought about going with her, we both knew it was never going to be my scene. I told her to call me if they needed a ride home.

Instead, I got a news alert the next morning that she was found dead in the alley behind Ryan Volkov's apartment building and a witness had seen him leave his club with her.

When my grief went from sadness to rage, I started looking. I started asking questions. I got the version of events that police were told, the version of events that Ryan told his friends, I got the story that her body told the medical examiner. When I started asking questions, I found out that Tamara was part of a pattern.

Ryan would take women back to his apartment, tie them up, rape them, hurt them, do whatever he wanted to them. When he was done, he'd let them go. Some needed to seek medical treatment, some tried to report him, but his father always made it go away. Some healed, some tried to, and some found that they didn't want to live with what had happened to them. I've found 12 women, not including Tamara. Eight of them are still alive.

What I know is that when Ryan untied Tamara, she walked into his kitchen, took a knife, and slit her wrists.

The blood was still on his floor when the police came to the apartment. Obvious signs of her body being dragged out to the elevator were there. Signs of her assault were everywhere, and clear indicators that she had been assaulted by Ryan were still present on his body and in the apartment.

He was brought in for questioning, and walked out four hours later. Never charged.

There was a large payment made to her family. Ryan normally attacked peasants - this time it was Tamara Fielding, whose father did business with his family in that way that all rich people in the same city are connected, and amends had to be made. Apparently, it had been agreed on by Mr. Volkov and Mr. Fielding that Tamara's life was worth $27 million. The cost of the shares she would've gotten upon her marriage.

I'm going to make them all pay, but I'm finally taking out the worm that started it all for me. The one who put in my head the idea to hurt those who hurt others, especially women, in that very specific way. It's been almost three years since she died, I've been killing for two, but this is the one that mattered.

After I kill him, I'll be able to let her memory go.

"It's not what you think!" Ryan breaks into my reminiscing. "I didn't know she'd do that!"

"Do what?" I ask in a sweet, high voice.

"C-cut herself - she was fine and we finished and she just - I didn't - she knew what was going to happen if she came home with me!" He strains against the rope and tries to stand up. I yank hard on the chain and he screams as his nipples are tugged away from his body, the skin stretched and taut.

"Ah, fuck! Bitch wanted to get fucked. All of you do. You're all dirty fucking whores afraid to ask for what you want, so I give it to you, you hear me?" He's screaming at me, spit flying from his mouth, wiggling to try and escape the rope around his wrists. "You all want to be fucked in every hole, every goddamn way, and it's not my fault if you feel shame after. She fucking loved what I did to her!"

"Then I think you're going to like what I do to you, Ryan." I straddle him and rearrange my hold on my knife. "Secretly, all men want to be hurt. You all want to show how tough you are in the face of pain."

I start carving the first line down his chest. He's getting a little too shouty, so I tear off a piece of my dress and stuff it in his mouth. It's not hard because he won't stop fucking talking, and it's to his own detriment. The more he moves, the stupider this will look.

When I finish, I blow on the wounds as if he was wood I'd carved and I need to get the dust away. In bold red letters on his chest, carved into his flesh: RAPIST.

"Ryan, I'm going to kill you now. It's going to be fast, and you probably won't feel much. Not because you deserve that mercy, but because Tamara would tell me you weren't worth any more of my time." His eyes blow wide with panic and he starts struggling against me. "You should be especially grateful because I'm waiting until after you're dead to cut your dick off."

Ryan starts to scream around the gag and tears stream down his cheeks. I jab my knife quick and deep in the little hollow at the bottom of his sternum, angling it up and over to hit his heart. I watch as the blood spills out of him, quick and thick. When his head slumps forward, I stand up and take in what I've done.

I'm not going to cut his dick off.

Staring at him, I do feel lighter.

I did something right today. I killed the person who hurt the best, purest friend I ever had outside of my own family. I killed the piece of shit who got away with raping her, harming and violating her body so badly she killed herself rather than process it.

I don't know how long I stand there, staring at Ryan Volkov's dead body, the demon I've been slaying over and over, until I was ready to confront him.

"Aster."

A jolt ricochets through my body, and I jump. Freelancer is standing in the entry, watching me. His hands are up, soothing the cornered wild animal that I am right now.

"We need to go," he says softly, walking toward me. His footsteps are soft, and he looks comforting in his dark jeans and black hoodie. The mask shines in the bright overhead lights of the apartment.

"I need to finish."

We look down at the body. "Why him? Why like this?"

"He hurt my friend. I wanted to hurt him in the same place. Take away his safe space."

I feel him looking at me, but don't return his gaze. "That's why you do it."

"Yeah."

"Okay." Out of the corner of my eye, I see him nod. He leaves my side and I hear him in the kitchen. When he comes back, he's got gloves on and is holding a bottle of cleaning fluid. In a detached way I watch as he sprays the body and the furniture down with bleach. He opens the body's mouth and removes the scrap of my dress. He picks up my shoes, and takes my hand.

I follow after him like a child. Ryan Volkov is gone. Tamara is gone. All that's left are empty shells, but they are bodies that will tell the stories of the people that animated them. I did the world a favor, but I still miss my friend.

For a bit, everything around me fades and goes black. Then my bare feet hit the cool, gritty blacktop and I'm in the alley behind the apartment building. I'm in the alley where he dumped her like trash, afraid to accept the consequences of his actions.

There's a high, keening noise that I don't know the source of until I realize it's me. I'm staring down the alley as if I could see her, find her body here, and tell her how much she meant to me. What a lifeline she was for me in a sea of awkwardness and outsiderness. There was a place for me in the underworld, and she helped me find it.

Freelancer wraps his arms around me, pressing my face into his hoodie. To my surprise, my arms move around him in return, feeling the strength of his body under his clothes, reveling in the sturdy way he stands, letting me lean on him and taking on the ocean of pain that surrounds me. I'm not crying, I'm just screaming.

Screaming into the void. Screaming for her. Screaming for every woman who has ever been treated like an object, who has had their autonomy violated, their choices taken away. I scream into his chest until my voice is hoarse and I can't anymore.

"Let me take you home, little monster."

Freelancer picks me up and carries me to his bike. He takes off his hoodie and wraps it around me, before putting a helmet on my head. I'm so outside my body I can't move, and he's taking care of me like I'm a child. Under the hoodie he's wearing a Henley, but the sleeves are pushed up slightly and I can see tattoos on his forearms.

He places me on his bike and then climbs on in front of me. I wrap my arms around him, the first voluntary move I've made since I saw him in the apartment. I hold on like I will leave the planet if I let go.

Time leaves me again, and then I'm in his arms, being carried up the stairs of my house in the dark. Everyone is asleep. No one even knows I was gone. No one knows how this night changed me. Freelancer puts me in bed, and that's the last thing I remember until morning.

17

Freelancer

Aster scares a lot of people, but until last night, she'd never scared me. I'd never seen someone I cared about hollowed out so thoroughly. I'd never held someone while they let go of that kind of pain. It reminded me again how deep Aster's feelings run, how well she buries them in the earth of her heart, and pretends they aren't there. She is a graveyard of buried emotions.

When she shows up at work the next day, I'm shocked, but I shouldn't be. Nothing would keep her from work when there was a crisis going on. She looks terrible, her face bare, and she's wearing huge clothes that she drowns in, as if she tried to wear blankets to work.

All day she sits in a corner with her laptop on her lap and doesn't speak to anyone. I bring her a hot chocolate from the coffee place downstairs after lunch so she gets some sort of calories in her.

Her family must have noticed something was off because at 5:00, her guard, Nino, shows up to drive her home. She doesn't talk to anyone on the team, just leaves.

It's unusual behavior for her, but none of us says anything. Not to her, and not to each other. Tella once joked that Aster would know if we talked about her behind her back. I think it's because everyone likes her enough, as surprised as Aster would be about that fact, to not kick her while she's obviously down.

I leave shortly after, back on duty.

Aster doesn't leave her room and I don't like it. She doesn't even come down to dinner. I watch Anora carry a tray up the stairs, presumably to Aster's room. My heart races and I can't stand not being able to see her. She's not even on her phone.

I walk around the back of the house to where I can see the light on in her window. There's a tree that I can try to climb that might be high enough, but I don't like it because if anything happens I might not be able to get down fast enough. But I have to see her, so I climb. The view isn't great, but it's enough.

She's sitting on her bed, staring at nothing.

I wait. I wait and watch as the lights downstairs go out. Until the lights in bedrooms and bathrooms go on and then off, and then silence falls.

The door to the patio is easy to unlock and slides open silently. There's a guard stationed in the front room, the only one inside the house, but he doesn't notice me. He's worried about the threats that might still be outside. I make it up the stairs without a sound.

There's still a tray of food outside her door, untouched. I can tell Anora put it together for Aster specifically, beyond bringing her what was served for dinner. There's a bottle of Mountain Dew, a bag of Sour Patch Kids, a plate with chicken, rice, and green beans, and then a whole sheath of Ritz crackers. It was an effort to get Aster to eat anything.

At least they can blame the issues at Designation. If they look too deep I'm afraid what they might find, although it'll be awhile before anyone knows Ryan Volkov is dead. Aster didn't seem to care if he was found, but I did. I called in a favor and had someone clean the apartment, and dump his body. It'll look like a hit - a very violent, personally motivated hit. I know the shit that guy and his family were wrapped up in, so it won't be surprising to anyone.

Aster's door opens silently, and she doesn't even move to look at me from her still perch on the bed. Without a word, I walk into the room and to her bathroom. I get a glass of water and hold it in front of her until she takes it and drinks it. Then I undress her to her underwear and tuck her underneath her blankets. Before I turn out the lamp next to her bed, her little hand darts out and wraps around my wrist.

She looks directly at me, and I know she can feel me looking back at her. My little monster gives me a small nod, letting me know she's okay, and then tucks her hand underneath the blankets and closes her eyes. I turn out the light, leave the room, and leave the house. I go back to my hotel room and try to get some sleep.

By the time the weekend hits, Aster has recovered. I've texted her all week, checking in, and she promised me that after a few solid nights of sleep she feels better. She tells me about her friend - Tamara - the one that set off her vigilante mission. It explains a lot of the things she watches that seem out of character.

Whatever demons she's exorcised, she's also talking to me again.

While I do miss touching her body, and the way we turn each other on, this connection is real and important too. It's not some abstract attraction to the monster in each other, it's to the other part of ourselves as well. I am interested in everything about her. I want to know what makes her smile as much as I want to learn all of the ways to make her come.

Someday, I'll be able to do normal things with her. When this is done, and she's safe, I'll show her my face and we can build whatever comes next. I've never had feelings for anyone - romantic, positive feelings - and there's nothing that could convince me to let her go. I didn't think I believed in soulmates, let alone souls, but she makes me believe in a lot of things I never would have imagined to be real or possible.

Aster is a piece of me. I think she feels the same.

Now I have to start taking steps to make our future possible.

Don knows I'm away for the night and he's got extra eyes on Aster. It's unlikely she'll go anywhere, and I decided that it was a better course of action to tell her that I needed to go away for the night. She's gotten quite confident knowing that I have her back, and I need her to know that she's on her own and to be careful.

I'm not above begging her to stay put and behave.

What will I get if I do?

Be a good little monster and you'll find out, I reply to her.

Then I get on my bike and start the long drive to my meeting with Clive.

18

Freelancer

Everyone who needs a contract knows Clive. He helps keep things anonymous, connecting code names to jobs and finding the right people to do the right work. I don't know how he got into it or how he built his reputation, but he's as fair as he is deadly. We pay him a portion of our fees, and he finds work for people who can't advertise what they do.

Clive found me 6 years ago, a scrawny but deadly 18 year old on the streets, working on the edges of an Outfit and taking care of people when they needed to disappear. I had a talent for hiding things - unsurprising given my upbringing. He took me, fed me, set me up to bulk up, and then put my skills to work. He's like a finishing school for criminals - we live on his estate and do what he says, and then he makes us both money.

He agreed to meet with me on the far side of Chicago, away from where anyone connected to Aster would be. Of course, being Clive, he found a house to meet at because he doesn't like being in public. The work he does makes him a lot of enemies as well as supporters, so he's abundantly careful.

I don't bother to knock, but enter the house. It's empty, clearly up for sale, but he's moved in a lamp, a table and chairs, and there's a bottle of whiskey sitting on top with two glasses. Clive relaxes in a chair, and smiles when he sees me, waving for me to take a seat. He's an older man, his hair is white and his movements are careful, but I've always wondered if he got plastic surgery to keep his face so intense and unlined. It doesn't even crease when he smiles.

His two usual guards are there as well, on alert even though they know me and know that I'm no threat to their boss. Their code names are Beefeater and Thunder. They're actually Liam and Fetu. I hung out with Fetu a lot, and he gives me a nod as I make eye contact before taking my seat. Before Aster, I missed being on the estate and being part of the brotherhood that developed there. Now, I'd never look back.

"Is there something wrong?" Clive starts.

"No. It's not an easy job, I'm not having any issues. I -" I swallow hard, struggling for a moment to tell him what's going on. "When the job is done, I'm out." That was easier to say than I thought it would be. Taking hits and jobs has been my life, the most productive and fulfilling chapter of it, that I never imagined I would leave. Except when it came out of my mouth, it felt like the right thing. It felt true and good. I know I'm making the right choice.

Clive's smile freezes on his face and then morphs into shock but it feels forced. "You've suddenly discovered you want to be a programmer? Someone like you can't ignore what they are." There's genuine concern in his voice and it makes me feel like I'm letting him down, even though he was very clear we could all be done whenever we wanted. We didn't owe him anything beyond the finder's fee. There were other of his trainees who had gone in and out of the life, and he always made room for them to come back. Clive never closed the door on an asset.

It should be a shock to me as well that I can imagine my life as a programmer by day, my woman's backup by night. I don't need to be the center of attention, or even the one in charge. She's more than enough satiation for my blood lust because I'll never ask her to stop - I couldn't. It would be wrong. All I'll ask of her is to let me be by her side or at her back.

"It's not that." I don't want to tell him about Aster, but I do at the same time. It's not like I fell for a hit, I fell for the client. I'm supposed to be keeping her safe and alive, and now I have more motivation than ever to do exactly that.

The silence stretches on, and when I look at Clive, I see something dawn in his eyes.

"You fell for Aster Sorrelle." It might be pity.

"Yes."

"Does she feel the same?"

"I think so."

Clive sits back and takes a drink from his tumbler. "You picked a good job to go out on. It's going to make you a fuck ton of money." He sighs and finishes his whiskey.

I swallow, thinking about how weird it is that I'll be taking her father's money and hopefully taking her. "I know."

I watch Clive carefully, trying to read how he's reacting to this. No matter how much he's reassured all of us that we're free, it still feels like I'm disappointing him. Or even rejecting all that he's given me and taught me. I would always be dangerous, but because of Clive I have power and control that I never knew before. It took me from being a thug to being an assassin, and to feel safe for the first time in my life. I don't want him to think that I don't appreciate what I've been given.

He surprises me when he leans forward and pats my leg. "Don't worry. I knew you weren't in the life forever."

"You did?"

"The way you grew up...some people, it turns them into machines, and others, it turns them into puzzle pieces. You didn't fit there, so you've spent the rest of your life trying to find where you fit. To find where you belong. I'm happy for you." This time I understand the look - it's pride. He was waiting for me to use what he gave me to find a place I wanted to be, and I did.

The thing is, I've done truly heinous things, and I've enjoyed them. The idea that I would want something as simple as love and belonging is ludicrous, but his words ring true. I've never wanted to be alone, but felt like I had to be. Felt like if my own family didn't value me, why would anyone else? Clive was the closest I came. I never thought I'd be in a place to connect with anyone, or that they'd see past who I became in order to survive, and who I choose to keep being because I'm fucking good at it.

Aster knows all those things and still lets me touch her. Trusts me to have her back and protect her. Asks me to believe in her and stand by her.

"What if I'm wrong?"

"You're not," Clive reassures me, "but if you are, you have a place with me."

I nod. We finish our whiskey in silence, and without another word, I leave. I have to get back to her, and get back on the job.

19

Aster

Ever since the day of the hack, Isaac and I started eating lunch together on the roof. No one says anything when we leave together, but I've seen looks pass between him and Dominic that I don't feel like addressing.

Things have calmed down. There haven't been any other attempts, and based on the laptop we got from the hard hack, we've been able to build up both internal and external security. It still feels like I'm missing something and that is beyond frustrating. I know that I'm starting to go into an obsessive spiral of working non-stop and never leaving my cave.

Isaac pulling me out of it to make sure that I at least eat lunch is both thoughtful and necessary.

We've fallen into a weird rhythm without talking about it with each other. I bring the veggies, he brings the protein, and we swap half our food. Sometimes he'll bring drinks, and sometimes it's on me. The first few times we didn't talk much, and now we can't seem to shut up.

It's not even all about work, although we do talk about what we're doing, coding, hacks we've heard about that were interesting or we might look at to assess our own defenses. How we got into programming, how and when we got in trouble for hacking, and what we think we could do to make Designation better, what the next products should be. Then we also talk about absolute nonsense, and it's been a long time since I could do that with anyone.

Today we're arguing about our favorite episodes of *Parks and Recreation*. It's one of the shows that I only watched because of Tamara, but I'm oddly attached to Leslie and Ron. You'd think I'd be an April kind of person but someone like Leslie is the sunshine to my cloudy day.

"How you can say it's anything other than "Ron and Tammys" is beyond me." I gesture wildly.

"Over "the Fight"? "the Bubble"? "Flu Season?!""

"Flu Season is only funny for one line," I challenge.

"Okay, I'll give you that one."

I finish the lemonade that Isaac brought us to share and slide down in the chair, stretching out my legs. Part of me is dreading going back to the team because we haven't come any closer to anything, even if we've protected what we can. It's like we're running in place, or holding a dam together with one finger while the pressure builds. Right now it's waiting for the next incident.

It could be another hack, another attempt on me, I have no idea. I hate not knowing and I hate not knowing how to protect myself or anyone else. I'm getting restless for control again, but after the mess I made with Ryan Volkov and the fact that Freelancer had to clean up after me, I think I need a break.

There will never stop being creeps out there and I will never run out of targets. Someone will always take advantage, or seek to take down people that they think are weaker or less human than they are. I'll show them exactly how much less human I can be. No one should have to spend their life recovering from something they didn't choose.

"You okay?"

Isaac snaps me out of my reverie, and I pull myself out of my chair to go and stand on the edge of the roof, looking down over the packed parking lot. There's a long field between the parking lot and the road, and it's almost weird we don't do more with all the land we have. The isolation is good for us though - it keeps other things from interfering with Designation.

I shouldn't be standing on the edge, but I think Isaac being here is keeping the worst of my immediate thoughts down. How easy it would be to jump. How it might feel to fly for a few seconds. My fingers curl and my nails dig into my palms. It would be easy, but it would be terrible. I focus back on Isaac.

"I guess. I feel like I'm wasting time."

"Because we're playing defense."

"Yes." I'm glad that he understands me.

"What could we be doing differently?" He gets up and stands next to me, and we're staring off into the distance together. I look at him out of the corner of my eye. His hair looks redder in the sun, a dark auburn. The light glints off his glasses so I can't see his eyes, but I know he's as frustrated as I am. His arms cross and I notice again that his shirt is buttoned at the wrists. Isaac never relaxes at work - this is as close as he gets.

"Well, I had an idea, but…" I trail off and consider if I should share my thoughts or not. It's not something that I do with anyone - even with Freelancer it takes work. Most of the time, I don't want to look wrong or stupid. I don't like to process out loud. Everything is tight and internal, gone over again and again in my mind until I've seen every angle and know that it's the move that needs to be made.

Not to mention, there's absolutely sexism in my industry. Not from my team, and not from our leadership, but I definitely dealt with it in college and grad school. I already keep everything internalized but when douchey dudes were waiting for any mistake, even a tiny one, as a reason to jump at you and call you out, it teaches you to be quiet and certain before saying a fucking word. Those same dudes would then try and fuck me. Right.

The thing is, I also can't do this alone, and I do trust Isaac.

"We could build a trap." I start explaining to him that I've started to build a mirror to our system. It's taking forever because I'm doing it alone and I don't want to take any shortcuts - I'm trying to make everything fresh and from scratch because then I'll also notice any existing vulnerabilities that I haven't seen when looking at the code. Sometimes I'll only notice an error in the writing of it. My eyes can't catch it the way the rest of my brain can.

Isaac jumps on board with enthusiasm, and starts asking all the right questions about how big and how far I want to take this, how we'd put the mirror codes online in place of the real one, and then the question that I don't have an answer for - are we trapping the hacker, or is this a way to trace them and maybe find out who they are?

Either way, this might be the only way we get them.

"I think you should take this to Owen," Isaac says. I notice that he called him Owen instead of Mr. Carver, or just Carver, like everyone else. "He might give us more resources and support to make it happen."

"What if I'm wrong?" I can't believe I said that out loud.

"It's better than doing nothing." Isaac and I turned to face one another in the excitement of our conversation, and we're standing close together now. I have to tilt my head back to look at him. My arms are crossed and he wraps his fingers around my elbow, giving me a little shake. I don't mind him touching me, and warmth spreads up and down my arm. It's surprising, and I can't move.

Isaac's face is serious as he looks down at me. "You're incredible, Aster. Scary and smart and single-handedly helping this place keep it's shit together."

"Thank you?" I don't know why that came out as a question and I'm starting to get flustered. Isaac smells really good and he has a very nice mouth, a full bottom lip and a sharp cupid's bow on top. It's framed perfectly by his facial hair, which he keeps clean and trimmed. Isaac takes care of himself, and it is attractive. Except that it makes me think of Freelancer. I've felt his mouth on my body, but never pressed against my lips. I want to know what it looks like. I want to taste it with my tongue.

He's looking at my mouth, and then back into my eyes. I take a step back, forcing his arm to drop and putting distance between us. Even without any kind of conversation or understanding, I belong to Freelancer. I have loyalty to him for what we have. If I would let Isaac kiss me, Freelancer would kill him. Also, as his boss, this is a big ass no no. I won't cross that line with an employee just because I'm curious and he has a nice mouth.

"Sorry." He turns away from me, his cheeks slightly pink.

"It's okay. I'm…seeing someone."

The way his eyebrows shoot to his hairline should be insulting but it makes me laugh. "How have you kept that a secret?"

"I keep all my shit on lockdown. Not even my family knows."

This time he frowns. "Is that healthy? Are you safe?" His concern is kind, and his questions worth reflecting on. Are Freelancer and I healthy? Absolutely fucking not. Our relationship is intense and obsessive, full of secrets and darkness, and a playground for our very specific, very dangerous kinks.

Am I safe? Yes. Safer than I've ever been on a physical and mental level. The weights that I carry around, my fears, my shame, all of it lightens with him. Freelancer never judges me, and always tries to help me figure things out, or keep my mind focused. Plus, I have this tendency to put myself in danger or walk on the edge of it, and for the first time I have someone who will catch me before I fall. It makes me understand why some people are addicted to being in a relationship.

"It's the happiest I've ever been," I answer Isaac. "Probably because no one is in my business." Then I give him a pointed look, reminding him that he's getting into my business with his questions. Isaac laughs and raises his hands in surrender.

"As long as you're happy." There's a twinkle in his eye I don't understand, but I don't talk anymore about my personal life as we pack up lunch and head back to the pod. It's flattering that Isaac is attracted to me - but it also solidified for me that my feelings for Freelancer aren't born out of loneliness or a need for connection. It's wholly about him.

I won't deny I feel a spark for Isaac, but I also feel like he's holding back. That's not enough for me.

20

Aster

We're in Anora's room on FaceTime with Alina. She's been planning a huge gala for the last few months and it's finally happening tonight. Even over the screen I can tell that there's something different about her. There's no doubt that she misses us, but she's happy.

I make Aro get out of the way so I can show Alina how to do her eyeliner. It's funny because the four of us clearly look like sisters, and take after our father's side of the family, but we're all a patchwork of features. Alina and I have the same eyes in different colors, deep with heavy lids, which makes eyeliner a bitch. Alina and Anora have the same mouth, although Anora's is always smiling and Alina's is always a frown. Aro and I both have dark, dark eyes and the shape of our faces is the same. Her and I look the most alike, although there's something pleasant about her that's missing from me.

It's odd to look at someone else and see your features in their face. To be the same and yet totally different.

I love my sisters. They're never afraid of me, only afraid for me. Probably not as afraid for me as they should be. We all keep secrets from each other, some of us are just keeping bigger secrets than others. Except maybe Aro, she's such an open book I can't imagine her even thinking that she should keep something secret. In a way, I wish I could be more like her because she never feels shame or fear about who she is.

That's why Alina and I have always gotten along. Somewhere inside, Alina thinks she'll never be enough, and I know that I'm a monster. We both work really hard to show the world one version of ourselves, even if it's for different reasons. Alina's always been supportive of my dark side but would work hard to pull me back when I got too far out of the light. I'm surprised how much I miss her - not because I don't love my sister, but because I didn't realize how stabilizing of a force she was in our house and in my life.

When Alina pulls back and shows us her completed outfit in the mirror, my heart squeezes. She looks beautiful, and happy. I want to see her happy, especially given all the shit going down with the Clayton businesses right now. Tonight should hopefully be a breath of relief for all of them - a gorgeous party for a good cause.

"She's totally in love." Aro sighs and starfishes on Anora's bed.

"Absolutely," Anora agrees.

"How do you know?" I think they're right, but I want to know why. I know because I know Alina, but I'm not always as good at understanding the way people I don't know as well feel. When I'm right about something, I like to pick it apart for future use and understanding. I want to know how we all know. Maybe it'll help me figure out my own feelings.

"The way she talks about him. You know Alina - for her to talk about what he wants, cares about, wanting to look good for him…she doesn't care how she looks, but she wants him to go crazy when he sees her." Aro rolls over onto her stomach. "She sent us a selfie with him the other day. Our girl is gone - she took a picture of her own face, have you ever known her to do that?"

No, that's very true. Anora gets photographed all the time because of the events that she does and because she's been the public face of our family for almost a decade now. When people hear the name Sorrelle, they think of dad and Anora. Maybe Owen, depending on how into computer security they are. He had a viral interview on YouTube a few years ago because he was a "hot nerd." We made fun of him about it for exactly one day before Anora shut it all down because it genuinely upset him.

Now we only talk about it behind his back.

Alina, Aro, and I don't post pictures of our faces on social media, don't go out and make spectacles of ourselves, all for our own particular reasons. Alina knows bodyguards need to be invisible, I don't want anyone to remember or recognize my face, and Aro is shy as hell. We're the odd people out in a world obsessed with documenting everything. I know that it bothers Aro sometimes because she wants to find ways to express herself. It's why she goes through phases experimenting with different art forms, but nothing sticks.

I kill people.

No coping mechanism is probably a better coping mechanism than that.

"Have you ever been in love?" I slide down on the floor next to Anora's bed, and take out my phone. They know that I'm listening, but I need to do something with my hands while we talk or I get anxious. I pull up Tetris, and start killing lines.

"No," Aro sighs. "I can't talk to people. I barely made friends, let alone a boyfriend. What about you, Miss Popular?"

Anora did date in high school but no one seriously that I could tell.

"Yes." Anora's voice is a whisper, and when I look up at her there's shock on her face, as if she can't believe that she answered, or that she answered yes.

"Oh my god!" Aro jumps up and whips a pillow at our sister. It hits her in the face and snaps Anora out of her trance. "Who? When? How come we don't know about this guy?"

Anora looks sad, and I don't like it. Whoever this dude is, maybe he broke her heart, and maybe I'll need to break some of his bones in return.

"It's complicated. We - there are reasons we can't be together. Legitimate, serious reasons," Anora is convincing herself as she tries to convince us. "I didn't want to fall in love with him." She shrugs and sits down on her bed, still holding the pillow Aro threw at her.

"You're still in love with him." My voice is soft, but she looks down at me and I can see it in her face. How much she's hurting over a person she made a choice to stay away from. If there's anything I will always do for my sisters, it's respect their choices. I might tell them if they're being dumbasses in private, but I'll have their back when they need it.

"It's not what I need. Maybe someday." I had no idea Anora was carrying around a hurt like this, although it does explain a lot of what she was like in the months leading up to her marriage agreement being finalized. I think she dodged even more of a bullet than we realized when Derick wanted Alina. It's a different chance at happiness for Anora, but it wasn't enough for her and her person to be together. I have so many questions that are none of my business.

Aro leans over and hugs Anora. I pat her foot. It's awkward, but I know Anora appreciates the gesture.

"I'm going to be in love someday," Aro says firmly, "and nothing is going to get in my way."

"Okay, baby," Anora says as she pats her arm. Aro's naivety is sweet, but too sweet for this conversation.

"I'm going to ask a question but you can't ask any questions," I growl out. Aro and Anora both turn their heads to look at me. Anora has a full face of make up and Aro isn't wearing any, and they look decades apart in age. Like Aro could be her daughter rather than her sister. For a moment I feel a weird uncanny feeling, like Anora is hiding more than I know - like the make up is a mask that I can't see past, and that I don't know the truth of her at all. I shake my head and focus again, filing that panicked anxiety thought away to examine later.

"How did you know it was love, not just lust?"

Anora thinks for a moment. "I would know he was there without seeing him. I could tell him anything without feeling judged, or sometimes without having to tell him at all. He could read me, and I could read him. I know I loved him because when I told him I had to let it go, let us go, he understood. He respects me, and that is at the core of who he is, and I love that. I love everything about who he is, and how he treated me as a result."

"Did he know anything about you that no one else does?"

Now she frowns at me, concerned by that question. "He can keep a secret."

Freelancer keeps my secrets. He knows me better than anyone, but I don't feel like I know him at all. Is it only lust?

I know he's there before I see him - his presence is like a wave in my psychic landscape. Even now I think if I tried to follow the feeling it would guide me straight to him. He's seen me at my worst, at my most vulnerable, and at my absolute darkest. Freelancer never looked away, and never judged me. I feel like he knows me.

If it's ever going to be anything more, he needs to break down for me too. We've talked about surface level things, but I need things to go deeper than that. He can promise me all he wants that he's not going to leave and that he's staying for me, but that might be built on a shaky as hell foundation. The tension and danger surrounding us is an aphrodisiac to psychos like us. The more unhinged, the hornier we are.

When the danger is gone, what will we have left?

That thought still echoes in my mind as I sit up in bed, watching episode after episode of a TV show I can't even remember the name of. I'm not even sure what's happening and I've been watching it for at least 5 episodes now. That might be why it got canceled after two seasons though.

The door to my room opens, and I sit up ready to be fucking pissed at whoever didn't knock when entering my domain, but it's Freelancer. He's wearing black jeans and a gray hoodie, his mask in place. The only thing I can see are his hands. They're familiar and capable, but now I'm feeling even more like there's a barrier between us. A literal one, yes, but it's more than that.

At first, I thought the anonymity and rawness of our connection made it deep. Now I'm afraid it was novel.

"I thought about kissing someone."

"I know."

I frown at him. "How do you know?"

He comes closer, leaning over me on the bed. For the first time, I find him threatening. "I know everything you do, little monster." Then he takes a few steps back and sits on the end of the bed. I guess we're having a chat.

"Are you mad?"

"No."

Now I'm really confused. "Why not?"

"We haven't made each other any promises. I'm not asking you to make them until this is done."

God damn it, human beings are frustrating. I huff. "Why not?" I ask again. I need to understand. This thing between us is intoxicating and aggravating. I'm as excited as I am confused.

"You don't even know my name. We can't tell your family there's anything going on between us. I can't be with you in public."

"I don't care about that."

"I know," I can hear the smile in his voice. "I have more bodies on my hands than you do. I have enemies. The more you know, the more dangerous you are to me, Aster. What if you decide that it's too much?"

"You'd let me walk away?" I scoff. Why am I offended? Isn't the freedom and the choice exactly what I want in the first place? The whole point is that I know enough to know if this is love, or could be love. Love is worth fighting all of my demons for. Lust is only worth ignoring them for awhile so I can get off.

Freelancer doesn't answer that question. He turns his head like he can't bear to make eye contact with me, even though I wouldn't be able to tell if he was looking into my eyes or not. The mesh mask looks alien in the regular light of my bedroom. He's alien to me right now, and I feel my flesh crawl and get itchy. The trapped and anxious feelings is sliding along my body, pumping in my veins.

"I will do whatever it takes so you don't want to." His voice is a fierce grumble, and I believe him. That's obsession. It's also not the same as love. Obsession means he'll keep me no matter what. As gratifying as knowing someone is obsessed with me can be on the one hand, on the other I want choices.

Before we can go any further with this conversation, my phone rings. It's not the usual tone - it's the one I have set to override when it's silenced and means it's a fucking emergency.

It's Kade.

"What happened?" I ask. Freelancer sits up straight and tenses beside me, waiting to be put into action even though he has no idea why.

"There was an attack at the gala - someone attempted to shoot Derick. They hit Alina."

My stomach drops to the floor and I think I'm going to throw up. "Is she okay?"

"She's fine - hit her shoulder. But I know she won't tell you and we also don't know what the fuck is going on, so I'm telling you. Keep an eye out, yeah kid?"

My research on Kade and his capabilities has been extensive enough that I let him get away with calling me kid even though I'm 22 years old. About to be 23. Kade just turned 30 but he's lived a fuck ton more life and seen more things than I probably ever will. I respect him, and even though he calls me kid, I know he respects me too. He wouldn't be calling otherwise.

"Got it. I'll let you know if I see anything interesting."

We hang up without saying anything else, and I take a few deep breaths.

"What happened?" Freelancer moves closer but doesn't touch me, accurately assessing my need for distance right now.

"Alina got shot," my voice cracks. I take another deep breath. "She's fine. It's fine. But I have work to do - you should go."

Freelancer stands and comes over to me. We stare at one another - or at least I'm looking up at him. Quickly, he swipes his thumb down the center of my lips and then leaves without another word.

21

Aster

I spend most of the night looking through everything again, and all of Sunday in front of my screens. It helps that I don't have to hack into any of Venture's things. After catching some of the infiltration that had already happened, Kade got Derick to give me full access to everything. There's no walls between me and their business now.

Everything looks secure, so whatever is going on the attack is not focused on Venture. That's always been my feeling, and it's been Alina's too, but this feels like proof. They went after Derick but didn't use it as a distraction to get to Venture, or get access to anything else that I have flagged. It was purely about attacking him, but instead they got to Alina.

I'm dazed and tired when I get into the office Monday morning. On the way to Designation, I told Owen what had happened. He can keep things quiet. He won't even tell dad, he promised.

"I need to use our resources to look into this. I don't want anyone tracking what I'm doing."

"What will you be doing?" I can see him share a look with Alonzo through the rear view mirror, but don't call it out.

"I'm looking into the people around them. It's personal. It's all fucking personal, Owen. I have to figure this out."

"Fine. Don't be stupid."

I scoff at him. "Don't insult me."

Owen grimaces, as close as he gets to a smile most of the time, and we drive the rest of the way to work in silence.

At Designation, I check in with the team and make sure they're all working on projects and analysis. Things have stayed quiet, so right now we're trying to catch up on all of the details and documentation needed to track the work we've already done. It'll help if or when we need to share what we're doing with other teams. There should always be a record and a way for someone else to pick apart what you've done.

I'm not saying that I'm planning for a scenario in which I suddenly die or disappear, but that's not not what I'm doing either. It's morbid, but it's my reality.

When I make sure everyone is on track, I catch Isaac's eye and move my head so he knows to come over to my station. I don't miss the way Dominic watches him as he comes over by me, or the way that he glares. This is not the time, but it'll have to be handled. I'm really trying to keep professional boundaries with Isaac - despite what happened on the roof - and Dominic's jealousy is unfounded.

"You have a project."

Isaac frowns. "Lay it on me."

"This is outside the usual. I got approval for it to be business hours from Owen, but it's...personal. To the family."

The frown deepens. "Why aren't you doing it?"

I sigh. "I've been over everything a hundred times. I think I'm too close. I need someone outside that has the skills and that I trust to see what I'm not."

This time there's a small smile. "You trust me?"

"Shut up. Don't make me regret this." I give him a list of names, the names that I'm most suspicious of that surround my sister and her husband, and tell him to dig through everything. I want to know what they buy online and where they bank, what they do with their free time, and what they do on their phones. Whatever it is, wherever it's stored, I want him to find it. I've already got most of it in a file in my personal server, but it might serve me better to have him start from scratch.

He might find something that I didn't.

Isaac goes back to his corner of our space, and I sit back down at my computer. I'm trying to fall into my own project and hope that it distracts me.

My phone buzzes on the desk next to me.

How are you, little monster?

Fine, I text Freelancer back.

Feeling the urge?

I think for a moment, assessing my mind and body. Since last night, I've been running on a weird kind of energy. Momentum moves me forward but I didn't take a moment to stand still until right now. Until he made me.

I've been unraveling the last few days, and last night made it worse. The moment when I had to contemplate that Alina might be seriously hurt, even dead, rattled me to the core. My brain immediately went into assault mode, telling me that I wasn't doing enough, I was missing something, Alina being hurt was my fault, I had to do more more more until everyone was safe because I was saving them. Nothing I could do would ever be enough.

I am crawling with rage, panic, and fear. My stomach has been a hard knot and I've barely eaten or slept. The desperate desire for control is making my muscles rigid and my body shake. Do I want to hunt? Absolutely. Am I in a state for it? No.

It's a bad time.

He doesn't answer for a few minutes, and that makes me edgier.

If you need it, I'll be with you.
Not yet.
When you're ready.

Wednesday morning, Isaac finds something.

When we huddle up in the corner with his laptop, he pulls up financial histories for multiple employees. Not of Venture, but of the Clayton household.

"What am I looking at?"

Isaac clicks through the screens, and then looks at me expectantly.

"I haven't slept in 4 days, spell it out for me," I snap.

"That's three months worth of finances that haven't changed. Jack Clayton, and two other employees - their bank balances haven't been touched for months. No payments, deposits, anything."

"Why is that important?" It's on the tip of my brain but I can't put the pieces together.

"Where is their money going? Where are they keeping it, and where are they spending it from? They're hiding their money - or at least, storing it somewhere that's not tied to their names."

"That's suspicious. Send it all to me."

Isaac does it with a few clicks of his mouse, and I immediately send it to Kade with an explanation for why I'm concerned. I don't want to bother Alina while she's healing and I don't want Derick to go off half-cocked. I don't know him that well - I know Kade, and I trust him.

"Anything else?"

"I think I figured out how whoever is skimming from the clubs."

"Go on." Derick and Kade have been going around in circles about that one for awhile now. Of course Isaac, who isn't emotionally invested in any of this, would see it when we couldn't. Emotions blind us. It's why I have to force them down deep when I work, when

I do anything, because otherwise I'll never get anything done.

Maybe that's why I like the wet work. I can be one or the other, the extreme version, and get something useful out of it. I can be emotional and cause pain as a way to get my emotions out; I can get vengeance on those who hurt others. Or, I can be clinical and detached and feel nothing.

Isaac pulls up a series of receipts. "This is the percentage they have to pay for every credit card transaction, but if you look - sometimes the percentage is different. Someone in the club, whoever was doing the books at the end of the night on these dates, would have to manually alter the percentage. Then they take the over-payment. The club is doing the same amount of business, but it looks as if they're losing money because more is being paid out here. It's smart. Who's going to check that detail, especially if it involves people they trust."

"You can't trust anyone," I grumble, and I'm already typing that explanation to Kade, along with the receipts that Isaac pulled. I already had copies of them in my server and never even noticed. I feel fucking dumb right now.

I need...I need to feel strong. I need to feel capable.

Isaac puts his hand on my thigh underneath the desk and I'm more shocked that I don't feel the need to run away from it than I am that he did it. "You can trust me, Aster."

We lock eyes in the darkened room, and there's an intensity in his that I've never seen before. There are layers to Isaac that I clearly don't know about, but that I might like to uncover.

I don't say anything, and go back to my station.

As if he knows, Freelancer texts me. Not only am I feeling murdery, I'm also really fucking horny right now. Not a good combination.

Whenever you're ready baby.

Fucking shit goddamn. I slam the phone face down on my desk and get back to work.

22

Aster

When Alina texted us that she was coming home to convalesce, I knew it was a mistake. My sister doesn't run away from a problem. She doesn't back down for anybody.

Anora was right that Alina was going to fall for Derick because I've never seen her act like this. I'm all for Alina being happy and in love if that's what she wants, but her fear is making her do the wrong thing. I don't manage to reach her before the plane takes off, so I do the next best thing.

I buy myself a cheap ticket (Chicago to Minneapolis) so I can get past security, and buy her one of the last spots on the return flight. She's going to get off the plane, they'll clean it, and then she's getting right back on. I refuse to let her fear make her run from a fight.

To say she's surprised to see me might be an understatement. Despite all the dark and crazy things I've done in my life, things that she knows about and has seen first hand, I've never seen her shocked over anything I've done. Things are changing for all of us, even for me.

When I tell her why I'm here and what she needs to do, she throws me off balance when she yanks me into a hug. After a moment, my body goes out of panic mode. I let Alina hug me.

Then it's time for my own confessions. We've left Alina out of it, and I've respected dad's and Owen's wishes on that. While she'll always be my sister and should be in on things about our family, the issue with Designation is work. She doesn't work for us anymore, and doesn't need to worry about things that won't impact her the same way anymore. Still, it's time she knows.

I tell her about the attempted and the successful hacks. I tell her about the physical attack on Designation, and I tell her without using any names, about Freelancer. In a way I'm also telling her about Isaac. Both of them have been helping me make our problems go away, or protecting things from getting worse. They're both helping me in different ways and I'm grateful for both of them.

I absolutely do not tell Alina about the threats against me. That's a one-way ticket to a sisterly ass-whooping.

"We'll figure it out. We're close. Freelancer and I are all over it."

Alina flinches and I realize what I've done. I pretend like I don't notice it and keep talking. "We've created some great stuff in response. My team is good."

"Are you doing anything for your birthday?" she asks.

It's in two weeks. I hadn't planned on it. I usually don't. As a kid, I didn't have any friends to invite to birthday parties, plus having a summer birthday in our crowd meant that no one was really around. They were all on trips, experiencing things before being stuffed back into the confines of education. Most of the time I spend my birthday relaxing. I'll take the day off work if it's on a weekday, but this year it's on a Saturday.

"No. Maybe I'll have a dinner. Something small."

"Just do something, okay?"

"Okay." I capitulate because I think it'll make Alina feel better.

It's time for her to get back on her way to Seattle. I watch her walk toward the gate, and then make my way out of the airport. I hope that everything is fine when she gets there, that she's in time to make the difference she needs.

There is something different about her now. Alina has always been tough, but there's a confidence now that was never there before. Something that radiates out of her, powerful and hard to look away from. Maybe it's that she doesn't need to hold herself back anymore. Alina can be herself all the time, and not have to go into invisible bodyguard mode. It disappoints me in myself that I didn't see how much Alina was holding herself down to be there for our family.

Who would I be without the constraints of our family?

I think about that question as I drive back the house, the insanity of the question keeping my intrusive thoughts away. I only think about crashing the car once, which is a record.

Without my family, or without my loyalty to them, I'd absolutely be a criminal. It's the care I have for them that keeps me mostly above board. Vigilantism aside, most of the work I do is within the boundaries of the law. Most of the crimes I commit with my computer are done in the name of my family's safety. When I go down to that room in the basement, it's to extract information that will keep them safe.

I jump in to situations, knife first, if it means that I keep anything bad from happening to them. I will cut first and ask questions if there's time.

When I get home, I don't tell anyone where I went or what I did, and they don't think to ask. Even Freelancer doesn't reach out, which is surprising considering he probably followed me to the airport and back. I wonder if he got a ticket to get past security, or if he assumed I was safe enough inside the airport. If he thought I was flying somewhere…but he didn't. How does he know me so well? How does someone I barely know continue to guess my thoughts and actions?

I pull out my phone and stare down at it, letting those questions bounce around in my head as I pull up my email. I have reports run automatically at work and get them emailed to me.

I close the email, and open my texts instead.

Did you mirror my phone?

The answer is immediate, and surprising. *Yes.* Not because that's the answer, but because he didn't bother trying to lie, or jump to a justification.

Why?

At first to track your location.

Then...

I wanted to be inside your head.

Part of me wants to be angry at him, but the other part is intrigued. It's kind of sick, but no one has ever accused me of being well. Something about me was so interesting to this man who's made for murder that he wanted to know the mundane things about me. The day to day stupid shit that I do on my phone. Another part of me wants to be embarrassed, but it's also kind of a shortcut. I don't even have to bother telling him certain things because he already knows.

What did you learn?

The three dots that he's texting back show for a long time. I'm thinking I'm about to get treated to a list. Even though he's going to be talking about me to me, it's really going to reveal more about him. The things that he thinks are important, worth remembering, focuses on paying attention to, will tell me the things that matter to him. Asking Freelancer outright will get me nowhere. He's got a wall up between us. No, that's not right. He's got a one-way mirror. He can see everything, I can only see myself. He'll only let me see myself.

I want to see him. I don't mean his face, although I'm curious about it, I mean who he is underneath. There's the killer, the hunter, the tracker - but why is he like that? Where did he learn his skills? What motivates him, what matters to him, does he get satisfaction from the work that he does? Freelancer is intriguing, and I can't deny the way my body reacts to his presence and his touch, but I want to know if there's more to us than that.

It's not going to stop me from indulging in the physical with him because I rarely get comfortable to engage with someone the way that I have with Freelancer. Even if this is temporary, I'm not going to regret it. If I decide to walk away, even if I have to fight him to do it, this will still have been worth it.

You like shows you can binge so you don't have to invest your emotions and overwhelm yourself. When you're bored you look up words - their definitions and then their synonyms and antonyms. I think it's because you like to be specific. You argue with people on the internet even though they won't care. You watch way too many cat videos. When you watch porn you like the foreplay more than the sex, and when you read it you like love stories. You like the start of things. I want to follow through with you - all the way to the end.

My heart flutters in my chest. Some of it is accurate. I also didn't expect him to be quite so honest about some of the things he's watched me do on my phone, but I also can't say that he's wrong.

I do like beginnings. When things are exciting and energy is invested in figuring things out. There's adrenaline there. It's keeping me hooked that's always the problem. At some point I know too much, and I turn away because there's nothing else to learn. It's part of the reason I'm afraid to get close to people. I don't want to hurt someone because they stop being intriguing to me. They stop being a mystery and my feelings disappear.

It's never happened because I've never let it.

I cut things off before I have time to learn too much.

It's lonely, but it's the right thing to do.

Freelancer isn't going to let me do that. Maybe he's what I've been looking for. An endless well of information, feelings, unexpected actions, new experiences, that will keep me hooked forever.

I might by cynical, and I might have the darkest of dark sides, but there's also a little bit of a romantic in me. If I find someone that I think I could love forever, I will give them everything I have. The amount of love I have to give would be a burden on the wrong person.

The hard question is: how do I know the right one when I find them? I've never felt anything like I do when I'm with Freelancer, but there's also this weird warmth building between me and Isaac. I've never trusted people as quickly as I seem to trust the two of them. Do I want the danger of Freelancer, or do I want the safety of what Isaac and I could be?

I feel like my head is going to explode. I shove it under my pillow and close my eyes to try and go to sleep. A call from Alina wakes me up, and I spend the rest of the night helping her save her husband.

23

Freelancer

I wake up to a series of alerts on my phone. The klaxon sound I have set for certain events echoes through the small room where I sleep, and it jolts me into awareness. In moments I'm fully awake and opening up my laptop to look into the messages. I kneel on the floor next to the small coffee table where it rests, and race through the alerts to see what's going on.

Someone sent new threats to Don, tried to hack into Aster's private server, and another attack was launched on Designation - specifically the personnel files. It was a coordinated attack because all of it happened or was initiated in the last 5 minutes. Whoever is doing this is not necessarily smart, but motivated, and capable of funding people willing to try to get what they want.

I start with the threat sent to Don, and open the flagged email. If it's something fucked up I want to protect him from seeing it. It's a photo of Aster in Owen's car, likely in the parking lot of Designation. There's a target over her face. It's accompanied by a message:

I will rip her away from you and watch her bleed. I will bury her where you can never find her.

So they're getting a little more graphic and specific. I send a quick text to Don, Owen, and Gailen. They have reason to be concerned - whoever is doing this is getting frustrated, and that makes them even more dangerous.

The rage that races through me is an inferno. My breathing is quick and erratic and my hands are shaking with the need to take this feeling out on the person who deserves it. To hurt anyone who would even think about touching Aster that way. I want to rip apart their entire life, followed by their entire body, and feed them to fucking coyotes.

While I will never regret what brought Aster into my life, I'm livid that anyone wants to punish her for what might be her father's sins. Aster's secret life seems pretty safe - if someone wanted revenge for that, they would be going right for her and not for her father. This is all about something else.

The absolute fucking audacity of my own brain to not figure out what the missing piece is pisses me off. I've questioned Don about everything Aster has ever been involved in for their secret shit as well as for Designation. I know everything there is to know about her, things no one else knows, and I still can't see what it is about her specifically that they think will give them what they want.

If it was about Designation, they should be targeting Owen. He has the power and the access, and is slightly arrogant about his own safety. They could probably take him in a well-planned attack, and wouldn't even need to bother with all their cyber attacks because he could get them in wherever they wanted.

It's got be about punishing the Sorrelles, and Aster is the tool they want to use to do it.

My phone buzzes again.

Was it you?

I stare at Aster's text, puzzled. *What?*

That tried to get into my server.

No. That was a hack. Is it safe?

She sends me an eyeroll emoji in response, so I'll take that as a yes. *I need to go out tonight*, she messages. *I can't take this anymore.*

I'll be there, I reply. Now it's more important than ever that I attach myself to her wherever she goes. They might not know her secret yet, but if they get pissed and obsessive enough they will. They'll know exactly how to bring both Don and Aster down - and they could get her sent to prison.

Given everything that she's been dealing with at work, it tracks that they would try and get into her private server, hoping for something there that would help them. It probably won't even occur to Aster that it was about getting her information specifically. To know what she considers important enough to keep in a private place.

I'm worried that the more threats that come and the more she feels like she's to blame, the more reckless she's going to become. I have to try and keep some of this from her. It's paternalistic as fuck, I know, but it's also true. She'd either put herself in danger trying to hunt them down, or sacrifice herself in order to keep her family safe. Neither is acceptable to me.

I'll be the one to step in front of the bullet, not her.

24

Freelancer

I wait for Aster on my bike, where she usually meets the cab that drives her into the city. It's a warm, wet night but the end of a week of rain means people will be out in droves on a Friday night.

When she comes up the incline and onto the road, I about swallow my tongue.

She's in a black romper that's so damn short I know that I'd be able to see the curve of her tight little ass peeking out. It has a deep V that goes almost down to her belly button and reveals the swell of her small, tight breasts. Her curly hair is down and wild, and her lips are painted black.

I don't know who we're hunting tonight but she's in full pretty predator mode. Anyone who looks at her will be drawn in and want to do whatever she says.

I hand her my helmet, and she gives me a smirk before sliding it over her head. I can feel the tension in her when she gets on behind me, pressing against my body and wrapping her arms around my waist. Aster is strung tight, on the edge of breaking, and I hope that this will clear her head.

If not, it might be time for me to fuck it out of her.

We haven't crossed that line yet. It hasn't been the right time, and honestly, I don't think I can fuck her without kissing her. I've tasted her pussy but I'm desperate to taste her mouth as well. I need my mouth on her when I take her, and I want to give her what I can of my face. Not just touching it, but sitting on it too.

Tonight we'll do something, I know it, because she gets off on the kill. So do I. The energy between us when we're getting off together is astronomical. We took a life and it makes us feel fucking alive.

When we get far enough from her house that it feels safe to slow down, I pull into a gas station to fill up.

"Where are we going?"

Aster takes off the helmet, and tells me the cross streets. I'm familiar with the area. She shakes out her curls and I'm mesmerized by their inky blankness in the bright lights. Her beauty strikes me all the time, and then when her eyes meet mine, the fire inside them already gets my cock hard as a rock in seconds. It's tempting to go behind the station and fuck those pretty black lips until she's all messy, lipstick all over my dick and her face.

Later.

"Who's the target?"

Now her eyes really glow, malice coming from deep inside their brown depths.

"Dirk Andresson."

"Dirk, really?" There's humor in my voice, and she smiles in return. It's pure fucking evil. "What did Dirk do?"

"Gets his victims drunk, unconscious, and then films himself. I had someone take it to the police but they said since you never saw his face, there was nothing they could do."

"Smells like bullshit."

"It is," she nearly growls. "So I guess I'll have to take care of it myself." Then she smiles again and I don't care how tiny she is, if I was the reason for that look and those intentions on her face, I'd run like the devil was after me. Aster is beyond a little monster - she's a demon. A demon that's already claimed my soul.

Before we get back on my bike, we make a game plan for inside the bar. Aster already has it all planned out in her head - she's studied his hunting habits, disrupted quite a few of his attempts, but she can't babysit all the animals all the time. I hate the idea of Aster as bait because I know he's going to put his hands on her, I know he's going to touch her in places that only I should be touching, but I also know that I'll do anything she asks of me. Even this.

Aster climbs back on behind me, wiggling her hips against my ass.

"Wet already, baby?"

"Maybe." She slides down the visor on the helmet, and I take off onto the highway. I don't go as fast as I'd like because the roads are still slick and she's precious cargo. I drop her off at the front of the bar and take the bike around back, stashing it in the alley for a quick getaway before I go in the back door.

It's the hallway where the bathrooms and storage rooms are, and it's packed even back here. There are lines for both bathrooms, people making out or more in the deeply recessed doorways, and bartenders running back and forth from storage when they've gotten low on liquor.

The body heat hits me like a wall as I get to the club proper. It's a massive dance floor writhing with bodies, and a bunch of big round booths on elevated platforms around it. There's a balcony VIP area, and people are looking down on the crowd from above.

I work my way around the room until I spot the booth Aster told me Dirk occupies. She's already made her way up to his table, sitting with him and his friends - a mix of men and women.

It's amazing to watch her performance, the way she gets everybody to look one direction and switches out drinks for an empty one, passing the full drink off to someone else at the table. Even from my distance I can hear her laugh getting louder, and the way she makes her gestures more exaggerated. She touches everyone around her, even Dirk from across the table.

With my view, I can see that underneath she's started running the toe of her shoe up and down his calf. Dirk is fixated on staring at her, even though she's not looking back.

One of his friends declares that they should dance, and while the rest of the group gets up to push onto the dance floor, Aster and Dirk stay behind. They talk quietly, or quietly enough that I can't hear them.

Dirk signals to the server and after a few minutes she brings them a tray of shots. I wonder how Aster is going to pull off not drinking them, and it takes me a few tries to see what she's doing. He closes his eyes when he drinks, and she slides her shot down and dumps it in a cup on the booth seat next to her. Dirk doesn't even notice, and thinks they've put down multiple shots together.

When he asks Aster to dance, it takes everything I have not to tear across the club and rip him to pieces. Dirk grinds on her, grabbing her ass and too high on her thighs to be appropriate, and slides his hand into the romper to rest on her stomach below her breast. I'm going to cut off his fucking hands when she's done with him.

For Aster's part, she starts leaning on him more and more heavily, letting her head bob like she's losing consciousness or extremely out of it.

Dirk is subtle. They start moving closer and closer to the entrance, only a few steps and sways at a time. If he was going to drag her out, or even pick her up and carry her, it would cause too much attention. This way no one is watching until they're almost out the door. It shows how practiced he is at shit like this.

I follow when he wraps his arm around her shoulder, tucking Aster close to his body, and walks with complete confidence out of the club.

Even though Aster is stumbling, no one even looks twice. I'm only a few steps behind them as they leave.

Once we're outside, I follow at a bit of a distance so it doesn't look suspicious. The street is filled with people walking to different bars and clubs so it doesn't stand out that I'm following. I'm far enough away, and stayed far enough from Aster, that she didn't see me without my mask.

When he guides her into the parking garage, I take the flexible mesh from my pocket and slide it over my head. It's not just protecting my face, it's like putting on a very specific persona. One that wants Dirk's blood.

From what Aster told me, Dirk takes the drunkest ones to his car and films himself assaulting them in the backseat. If they aren't quite drunk enough he takes them home and gives them more drinks. Looks like Aster made all the right moves to be put in the backseat.

She doesn't need me, not yet, so when I see his car, I arrange myself behind a pillar. I can see everything and get there quick if she needs me, but I'm hidden enough that Dirk won't notice me. I'm here for the show.

Dirk gets the back car door open, and flops Aster down inside. Her feet don't even touch the ground because she's so short, and the sight of her dangling there with the appearance of vulnerability makes me fucking sick. It makes me sick for every woman he did this to, thinking they were objects for his use instead of human beings with autonomy and choices. I know what it's like to feel like all my choices were made for me, and I didn't get a say in what happened to me. I can't even imagine how much worse it is in a sexual context.

Predictably, Dirk takes out his phone. I watch as he runs his hand down her body - across her throat, down the valley between her breasts, her soft stomach, and then over her crotch. When he leans into the car and over her body, the show begins.

Aster brings her legs in close to her body, presses her feet to his chest, and pushes. Dirk goes flying back, smashing into the wall. Of course he parks in a corner, protecting himself from view.

It's like watching a snake coil and strike when Aster slides out of the car and attacks him. She hits him with quick, sharp jabs that hurt, and then a solid blow to the solar plexus that makes all the air leave him in a whoosh. Then she goes for the nut shot, which makes me cringe automatically even if I have no sympathy for this piece of shit.

When he drops to his knees she whips out her knife. I have no idea where she kept it since there doesn't appear to be a lot of places to hide it in that romper, but it's at his throat in a quick second. It rests comfortably in her hand, a tool poised to be used the way some people might hold a pen. Watching her lethal competence is getting me hard.

I start walking over, wanting to hear the final moments.

I pick up his phone from where it dropped on the ground when she attacked, and it's still recording. I aim it at Dirk's face.

"Tell the camera what you were going to do to me."

Dirk is pale and crying. It's fucking pathetic. "I was going to take you home. You were drunk," he whines.

Aster slashes down his chest. Dirk's shirt rips open and a line of blood appears. He cries out, and I laugh. It seems to make him even more terrified. Good.

"What were you going to do to me, Dirk?"

"Nothing," he gulps.

"Why did you touch me then?"

He has no answer.

"Were you going to rape me, Dirk? Film yourself fucking an unconscious woman in the back of your car?"

"I'd tell her the truth," I advise him. He looks at me, then back at Aster, doing some mental calculations. Right now, he probably believes that if he confesses, he might live.

"Yes." He hangs his head.

Aster slashes him again and he screams. "Yes what?" she demands.

"I was going to fuck you and film it."

"You've done it before?"

Dirk nods.

"Right now," she purrs at him, "you're going to try and promise me that you've learned your lesson, that you'll stop, you'll never do it again." Dirk looks at her with hope in his eyes, nodding profusely. He's mistaking the benevolent smile on her face for mercy.

"But you're a predator - it takes one to know one - and I can't let you live."

"No-" Dirk starts to speak but it's cut off by a gurgle when Aster slices the knife deep and hard across his throat. Blood spills down in a thick, dark sheet, flooding across his shirt, his pants, and down onto the concrete of the parking garage floor. It's incredibly satisfying. He slides down the wall, and then slumps down onto the ground. I pocket his phone. I'll delete the video later.

Aster cleans her knife on his pants and then tucks it up the leg of the romper. I wait to see what she'll do next.

I stand still as she stalks over to me, tiny but powerful, and presses me into the wall. We're in a corner, protected from view.

The moment she drops to her knees in front of me, I'm hard and ready to go. Aster gets my cock out of my jeans and wraps her soft, warm hand around me before putting the head in her mouth. It's so fucking warm. All my self control goes to holding back from fucking the shit out of her face, so I can let her take what she wants from me in this moment. I know her mouth gets sensitive, and I know she gets enjoyment from this too.

I'm still going to bend her over the bag of shit's car and make her come on my fingers though.

When she takes me into the back of her throat and swallows, the muscle working around the sensitive head, I can't fucking stop my hips from thrusting forward. My hand dives into her soft, wild curls and I grip her hard, finding a rhythm we can both handle as I slide in and out of her silky, wet softness. Aster moans around my cock, digs her fingernails into my thighs, and from this angle I can watch her squirm as she gets turned on.

She releases my cock with a wet pop. "Do it."

"Do what?" I need to hear her say it.

"Fuck my mouth."

"Ask me nicely, little monster." I yank her head back by her hair, stretching out her neck. "I know you're in slut mode but manners, baby, manners."

"Fuck my mouth, please." She rasps, licking her lips.

"Good monster." I relax my hold. I watch her lean forward and slide my cock between her lips again. Her lipstick remains intact at the moment, and I'm going to change that. Aster looks up at me, aroused desperation on her face as she keeps eye contact and works me further into her.

My restraint snaps. I keep one hand in her hair and wrap the other around the base of my cock, and then I start to move. It feels incredible. She's so wet and warm, and watching the way her eyes flutter shut as I pick up the pace, the head hitting the back of her throat and causing a rush of saliva that makes me moan into the empty space around us. It echoes off the concrete.

Aster slurps at my cock, trying to keep up with me. I'm going to punish her mouth and come down her throat, and then I'm going to reward her by making her scream and come until her legs are shaking.

My orgasm is coming fast, and I don't warn her. I push her down to her limit and hold her there as my release explodes out of me and into her throat. Aster moans again, and swallows around me, taking it all.

I don't give her time to recover. Instead, I slip from her mouth, grab her under the arms, and throw her across the trunk of the car. My hand slides up under her romper and I meet the bare, velvet skin of her pussy lips.

"Naughty girl, Aster," I growl as I tease her. She's already soaked, the smell of her pussy reaching me easily through the mask. I take my hand out and reach around, sliding my fingers into her mouth. She sucks at them eagerly. My fingers come away smeared with black from her lipstick, and the satisfaction at mussing her up is primal.

I yank the shorts aside again, and slide those same two fingers into her hot, needy pussy. Aster cries out immediately, backing her sweet little ass up, chasing the feeling. She moves her ass back and forth, fucking my fingers, and it's the hottest thing I've ever seen. I shift so my thumb can rub against her clit as she gets herself off.

"Come all over my hand. You've earned it. Fuck it gets me hot watching you kill, baby."

"Yeah?" Aster moans, moving faster and grinding harder.

"You're dangerous."

She's getting close because I can feel her pussy squeezing my fingers and she can't answer me except in unintelligible sounds. I let go of her shorts to reach up and wrap my hand around her throat, holding her steady. She's about to fucking explode.

Aster continues to move, and then I start to move back. I slide my fingers in and out of her, moving fast and pressing in deep, fucking her hard. The wet sounds of her arousal join the echoes of her moaning, her pussy beyond wet and primed to come.

"Fuck!" Aster screams it, long and drawn out, as she clenches around my fingers, pussy working through her orgasm. When I feel her relax, I slide my fingers out of her and pull her back against my body.

I wrap my arms around her, swaying gently as she leans back against me. My cock is still out and its getting hard again, tucked against the top of her ass. I don't care. This is the moment that I really want.

Holding her, soothing her, recovering with her after the emotional high of a kill and the adrenaline rush of an orgasm.

We stand like that for a long time, longer than is safe considering we're next to a dead body. Then we walk out of the garage, and I take her home.

25

Aster

I feel better.

It's going to sound crazy, but killing with someone else feels better than killing alone. Even though I did the dirty work, so to speak, knowing that Freelancer had my back felt good. It felt right. Knowing that he was there - not only to protect me but also to enjoy me - was hot. In some twisted way, he's proud of me.

Someday I'd like to see how he works, too. I want to see Freelancer unleashed.

My feelings are complicated though. When I get into work Monday, Isaac is already there and waiting for me. He looks excited, and seeing the fire in his eyes makes me happy. It makes my stomach flutter. I don't like having feelings that are complicated but right now they are.

Freelancer makes me feel something dark, heavy, and sexual. With him, it's the darkest, most brutal side of my personality. We dive into the dark together and he never judges me for my needs.

Isaac brings out something lighter in me. I'm attracted to him but I also enjoy that he makes me smile. That he pushes my walls without pushing my boundaries beyond where I'm comfortable. He's also comfortable around me, which I can't say about many people, and I like that we can open up to each other about our lives. I can tell him about the normal stuff and it makes me feel normal.

I sit in what's become my new regular spot in the pod, next to Isaac. "It's ready."

I sit up straighter. "Seriously?"

"Yes. I had Thor and Tella look through it, and then also had Marie give it a try - I didn't tell her what she was looking at and it took her a minute to believe it wasn't real. Our mock base codes are a near perfect version of the actual system. Without the key information. If they access it, we'll be able to trace them back. It will give a physical location to track down."

"Should we go live tonight?"

"We know the access point they last used and we haven't closed it - this might be our only chance."

My grin is giddy and a little relieved. We're making progress. This is a distinct, offensive move that will help us protect Designation. It's nice to actually be doing something, instead of reacting to the things that keep happening. Plus, when I find the bastards who are fucking with us I'll make them regret ever being born.

Isaac and I both grin with excitement, and on impulse and instinct we come together and hug. It's weird that it's not weird. I'm feeling good about something and I don't feel uncomfortable with him touching me.

A throat clearing snaps us apart, and Isaac looks as guilty as I feel when we turn back to look at Dominic. He's glowering at the two of us, but doesn't say anything before stomping over to his station and getting to work. No one is usually here this early - it's not even 8 yet - and we weren't even doing anything wrong. It was a freaking hug.

"Boss?" Dominic rumbles from behind me.

"Yeah?" I get up and go over to him, leaning on the desk. Dominic is a big dude. Isaac is tall, but he's wiry even though he's muscular.

Dominic is broad, his musculature more obvious, and his stance a bit more physically imposing. Still, all that muscle comes from lifting in a gym not actually kicking ass, so I have no doubts that I could cut him down if needed.

Why am I thinking like that about Dominic? He's not a threat. He's my employee. My teammate. What the fuck. If this is how I'm going to be thinking I need to put distance back between me and Isaac.

An awkward silence falls between us while Dominic glares at his computer and Isaac stares at his, pretending like he's not listening to us.

"I think I found the identity of the hacker."

"What?!" I stand up and turn, leaning over next to him.

"See this line? This is the signature. I knew I'd seen it before - it was part of that hack on federal loan info last year, remember?" I do remember, because we got a bunch of new government contracts after that hack in order to beef up their security. "Their handle is Sn0wWh1te. I've seen them around before."

"So have I. How did we not recognize it earlier? The signature is right there."

"We were looking for a black hat. SnowWh1te is a gray hat."

"Why would someone like that attack us though? Designation has a good reputation."

Dominic frowns and shakes his head. "I don't know."

We sit in silence for a few minutes, all of us digesting that information. Isaac turns around in his office chair, looking at Dominic until the other man returns his gaze.

"Do you still talk to him?"

"Still talk to who?" I look between them. I'm missing information and I don't like it.

"My brother," Dominic rumbles. "He's a black hat. On and off the grid for years. A little bit of jail time, too. And yes, I can reach him if

I need to, but he isn't going to do shit for us." Isaac opens his mouth but Dominic stops him. "Or for me."

"Clear this up for me, jerks."

"We could try and use my brother to get in touch with SnowWh1te and find out what the hell is going on."

I shake my head. "No. We're not going down that road. We know who they are, know what to look for, and we have other plans in place. None of that bring in the criminal to solve the crime bullshit. It's clear you don't trust him Dominic. I'm not putting you in that position."

"Thank you," he says, and makes eye contact with me for the first time since he arrived today. A sad understanding passes between us - he might have feelings but they are not returned on my part. It's not that I'm choosing Isaac - we're not together and I have an obsessive murderer pursuing me who would probably kill him if I did - but Dominic isn't even part of the equation for me.

"Let's get to work."

I take my laptop and curl up in my dark corner, and start studying everything I can find on this hacker who is messing with my livelihood and my family.

I'm the last member of my team still at the office, and I'm snapped out of my deep dive by Nino walking in the door. Since everything, I'm never allowed to leave by myself, and I'm not allowed to stay after it starts to get dark. That's pretty late in the summer, but the guys are under orders to get me out by 7:00pm.

I honestly have no idea when everyone else left. There's a cold cup of coffee on the table in front of me, and I can't recall if I got it myself and forgot about it or didn't notice someone leaving it for me. When I'm totally focused on a project, everything else can fall to the side. I try to get adequate sleep, but beyond that I exist on sheer obsession.

"Time to go, Aster," Nino says quietly, trying not to piss me off with his presence. Lucky for him, he's not. What I studied on our hacker nemesis today has given me lots of pieces of ideas about how to defend against them. They haven't come together yet, but give me a few days and something will emerge. My mind works in mysterious ways, even to me.

Without responding, I pack up my stuff and grab the cup of coffee.

Nino shadows me as I stop at the break room and dump out the cup and stick it in the shared dishwasher. It's mostly full so I start it up, trying to be considerate of everyone else on our floor.

He's looking around, calm and vigilant, and I can tell that he's a little on edge. Whatever is going on, it's got everyone nervous. I must be missing something because as far as I can tell, it's a series of hacks and a sloppy kidnapping attempt.

We walk through the mostly empty lobby, and my car is parked in one of the closer spots. Owen must've warned them I was in serious work mode and had Nino plan to stay behind. It makes me feel guilty that everyone is maneuvering around me, like I'm not capable of organizing and handling these things for myself - I have to be handled. They might see me as a weapon, and be afraid of what I'm capable of, but someone has to set and aim me.

It makes me feel like a child.

It also makes me feel protected.

I know people love my sisters, even Alina, because they are capable of showing love and affection freely. They can talk about their feelings, good and bad, and demonstrate that they care about others. They can touch people without having to prepare themselves, or be under the influence. It's natural for them to smile, laugh, or express sympathy. It's easy for other people to care about them.

That's not the case with me, and I know it. My sisters love me mostly because they think they have to - I think Aro genuinely loves me but it's because I have the least amount of barriers with her. Even with dad I think it comes from a place of responsibility and guilt to take care of me. I don't think he looks at me and feels love or affection. He feels duty.

I guess when you've been a grumpy, murdery little shit your whole life that's the best that can be hoped for. Dad would never let anything happen to me, and this is the proof.

The sun is still decently high in the sky, reflecting off the window of the car and nearly blinding us. I follow protocol and let Nino exit the building first, his head on a vigilant swivel, his eyes scanning quickly. He signals that I can exit the building and we start walking.

We both hear footsteps running toward us, and turn as one. Nino lifts his gun in a smooth, practiced motion.

"Birdsong! Birdsong!" It's Freelancer, masked, running towards us and pointing toward the roof of the building. It takes me a moment to remember what that's code for, but Nino knows.

He shoves me to the ground and moves so his body is blocking mine, and then turns, aiming his gun at the roof of the building.

Birdsong is code for sniper.

Freelancer slides to the ground next to me, trying to drag me up and away. I let him do it.

"Nino!" I yell, trying to get him to step back with us and behind the shield of the car.

It's too late. I watch him fire, three shots, and follow their trajectory up to the shadow on the roof of the Designation atrium. One louder, echoing shot fires, and Nino's head is gone in a spray of bloody mist.

"Come on, Aster, we have to go." Freelancer drags me to the car and throws me in the backseat, takes the keys from my hands, then gets behind the wheel and screeches out of the parking lot, probably destroying my wheels with the amount of smoke we're leaving behind. I'm not sure why I'm thinking about that right now.

Nino died for me.

"Call your father," Freelancer says. It takes me a minute to process. My brain is already mush from the work day and now the shock of a straight up murder attempt is more than I can compute.

Slowly, I take my phone out of my pocket.

"On speaker."

Dad answers. "Aster?" I never call him so the panic is earned. If it can't be said in a text I don't bother saying it.

"Sir," Freelancer speaks, "there was an attempt. Nino's gone."

"Fuck." Dad almost never swears. "Aster, are you alright?"

"I'm alive." The most honest answer.

"Okay." His voice is soft, and reassuring. Dad's always like that. Freelancer reaches over and squeezes my thigh, trying to calm me with his touch. I squeeze his hand and then lift it off of me. I don't want to be touched right now and I'd prefer if he had two hands on the wheel while driving like a bat out of hell.

Touch is something that affects me. Every time I think of Nino, I'm going to feel exactly where he pressed against my shoulder to push me down. The feeling will be burned into my sense memories forever. I will always know that was the last interaction we had before he gave his life for mine.

The world I live in is so fucking fucked.

When we pull into the house, I get out and walk to the door, and then straight over to dad's office. He's on the phone when we walk in, and Owen is pacing in the corner growling at someone on his cell phone. Gailen and Alonzo are nowhere to be found and I suspect they are dealing with what we left behind at Designation. Who we left behind.

Fucking Nino, doing his job. I'm not worth anyone dying for, let alone him.

"You're on lockdown," dad says, snapping me out of my anger spiral.

"What? There's too much work to do! No. No - I have to be in the office. I don't have anything I need."

"I'll have whatever you need brought here."

"My entire team?"

Dad gives me a look. "Don't be ridiculous."

I huff but nod. Without saying a word to anyone, or even glancing at Freelancer, I leave and go to my room. There is no way that I can be rational right now, and everything they say will set me off. With each passing minute they'll learn more information and another burden will be added to the already massive guilt I'm carrying.

For a moment I stand there, taking deep breaths, the itch crawling along my skin to kill everyone and everything until I am baptized in blood and anger.

Instead, I close my blackout curtains and crawl into bed.

26

Aster

I feel a finger run across the top of my foot.

As I come awake, in the pitch dark, I know that it's Freelancer touching me. His finger trails up my leg, over my knee, and along my thigh until it meets the shorts I'm sleeping in. Then he flattens his hand, the palm pressing in and over my skin. Across my stomach, between my breasts, until it's wrapped gently around my throat.

"Hi," I whisper into the dark. After what happened today I felt alone - I wanted someone to be there and I wanted to push them away at the same time. It was hard not to text him and demand he leave the job to be with me, but that would draw too much attention. The last thing I want right now is my family interfering with what I have with Freelancer. I need him so much. I need him right now.

"What do you need?" His voice sounds different, and I realize that he's not wearing his mask. We're in the dark, I can't see him, and a barrier between us has dropped. For now.

"You." It's vulnerable, honest, and difficult to say. The word strangles in my throat but I push it out.

His hand flexes around my throat as he hums, and my pussy clenches in response. I need to be brought down to my basest existence right now. To being a primal animal. Wetness floods my panties and part of me wants to dive at him and attack him, ripping at him until he's inside me. The more patient, sane part, is waiting to see where he takes this.

Freelancer leans close. I can feel his breath on my face.

"Open your mouth."

I do as he says, and a shocked gasp escapes me when he spits in my mouth. His saliva tastes like him and slides down my tongue. I swallow on a moan.

"I want to kiss you, little monster."

I nod against his hand. I know why he's asking. I've talked to him before about how sometimes kissing makes me uncomfortable, or that I haven't wanted it in the past. To be fair, I've told him lots of things about what I like and don't like. Torturing him with my sexual fantasies and appetites, taunting him into action. Finally, it's worked when I need it the most.

Freelancer slides his tongue into my mouth, taunting my lips, tongue, and teeth, working all those sweet sensitive nerve endings before sealing our lips together. It's absolutely filthy, and I think that's why I like it. He tastes so damn delicious.

The other thing I realize is that our mental closeness makes me more comfortable with physical touch from him - not only sexual touch but touch of any kind. Ever since I fell apart in his arms after killing Ryan Volkov, I've been coming to the realization that I'm more comfortable with him than I've ever been with anyone.

My hands reach out for him, and I meet the smooth, bare skin of his torso. My fingers trace the muscles beneath the skin, familiarizing myself with the landscape of his body. There's so much it overwhelms my senses in a way that I like - the dips and ridges of his abs, the smooth slope of his pecs, and I trace my fingers along his collarbones before sliding them up into his hair.

It's soft. So soft, and I'm so sensitive right now that the pleasing feel of it sends a shiver through my body. I tug on him until he follows, moving onto the bed and his body over mine. He fits perfectly between my thighs, and I can feel his hard cock beneath his pants, pressing into my center. I lift my hips and grind against him. We haven't been physical with each other in days, so much has happened that hit me hard, and this is an overload for me. I like it.

He breaks the kiss. "Do you want me to fuck you, little monster? Feel you take this cock like a good girl?"

"Yes," I answer. He licks my lips, and then pulls away. I feel his hands trail over my skin as they lift my tank top, and I take over and pull it over my head and off my body. When his tongue teases my nipple I cry out and cling to him, trying to pull him down and against me. He sucks at one nipple and then the other, hard and deep and then with a little bit of teeth. The edge of pain feels good. He grinds his hips down into me, sending sparks from my pussy to the rest of my body.

"Your skin tastes so fucking good," he tells me, and kisses down my body until he gets to my shorts. Freelancer yanks them down and off me, shorts and panties in one pull, throwing them into the dark. His mouth attacks my pussy like he's starving for it. He sucks so hard at my clit I'm on the edge almost immediately, driving my hips into his face and chasing the feeling of release. He groans into my skin and the vibration of his voice increases the intense feeling.

When he slides two fingers inside me, I have to slap my hands over my mouth to stop from screaming out. He's fucking me rough and deep with his fingers, alternately sucking and nibbling at my clit, and I think this might be the biggest orgasm I've ever had, if he lets me get there.

"I could eat you forever." He licks my clit with the flat of his tongue, letting my body relax. I know he's doing it to make everything more intense later. Edging me again. "Never tasted anything that made me as happy as you."

My heart flutters in my chest and I comb my hands through his hair, letting my nails tease his scalp. Freelancer presses into me and resumes his attack on my clit. Everything behind my eyes goes white as I start to come, my hips thrust off the bed and into his face, my thighs shaking from holding myself so tight as I do everything I can not to scream out into the darkness and make the whole house hear how good I feel.

When I come down, he slides back up my body, holding me close. His nose bumps mine.

"Open," he says, and I do, poking my tongue out to touch his lip so he knows. Saliva slides into my mouth, and it tastes like me and like him and I love it.

"I want to taste you," I murmur against his mouth, kissing him everywhere I can reach - his lips, his chin, his nose, his neck. When I breathe against his neck, his hips roll, and I do it again. I lick and suck and bite, enjoying that way he squeezes me and presses into me as I tease him. "Let me suck your cock. I want to be on my knees for you."

"Fucking hell, little monster." Freelancer moves off of me and I sit up, feeling that he's on the bed with his legs hanging off. I slide onto the floor and kneel between his legs, undoing his jeans and sliding everything off of him and onto the floor. We've never been naked together, and the thrill of it gives me a shiver.

His cock is hard and hot, and pulses in my hand. I'm ravenous for him, and don't tease. I open my mouth and take him in as deep as I can, deep until I gag and spit floods out of my mouth and down his shaft. It's all over my fist, dripping down to his balls, and I love the way he groans as he feels it. I slide up and down with my mouth on his smooth, warm flesh, my hand following my lips as I work him, going deeper with every stroke.

I don't want to stop - I want him to come in my mouth again and I want to taste him, but I also want him to fuck me.

"Finish me off, little monster," he says like he's reading my mind. "Swallow me down that pretty throat. Nothing could stop me from fucking you tonight, and I know what a little slut you are for my come."

Fuck fuck fuck. I almost orgasmed right there hearing him say it. I do have a sensitive mouth, and get extremely turned on from performing oral sex. I groan around his cock and he buries his hand in my hair, fisting it as I move up and down on him, sucking hard and enjoying the flavor of his skin.

"Take it, baby," he groans, seconds before I feel the flood of his come across my tongue. I swallow, sucking soft and deep as he presses into my mouth. He's salty and hot, and I take it all.

"Such a good little monster." He strokes my cheek when I slide off of him. "How do you want me to fuck you first? Missionary so I can kiss you and we taste ourselves while I pound that pussy? From behind so I can play with your clit and make you scream? Or do you want to ride me, baby, and dig those claws into my chest while you come?"

"Kiss me," I say, and sound desperate. I am desperate.

Freelancer picks me up and throws me down on the bed, climbing over me. I feel the hot head of his cock at my entrance, and then he's sliding easily into me. I'm so fucking wet, and he glides in, a perfect fit making me feel full in the best way.

I bury my hands in his hair and pull him to me, our mouths meeting in sloppy wet kisses. I can taste his come still, taste myself, and the flavor that's just him - his lips, his tongue, his spit - and the slide of our tongues gets me even wetter. Freelancer starts to slide his cock in and out of me, working me slowly. His hips grind into my clit every time he bottoms out inside me.

I wrap my arms around his neck, pulling him to me because even though he's literally inside me I want to be closer. I want to crawl inside his body and live there. I want to rip each other to pieces and sew them back together, inseparable. He bites my lip and I moan, thrusting my hips and enjoying the decadent feeling of his cock going in and out of me.

"You're mine, Aster. There's nowhere you can go that I won't find you, fuck you, and drag you back. In that order."

"Are you mine?" I ask, embarrassed by my insecurity but also feeling as possessive of him as he does of me.

"I've never been anybody else's," he groans, "I've been searching for you my whole fucking life."

I moan, overwhelmed by the emotions and the physical sensations. He starts to move faster, the sound of our bodies smacking together echoing in the room. One press of his hips and swipe of his tongue against mine and I'm coming again. I cry out and whimper into his mouth, and he eats up my sounds and my breath as I come.

Then he rolls us over, and when I'm on top he slides even further into my body.

"Fuck me. Show me how much you love my cock and make me come inside that perfect pussy."

I brace my hands on his chest and start to roll my hips, sliding up and down on him until I find the right pace. I work his cock in and out of my pussy, sliding up and then slamming my ass down on his hips. He groans and holds onto my hips, fingers digging in and I know he'll leave bruises. I go faster, rolling and sliding, responding to the noises that he makes. Every movement gives me incredible pleasure because I'm already so sensitive.

"Come inside me," I whine, building up to my own orgasm as I fuck him. "I want to feel you." I slam down and cry out, slapping one hand over my mouth as my orgasm hits. My pussy spasms around his cock and I try to keep moving, keep pumping him as the pleasure ratchets through my body, like lightning along my skin. I keep going as the pleasure hits me in waves, and then he slams my hips down and groans, hips pumping shallowly as he fills me up.

When we're both back on earth and breathing again, he sits up and pulls me to him, kissing me fiercely. I can feel his come leaking out of my pussy, covering both of us.

Freelancer rolls us over, and slides out of me. I hate the feeling. Then he's sliding two fingers inside me, pressing against that spot that drives me crazy, fucking me with both our come. I'm surprised when he leans forward to suck on my clit again, given the fact that he's probably tasting his own semen. That's unbearably hot, and I'm going to come again.

"One more time, little monster."

The rough sound of his voice does it, and I tip over the edge, both hands slapped over my face as I scream into them. My body is so incredibly sensitive that even the pleasure feels a little bit like pain.

I'm utterly spent.

Freelancer climbs on to bed beside me and wraps his arms around me. I do what feels right and snuggle my head into his chest.

"When can I see you?"

He knows what I'm asking. "As soon as it's safe."

"But won't you have to leave?"

"No. I'm never leaving you."

Then I fall asleep, dripping come and restored in body and mind.

27

Aster

The second I think anyone is in the office in the morning, I call. I'm glad it's Isaac that picks up, and it's also totally unsurprising. He's always there early like I am.

"Hey boss," he drawls. "Where are you?"

"Don't ask questions, just do what I say."

"Kinky," he laughs, and I can't help the slight lift of my lips.

"Shut up. I have to work from home for awhile, and I need you to get some of my stuff together." I start listing everything, where it is on my station, and where my spare bag is so it can all be transported safely.

"Do you want me to bring it over?"

"Yes," I answer without hesitation. Otherwise he'll have to give it to Owen and I'll lose an entire day of work. If Isaac brings it over, I'll only lose a few hours.

"Be there soon." He hangs up without saying anything else, and I realize he didn't ask where we live or how to get here. I mean, it's not like people who work for us aren't aware of the estate, but most of them don't know where it is. I file that away to think about later.

To make time pass a little faster, I go into my bathroom and take a long, long shower. I deep condition my curls, and go through the routine I skip more often than I should to make them curl nice and soft instead of frizzing out. My body is a little sore from Freelancer last night, but he also gave me a lot of relief.

The itch for violence is under control for the moment. My need for vengeance and answers has sharpened into obsessive clarity. This is about me. It's about my family. It's about Nino. I can't have let him die in vain - I never should have been at Designation that late. I never should have put him in that position. I owe him a debt that I can never repay.

When I'm done and dressed, I march down to dad's office. I know now that whoever is after us no longer wants me alive, and that means they figured something out about accessing Designation that they feel they no longer need.

The depth to which I am vulnerable and in danger right now has sunk in. I was furious with dad last night for putting me on lockdown but I know it's the right thing to do. No matter how careful I would be, the safest place is right here, secure. I won't have any more of our men put in danger because of me, or bring the danger around the innocent people at Designation.

I open the door hard enough that it slams into the wall and bounces back at me. Dad and Gailen look up at me, caught off guard but neither are surprised when they see that it's me. Gailen at least looks a little bit ashamed. He's been annoying as hell lately and maybe if he hadn't kept getting my back up so I'd run away, things could've been different.

"So now what? I'm trapped here, what the fuck do I do now?"

"Don't speak to me that way, dear." His tone doesn't change from being soft and fatherly. "Can I help you with something?"

"Where are we on finding the sniper?"

"Still looking," dad answers. Gailen frowns.

"Are you going to let me question him when we find him?" I know

I've hit my mark when Gailen looks away and Dad's frown deepens. That was going to be a no. They don't trust me to hold it together and get answers instead of exact revenge for Nino.

"It doesn't seem necessary. It's more important that you focus on your safety. Take precautions."

"Precautions got our men killed!" I kick the chair in front of his desk. Gailen immediately moves to right the chair, and to be a petulant ass, I kick it again and stare him down until he sits and leaves it knocked over.

I glower at him, but dad remains unmoved and unafraid. He's one of the only people I can't intimidate because he knows I'd never hurt him. Physically, anyway. I'd have no problem disobeying him and risking myself regardless of how it would make him feel. If it was the right thing to do, then it's the thing that needs to get done.

"You can't be involved anymore, not like you have been."

"Why not?"

"I need you at Designation. It's safer if that's your focus. I will not let you act as if nothing is happening. I will not use you as bait."

"Do we have any ideas?"

"No," dad frowns, "they are proving as illusive as our hacker."

"That doesn't make me feel any better."

"Me either."

We've reached an impasse. Dad isn't wrong - I shouldn't be bait. That's a bad idea and leaves too many possibilities for error. If something happens to me, we lose all our leads.

So I have to keep focusing on the hacker, and now I have to do it from home. Whoever is hunting me is not going to stop either approach, and this is probably the safest place for me to be.

The doorbell rings and I stand up to get the door.

"Aster!" dad calls after me to stop me.

"They aren't going to show up at the door and shoot me in the face!"

"You don't know that!"

I roll my eyes as I open the door. It's Isaac, like I suspected when I heard the bell. I take a step back to open the door further and let him in. He's got my bag, as well as a large monitor. He thought of everything.

When I give him a genuine smile, I hear Gailen swear behind me.

"The fuck are you doing here?" he snarls.

"I'm Isaac," he steps inside and nods at Gailen. "I work with Aster. I'm bringing her what she needs to work at home. Where do you want this?" He turns to me.

We both ignore Gailen as I take a few steps back into the house and Isaac follows. We go up the stairs and down the hall to my room. Aro pops out of hers when she hears me coming, and stops short when she sees that someone is with me.

"Hello," she draws it out in hesitation. "Who are you?"

"Isaac. I'm helping Aster." He lifts the monitor.

"Why?" Aro looks confused.

"I'll tell you later," I raise my eyebrows at her so she gets the hint that it's not something to talk about in front of civilians.

Aro nods. "Okay…" she steps backwards into her room like she's rewinding herself and closes the door. Isaac chuckles lightly and I feel both relieved and a tiny bit jealous.

When I open the door, it occurs to me I've never let anyone other than my sisters into my room before. Well, Freelancer but he came in without permission on those occasions, and probably other times when I wasn't even there. There's nothing for me to be embarrassed about, but I feel self-conscious nonetheless.

My room is tidy and blank. The walls are painted dark gray, my bedding is black. There's a single, large painting on one wall. Aro made one for all of us. Mine surprised me, but I still kind of like it. It's shades of white and cream, with more variation than I'd ever think, painted in smooth, straight lines. Then, of course, splattered with dark red paint. It's me, as she sees me, and I like how it makes me feel. There's a TV, a dresser, and a desk that's empty.

Isaac looks around quickly, then walks over to the desk. He sets down the monitor and goes about setting up a work station for me there. He even brought a dock so I could use my ports the way that I like. I watch, amused, as he acts as my personal IT support and gets everything up and running. When my monitor turns on and the login screen appears, he turns to look at me.

"What?" He looks bemused.

"I could've done that."

"I know." Isaac shrugs and walks over to me. "I wanted to do something nice for you."

"Thank you," I sigh and give him another small smile. "I'm sure I'll be calling you plenty, demanding you do things for me from Designation."

"I live to serve," he says, something suggestive underneath the statement. We lock eyes and there's heat there, but I break the connection first. I'm torn up emotionally on many levels right now, and I think the heat I've been experiencing with Freelancer is carrying over into other aspects of my life. I've never felt so many things at one time and I might be losing control of the tight lid I keep on feelings.

The thing is, there might never be anyone who fits with me like Freelancer. Isaac might make the most normal and innocent parts of me happy, but Freelancer...he sees and accepts all of me. Even if it means we will spend most of our lives walking in the dark, I don't think I can ever give up a connection like that. I don't know what it means for my future, but I plan on indulging in it for the present.

Isaac sighs and puts his hands in his pockets. "Talk soon?"

"Of course." I turn and guide him out of the room, down the stairs, and back to the front door. Before leaving, he turns and takes my hand.

"Anything you need, Aster."

"Thanks, Isaac." I watch him walk to his car, and don't step inside and close the door until he drives out of my sight.

When I turn around, I nearly run smack into Gailen's chest. I take a step back but he's already caught me, hands caged around my biceps. I look up at him, the way that I have to look up at everybody when they get too close. It's frustrating, and in this moment feels especially patronizing. His grip is firm and slightly uncomfortable.

"Why was he here?"

"I'm on lockdown, I needed my stuff."

"Why him?" Gailen looks up and past me, as if he could still see Isaac driving away.

"I trust him, he knows my work, and he was there when I called."

"You called him?"

I frown. "I called Designation. He was the one that answered."

Gailen's body relaxes. "Alright. You need anything else, you come directly to me, okay?" Then he reaches up and runs a thumb across my cheek, staring at me intently. It takes everything I have not to violently recoil and kick him in the balls.

I don't even acknowledge what he said and move away from him. Anora calls out that breakfast is ready, so I use that as an excuse to leave this weird fucking conversation. He's always overprotective, that's his job as the head of security, but I could send him to Designation with an exact list of what I needed and he would only know half the things I was talking about. It took me a week to train him how to use a VPN and even then he kept forgetting.

Anora is the only one at the table when I walk into the room, and I sit down and grab a waffle from the stack. She raises one delicate eyebrow, since I'm not usually much of a breakfast person, but I also need to stop myself from boredom snacking today so a hearty breakfast might help. Without asking, she pours me a cup of coffee and hands it over.

174

"I hear you'll be home for awhile."

"Yeah."

"I'm sorry about Nino." She lifts up her hand as if she's going to reach out and grab mine, but then thinks better of it. "He had no other family but us, so I thought I'd ask you if you wanted to have a service."

That catches me off guard. I knew that Nino had no one else. He'd been with my family since he was 15 years old, a tough kid living in a group home with reflexes like a cat. Alonzo had vetted him and trained him, and he'd been personally chosen by Alina to be my specific guard when needed. When I asked her why, she said it's because he's the only guard on staff who would catch my knife before I'd get it far enough in to kill him.

We'd talked plenty of times, about all kinds of nothing. The thing I absolutely knew about him was that he hated being the center of attention. Nino wanted to be told what to do and then do it, no fanfare, no call outs, no special remarks.

"A burial. Something simple."

She gives me a soft smile, the only kind I've ever seen on Anora's face, and nods. It occurs to me that I've never seen my oldest sister express joy. Anora has resting sweet face - always pleasant, innocent, inviting. Her smiles come easily but they're never big. I've never seen her face radiating delight or excitement. In fact, when it isn't her resting smile, it's mostly anxiety and concern.

I'd suspected she didn't want to get married, and assumed that some of that tension would dissipate when she was off the hook, but clearly not. I play a game on my phone but watch her out of the corner of my eye. She's picking at her food more than she's eating it, and her movements are jerky. Anora is flustered.

Before I can ask anything, Aro skips into the room and plops down in her seat next to me. I watch as she stuffs three grapes in her mouth and then puts two waffles on her plate and drowns them in syrup.

175

After she swallows the grapes, she turns to me. "What the hell is going on?"

"Someone is trying to hack Designation, trying to kill me, and…" I swallow.

"Nino was killed last night," Anora finishes for me.

"Shit!" Aro bursts into tears. It's very loud and I instinctively move away from her and her big emotions, and then feel shitty about struggling to deal with it. On the other hand, she wasn't there. Aro didn't have to see someone die in her place.

I stand up quickly, knocking my chair over and running out of the room.

"Aster!" Anora calls after me, but she's busy trying to calm Aro down.

I don't stop running until I'm in my room with the door locked. I close the blackout curtains, turn off the lights, and settle myself in front of my screen to disappear into the digital world. There are a lot less emotions involved there. I don't have to look in anyone's eyes and see the blame there - I see it just fine when I look in the mirror.

28

Freelancer

Clive finds the sniper.

I give the information to Don, because I'm not willing to chase him down and be that far from Aster right now. I can tell that she's shaken up, and on edge in a different way. Getting vengeance isn't going to clear the feeling she's fighting right now. There is nothing that will help this one except time. It's been almost a week and I've seen her in the rest of the house less and less.

I've never had anyone die for me, but I can imagine it doesn't feel good even if she's grateful to be alive. Knowing Aster the way I do, she's fighting with the part of herself that thinks she didn't deserve to be saved. I also know she's struggling with reliving the memory, because she's been playing meditation videos on YouTube and researching how to have dreamless sleep.

That's the part I think I can help with.

I watch the Sorrelle house as things go quiet. The staff take up their usual rotation on the grounds, but I'm already inside so the night security sensors won't detect me. When Gailen goes into the office to settle in for his night shift, I sneak in through the back door.

Aster is still awake, but the rest of the top floor is silent. Her door is locked, but it doesn't take much for me to pick it. She's probably got her headphones on because she's trying another meditation video right now - this one purports to help people have lucid dreams in order to control their nightmares.

The second I open the door, a knife comes flying through the semi-dark. It barely misses me, embedding itself in the door frame next to my head.

"Go away."

"No." I remove the knife from the frame and walk over to her. Aster has resumed her position laying on the floor, with her eyes closed and headphones on. She's laying with her arms at her sides, palms up, and legs bent so her feet are flat on the floor.

"Why are you here?" Her lips barely move when she speaks.

"I wanted to check on you. You seem tense again. I was hoping I'd taken care of that." There's a smirk in my voice that I can't keep out. To be truthful, I have no intention of doing anything sexual with Aster tonight. Even the other night might have been pressing things when I shouldn't have, but I could tell she desperately needed the distraction.

Tonight isn't for distraction. Tonight is for comfort.

Aster gives up on her meditation and sits up, removing her headphones and tossing them away. She glares up at me. "Don't you sleep?"

"I'm supposed to - technically, the second you go through those gates, I'm off duty."

"But?"

"But the first few weeks I did general recon and caught you sneaking out. Watching you means I'm never really off duty."

Her glower deepens. "Just stick a tracker in my ass and be done with it."

"You jest, but I would if you'd let me. You're in danger, Aster. Me following you wasn't enough to make you see it, but maybe this will. This is in the real, analog world."

"Fuck," she puts her head in her hands and breathes deeply. "I hate this."

"I know."

"You can't help me. I don't want to go out, I don't want...I don't want anything except to forget."

I sit down in front of her, staring and waiting until she finally looks up and looks back at me. My chest aches with the desire to take off my mask, to reveal this last truth, but I know that the moment I do all of the trust that we've built will be shaken. I don't have time right now to rebuild it and also help her. Helping her is more important, and protecting her will always overrule any other desire I have.

"No you don't. You will never forget, and you should never forget. Nino made a choice, and his choice was you. Did he love your family?"

"Yes," she whispers. "We were all the family he had."

"You treat most of your men like family, don't you?" She only nods in response. "Give me a memory of Nino."

Aster thinks for a long time, staring off into the middle distance. I can practically see a slideshow of different memories across her eyes until she finds one she's willing to share with me. It's not that she struggled to think of a memory of Nino, it's that she's careful about what she's willing to talk about with me. With anyone. Aster doesn't share her emotions, which gives some the impression she doesn't have any, but it's more that she holds things so damn close.

"We do Secret Santa at the holidays - all of us and the staff. It gets a little ridiculous - you get 2 small presents and then 1 bigger present. Dad throws money in too, that if you correctly guess your partner before the reveal, there's cash prizes based on time and order." Aster smiles down at her hands, a small lifting of one corner of her mouth. "It's $1000 if you guess your partner before being given a gift. Two years ago, I got Nino. He fucking guessed before I gave him a present and won the money."

"How did he know?"

"He said it was the expression on my face when we drew names. I "lifted an eyebrow in amusement"and we're not allowed to keep our sisters' names if we draw them. Nino went all the way through guessing it was me to guessing what I got him and he was fucking right." She scoffs in mock disgust. I wait her out, knowing she'll finish the story when she's ready.

"I swear to god, every car ride he would not shut up about wanting a dock for his phone. You bet I got him a fucking dock." Aster's voice doesn't crack or change at all, but the first tears start trailing down her cheeks.

"Alonzo broke it a month later. I stole his protein powder over and over until he replaced it." Her lips curl between her teeth and she clenches her jaw, trying hard to hold back the storm brewing inside her. The problem with holding her emotions in so tight is that when they need to escape, she won't let them. I have to force her to let it out.

We sit there on her floor for a long time as she cries silently for her friend. The only light in the room is her TV screen, flooding the room in blue light. I wait until I hear her take a deep breath, and wipe the tears from her face with the sleeves of her hoodie.

"I see it when I close my eyes."

"I know."

"It won't go away." She turns to me, and for the first time, she shows me her pain. The deep well of hurt that's burrowed inside her over Nino, over all of this that's going on and seems to be centered around her.

"I've done worse things. I've watched people die and I've been the one that got them to the threshold. Why does it haunt me?"

"Have you ever done that?"

"Done what?"

"Used a sniper rifle."

"No. I prefer knives."

"It feels impersonal, distant, and shocking in its suddenness. Not to mention, his loss was personal and you didn't just hear about it, you saw it. It's different."

The silence falls between us again and she leans her head on my shoulder, giving up, just a little.

"I'll stay with you. All night, if you need it."

Aster nods and stands. She walks over to her bed and pulls back the covers, then climbs inside. I move to stand on the other side of the bed and slide off my shoes, waiting for her to get situated. After I lay down beside her, I wait.

I'm not surprised when she turns off the TV. We're plunged into full darkness.

"Take off the mask," she whispers. I oblige, removing the mask and the hoodie. Aster feels for me in the dark, her small hands running over my chest, up my neck, into my beard until she's cupping my cheeks. "Thank you."

I feel her moving closer and let her pull me in, and relish the hesitant way she presses her mouth to mine. It's an achingly sweet, sad kiss. It's a kiss for comfort, and that's something Aster doesn't know how to do. Aster doesn't do intimate touching, but she wants to touch me. This is how she acknowledges that my presence and my touch give her comfort, and show how much she trusts me. Aster's trust is precious, and I will do everything I can not to break it - breaking it a little is inevitable, but I won't stretch things more than I have to.

I kiss her back, but don't take control. I take each of her soft kisses, and then the tender press of her forehead to mine, our breaths mingling, another reminder that we're alive.

Aster shifts away, letting me go. Then surprises me again when her hand slides along my arm until her fingers can weave through mine. I stay like that, holding her hand, until she falls asleep.

29

Aster

Freelancer comes every night. We don't do anything, we barely even talk most of the time, but when he's with me I either don't dream, or if I do when I wake up I'm not alone. Even the mask is comforting - I don't have to worry about reading someone else's face and see how they're taking my freak outs. I don't have to be afraid that I'm too much or a burden because even if he feels that way, I can't see it, and it's not in his actions.

When I need him, he lets me find him in the dark. It's the first time that seeking out physical affection instead of physical aggression has made me feel better. I think it's the first time I've allowed myself to be comforted since I was a kid.

It says a lot about how fucked I truly am in the head that I can only be comforted by a faceless person, or in the dark. Am I hiding my reactions from them, or hiding from their reactions?

I'm deep in creating a new algorithm that would log access locations and create data points. Then if anyone is trying to spoof an existing user to get into the system, I'd be able to be more precise about locations. Logging in next to someone's house or business versus actually being in the house or business would become clear.

There's a knock on my door followed by a whiff of perfume that announces it's Anora.

She comes to stand next to my desk, waiting patiently until I acknowledge her. Out of pure piggishness, I don't.

"We're throwing you a birthday party."

My hands freeze on my keys. "No."

"Yes. We need a morale boost, badly, and I think cake and drinks are the way to do it."

"We can't have people and vendors here when there's a literal threat on my life, Anora."

She flicks my ear and I look at her, stunned. There's a deep frown on her face. "I fucking know that, Aster. I'm not talking about some big ridiculous blowout that you'd hate. I mean the family, your team from work, that's it. Big meal, big cake, yard games."

I keep staring at her. "Why?"

"We need a reason to celebrate right now, and considering someone is trying to kill you, let's celebrate that you're alive."

"I'll think about it." I'm leaning toward yes but I'm not sure.

"I need to know by tonight."

"Fine." I turn back to my computer and start typing in nonsense but Anora wouldn't know the difference. I just want her to get the hint to leave. It takes a long time before she finally leaves the room. I stop, delete the nonsense, and call Alina. Even if she is all loved up and convalescing with Derick, she'll be honest and clear with me.

"What?"

That is how we answer the phone the majority of the time. "Anora wants to throw me a birthday party."

"When you're on lockdown? That's a terrible idea." I can hear Alina going into bodyguard mode through the line.

"That's what I said, but she said a small thing - family, the guys, my team - because morale is low."

"Well then if it makes you feel any better, it's not about you. You're the excuse, not the reason." That does make me feel better. I could ghost my own party at some point and no one could hold it against me. It wouldn't be the first time I ditched my own birthday.

"So you think we should?"

"Yes."

"If we all die, I'm going to blame you."

"Fine."

"Derick alive?" I feel like I need to do my duty as her sibling, and because despite the fact I've only met him once, I am rather fond of him. Venture is fun to work with and he's never questioned anything that I've done for him inside and outside of the company. Full marks for brother-in-lawhood. Plus, it's because of him I know Kade, and I might actually consider him a friend.

Alina fills me in on their recovery, mostly his, her bullet wound is almost completely healed. Derick's got some stab wounds but his problem is the concussion. I did a lot of googling after her wild night rescuing him. He's almost through the protocol, and they're planning a honeymoon.

At least someone gets to breathe.

"You good?" Alina asks.

"I'm fine," I scoff automatically. Silence falls between us, and she waits me out. "I'm angry, more than anything."

"Angry is okay. As long as you channel it in the right direction."

"Yeah. I'm going now."

"Okay." She starts to laugh and I hang up the phone.

Then I get up and walk down the hall to Anora's room. When I raise my hand to knock on the door, it opens before I can and Owen is standing in front of me.

"Forget your way?" His room is right across from hers. It occurs to me it's kind of weird that he still lives here, but at the same time someone is trying to murder me, so maybe being together is safer overall.

"I had some things to discuss with Anora." Owen doesn't say anything else, and pushes past me into his own room. He slams the door behind him.

I walk into Anora's room but she's not there. It's only been 15 minutes and I never figured her for the person that could get up to all that much in a short amount of time. After a second she steps out of her bathroom, wiping the corner of her lip like she's just reapplied her lipstick.

"Aster!" she jumps back and presses a hand to her chest. Not the first time I've gotten that reaction from someone.

"We can have a birthday party."

Anora smiles. "Great. Do you want-"

I hold up my hand. "I don't want to make any decisions. The best present you can give me is not ask my opinion."

"Got it."

"What was Owen doing in here?"

Anora turns red, which piques my interest. "We had to talk about some things. Socialite stuff." She waves it away like it doesn't matter to her even though we'd get frowned at for ever referring to the things she does as "socialite stuff." I leave it alone. I could probably hack into her cloud and find out anything I wanted, but sometimes when I go looking for something it's more than I ever wanted to know.

"Okay then."

I walk back to my room, resisting the urge to be a nosy little sister.

30

Aster

Tonight, I'm on edge for a different reason. It's after midnight, the house is quiet, and I'm waiting. The itch is running beneath my skin but my common sense is still overriding it. I can't go out and kill, so I'm going to stay in and fuck. I'm going to rip Freelancer to pieces, then break myself apart, and hope that it settles the humming inside me to exact vengeance.

I don't bother locking the door anymore, not until after Freelancer gets here. He enters the room without a sound, a dark, sexy presence that immediately awakens my entire body. He closes the door, locks it, and then leans against it. I bite my lip when he tilts his head, predatory and strong.

It almost makes me willing to beg.

Almost.

Without saying a word, I start to strip. My hoodie over my head, the soft cotton tickling my skin. I drop my shorts, the material cool as they slide to the floor. I'm not wearing a bra and my nipples are already hard in the cold air. All that's left is the little black boy shorts that I know make my ass look good. Even from across the room I can see and feel the escalating tension in Freelancer's body.

I turn away from him and move to sit on the end of my bed.

"Turn off the light, take off your clothes."

Freelancer stays still for long minutes, but I know this game. He's going to do what I want, but he has to keep some measure of control by moving at his own pace. He reaches out his long arm, his defined fingers spreading, and flicks the light switch. The room descends into darkness.

Every sense in my body is on edge as I stand up and listen as he removes his clothes. The shuffling of the material against his skin and then the floor. By the time I reach him and put my hand on his chest he's naked. His skin is smooth and warm, and when my fingers travel over him, he hisses when I pinch his nipple.

"We're playing it that way, huh?" his voice is gruff in the silence.

"I want to touch you. Let me."

Freelancer stays still as I do exactly that. My palms smooth up over his shoulders, to his neck, and I drag my nails through the scruff on his face, and then up into his hair. It's a little long and crazy soft. I press my body against his, stealing his warmth. He groans when I press my hips into his, feeling his erection against my stomach.

Keeping my hands on him, I slide around until I'm behind him. I pepper soft kisses across his back, from shoulder blade to shoulder blade, and tease his abs with my nails as I do. I press my body into his and reach down to grab his cock. With each stroke he pulses in my hand, but I don't change my pace. I keep moving fast enough to feel good but slow enough to be torture.

"Are you going to fuck me tonight?" I ask, deceptively calm.

"If you'll let me," he growls. I cup his balls and he bows over.

Before he can take back control, I move around him and drop to the ground, gripping the base of his cock. He's tall enough that I barely reach him when I'm on my knees, but it's close enough to do what I want. The velvet skin of his cock slides along my tongue and I moan, loving the taste of him. This isn't me sucking his cock to get him off, it's me purely and carnally enjoying the feeling and flavor of him in my mouth. I want to get to a sensory overload, an adrenaline explosion, and hope that it's enough.

I tease him with my tongue, swirling around the head, pressing hard against the bottom ridge, and taking him as deep as I can. It's delicious and arousing. My panties are fucking drenched from the fun of it.

"I can't take much more of this little monster. It's the best fucking torture."

"Good boy," I say, before resuming my consumption of his dick. "Tell me what you'll do to me if I let you."

"I'm going to kiss you so hard and so long - ah - that you can't breathe." I start taking long, deep strokes with my mouth to see how well he can keep talking while being pleasured. "Then I'm going to bend you over and eat your pussy and ass, fuck, until you come on my face. Fuck - ah - then I'm going to fuck you with my fingers with a hand around that naughty fucking throat. Fuck, Aster - I'm going to pound that slutty little pussy so hard you won't be able to fucking walk tomorrow."

Freelancer leans down and grabs me under my arms, lifting me into the air until I wrap my legs around his waist. We attack one another, a tangle of lips and teeth as he walks back in the pitch dark until we're tumbling onto my bed. He grinds his cock against my covered pussy driving me crazy as we writhe against each other. I dig my nails into the skin of his sides, and he lets go of my lips to bite into the skin of my shoulder.

It takes everything I have not to cry out, and I get even more aroused by the idea of the mark that's going to be left behind. I dig my nails in deeper, leaving marks of my own. Part of me means it when I feel like I want to rip him open and crawl inside his skin. I can't get close enough, get enough, I want pain and pleasure, and I want to feel like we're sharing the same lungs all the time.

When he moves off of me I actually fucking whine, not wanting this feeling to stop. I need him tonight. I need to feel that energy and connection that I only get from being with him. The last few nights he's made me feel safe and like I'm not alone. I've never met anyone whose company didn't drive me insane after a few hours. Even when he would talk about himself, I never felt like I had to figure out how to respond to him. I could listen without saying a word and he never wondered if I was being inattentive because I was still and quiet.

I let out an unexpected giggle when he flips me over and pulls up my hips. It quickly dies into a long moan as he rips down my panties and starts to eat me out. His tongue is voracious, driving straight into my entrance and devouring what's already there. In teasing strokes he lightly taunts my clit with the tip of his tongue.

"Little monster, did sucking my cock get you all wet like this?"

"Yes," I moan.

His hand slides up my thigh and takes the place of his tongue rubbing against my clit. I bury my face in the bed when he starts licking across my pussy and up to my ass, swirling his tongue around my tight hole before doing it again and again, the speed of his licks picking up as his fingers press harder and faster against me.

"Gonna come," I lift my face to say before burying it in the blankets again. Freelancer keeps his pace steady, and then lightning shoots through my limbs. My toes curl so hard it hurts as everything around me goes white and silent, the orgasm muffling my ability to see, hear, and even breathe. I gasp for air as the feeling overtakes my body, but he doesn't let up.

I haven't even caught my breath yet when he stands, slides two fingers inside my pussy, and then wraps his hand around my throat. I'm yanked up and against him as he brutally fucks me, the wet sounds of him sliding in and out of me turning me on even more. He puts pressure on the sides of my throat, cutting off my blood flow without cutting off my air, and I know that when I come this time he better cover my mouth.

Freelancer lets go of my throat and the blood comes rushing back, and I can feel my pulse pounding inside my head. When he reaches down to pinch my nipple, I detonate with a strangled scream. My pussy squeezes around his fingers but that doesn't stop him from railing into me, and I turn to bury my face in his neck, whimpering as I come, my body twitching and writhing with pleasure.

He lets me go and I slide down to the bed, limp with the power of my orgasms. Freelancer leans over me and moves my legs up so my ankles rest on his shoulders. As his cock slides inside me, I moan again at the invasive, filling sensation. In this position he's so fucking deep. I might be physically drained, but I need more from him.

Always more.

His big hands wrap around the top of my thighs, and he starts to move. Freelancer is fucking me with absolute brutality, his hips snapping and our skin slapping together until the meat of my ass is starting to hurt from the pounding he's giving me. I'll be lucky to be able to sit tomorrow, let alone walk. I can do nothing but lay there and take it, let him use me as a hot, wet hole for all the torture I put him through. The thought of that gets me so fucking hot - I know it's fucked up but I don't care. I love that I can make him break the leash he keeps on himself. I'm not afraid of what he's like without it.

When his hand slides around to toy with my clit I try and reach down and stop him.

"I can't take anymore."

"You can and you will, Aster. I'm going to fuck the thoughts right out of your head."

"Please," I beg, not sure if I'm asking him to do it or to stop. It doesn't matter, because he's going to keep doing it.

"Tell me you need it, little monster. Stop lying to me that you don't want to come until you think it might kill you." The pounding is relentless, and the pleasure shooting through me is bordering on ecstatic pain. "I'll get you there, baby."

"I need you," I moan and press my hands over my mouth. Freelancer pinches my clit and I release, every muscle in my body tightening, my back arching off the bed as I scream into my hands. I can feel myself clenching on his cock, unable to control the spasm of my muscles.

Freelancer lets my legs go and lays down between them, his face close to mine. I might not be able to see him, but I can feel him. I can feel the way his heart is racing alongside mine, the pulses of our chests pressing against one another.

"I'm not done with you yet. You're going to be my good little monster and beg me to come in your pussy."

I'm silent, and Freelancer lifts his chest until he can reach a hand between us. He pinches my nipple and my pussy clenches.

"Beg me."

I shake my head and he pinches me again while sliding deep and grinding his hips into my clit. My legs are shaking and I'm sweating, and I'm afraid that I might actually come again and it will get very close to killing me.

Freelancer stays deep, grinding hard. "Beg for my come, Aster."

"No," I whimper. Freelancer grumbles and moves, wrapping one arm behind my neck and the other around my waist. Before I can figure out what he's doing, he changes the movement of his hips. He's pressing my body hard against him, my forehead hard against his shoulder, as he takes shallow, sharp thrusts. Each one feels like a slap right to my pussy, and I think I might be starting to blackout.

"Beg me."

"Give it to me," I finally break, both chasing and afraid of my impending orgasm. "I want it. I want it." His thrusts are erratic and I know he's close. "Please, please come in my pussy."

"Fuck," he groans as he captures my mouth, sliding his tongue along mine in a sloppy, erotic kiss as his cock presses deep and he grinds hard. I freeze and hold my breath so I don't scream, my senses dulled as I come. I can feel him pushing into me but the pleasure and pain are so strong I think I've left my body. As I come down, Freelancer cradles my face in his hands and kisses me. We don't stop kissing, grinding and touching each other, soothing our bodies as we come back to them.

We've made an absolute fucking mess of my bed, which is the downside to black bedding since bodily fluids always show up white. I don't care. This was worth it. The weight that was on my chest has lifted some, and that's an immeasurable gift. I've never been able to get the itch out of my skin any other way before.

I feel like I'm back to myself, but I'm also becoming something more. I'll think about that later.

Freelancer kisses my forehead. "Do you want me to stay tonight?"

"No. I think...I think I'm okay now."

"I could stay anyway."

I smile in the darkness, but only because I know he can't see me. "Okay."

After trips to the bathroom for both of us, we crawl into my bed, still naked. There are knives under both of our pillows. Freelancer wraps his arms around me and pulls me close, hugging me from behind as he presses his face into my hair for a moment before settling in to sleep.

If I wanted, I could turn on the light. I could ruin his secret identity in a second, expose this thing between us and figure out if it's more than a guard and protectee situation. I'd force us to move forward.

It's tempting, but his trust in me is worth more than that knowledge. For now.

31

Aster

Here I am, having a fucking birthday party. I'm 23 today. Hurray.

Though given recent events, I am more grateful than usual to be alive. A fact that Alina kept texting me as I complained to her while getting ready. I have actual reasons to recognize that I made it another journey around the sun. More than I've had before.

Every time the thought that Nino won't have another birthday crosses my mind, I shove it away. I try and remind myself that he would not begrudge me being alive and having a birthday. I try to imagine that he'd be here, fucking with me, and if there is something after he's watching it all and laughing his ass off at my discomfort. I don't acknowledge my last memory of him. I don't let myself feel the press of his hand on my shoulder.

Anora had the staff set up a big awning with tables underneath full of food. There are different lawn games set up in the shady areas, there's a table covered with a sheet that I have a sneaking suspicion is hiding super soakers, there are seating areas strategically placed, and the guards watching the perimeter are all dressed more casually than usual so not to set off the civilian guests.

My team is here and it's nice to see them. Tella and Manuel are talking happily with Anora and my dad and I can tell they are delighted I let them throw this party. Dad also likes to meet employees in another context and I've never let them invite my team to anything before. Dominic, Isaac, and Thor are grazing along the food, talking to one another. Gailen glares over at them and I don't know what his problem is. Alonzo, Owen, and Aro are in one of the seating areas, not talking, just sitting. I think Aro is sneaky reading a book on her phone.

Anora, being annoying, is making me sit in a throne of honor. I'm in a big wicker chair, that dammit is comfortable, next to a table piled with presents. The amount of pastels in the wrapping paper makes me cringe, and don't even get me started on my birthday cake. The weather is nice for early September - a perfect day where it's cool enough to be comfortable but warm enough that no one needs layers. Soon it will be Midwestern fall, and I'll be in my happy zone.

Yes, I am a basic white bitch who loves fall, okay?

"Alright, everyone!" Anora gets the group's attention. We watch her as she walks over to the covered table and whips off the sheet. Just as I thought - super soakers. "We're going to play capture the flag. I've got everyone's names in a bowl and we'll pick teams. Aster, do you want to be a captain?"

"Sure," I stand up from my throne and walk over to the table.

"Versus?" Anora prompts.

I look around the party at the guests, even though I already know. "Isaac."

He smirks at me. "Game on, li-" he stops himself and laughs. Then he approaches and stands across from me where Anora is digging through the bowl and removes our names. We pick teams quickly, dad and Gailen both declining to play.

I've ended up with Manuel, Thor, Alonzo, and Aro. Isaac has Dominic, Tella, Owen, and Anora. We're fairly evenly matched, I think. My team groups together and we each grab our water guns.

"Okay, Alonzo, you go place the flag behind the guest house and keep an eye out. Aro, set up in the gazebo like a sniper. Manuel, you, me, and Thor are full on attack going for the other team's flag. In water wars there's no out, you just keep going until you have step back to refill your water. If your gun is empty, you can't keep going. Got it?" Water gun capture the flag may be a bit of a family tradition.

I watch as Isaac divides up his group as well, but he sends them off in pairs so I don't know which ones have the flag and which are setting up to go for ours.

Alonzo headed in the opposite direction of the guest house to throw them off, and he'll circle back and place it where we want. To start, I have us go to the gazebo, looking around for where Isaac might think to hide the flag. I know a lot about how he thinks because this game is strategy and problem-solving - so is hacking.

He'll go for some place obvious as a lure. Where the flag can be seen and we'll have to make a gutsy move to get to it, leaving us open to be hit and have to hit back, potentially running out of water.

Gailen blows an air horn, agreeing to be involved at least to that extent. He's been super touchy since I got put on lockdown. It's been two weeks and I can barely stand to be in the same room as him. He either glowers at me, holding a grudge for some unknown thing, or he's asking me weird, invasive questions about work or what I'm doing. It's out of character for him, even if my life is in danger, and I'm seconds away from threatening his life or threatening to go to dad to get him to fucking stop it.

Alina said I should tell him to shut the fuck up and not involve knives or dad, but she has more patience than I do. Slice first, questions and apologies later.

Thor leads our group, Manuel is in the middle, and I bring up the rear keeping an eye on our backs as we start circling the grounds trying to see where the other flag is.

Tella comes running out, screaming to announce her arrival, and we turn and start pummeling her with water - Manuel misses, which I think is on purpose - but Tella gets him straight in the face as Thor and I get her. I start backing away, using that distraction to keep looking for the flag. When Tella runs out of water, Manuel needs more as well.

It's Thor and I going through the trees and flowers, and he points to a small seating area at the back of the yard. It's a brick platform surrounded by trees with a nice bench on it - the flag is on the bench. Other than the trees, there's open, rolling grass between the trees where we are, and the area. Just as I suspected it would be.

Thor snorts. "Of course. Trick them into thinking there's minimal protection." We exchange a look and shake our heads.

"Take more of them out, split, or go for it?" I ask him.

He thinks for a moment, looks back at me, and then looks around. We can hear the shrieks and laughs of everyone else as they continue to play. I have no idea how our flag is doing but I haven't heard the air horn, so far so good.

"Go for it. If we get it and get caught, the flag stays where it drops. Why not?"

"This is why I wanted to work for you," Thor says and cracks a smile so tiny I almost miss it. Good to know he's not entirely miserable working for the dysfunctional family that is my team.

Without another word, I start booking it across the lawn. Thor is faster than I am, simply because his legs are at least a foot longer, and passes me quickly.

Much to my absolute shock, Anora and Owen bust out from behind the trees and start spraying us. I've never seen her look so vicious, and it's the most entertaining thing to happen all day.

Thor and I run out of water before they do, and book it back through the trees to get to the hose to refill our guns. Isaac is there, filling up. Manuel and Tella are standing nearby, both guns refilled but not rejoining their respective teams.

"Find our flag?" Isaac asks.

"Did you find ours?"

"Not yet," he raises an eyebrow.

"Guess I'm not as obvious as you," I taunt, wasting time with some smack talk.

"You think I'm obvious?"

"I know you are." Thor takes my gun and starts refilling both of them. "I knew exactly the kind of place you'd put your flag - easy to see, hard to get to."

"Oh, unlike you, who'd hide it somewhere subtle and random, but mostly unprotected."

Shit, he is correct. The good thing is, he doesn't know our property well enough to know what kind of places would fit that description. Isaac has only been here to drop off my stuff two weeks ago. Other than that, this place is foreign to him.

Except I see a light in his eyes like something has dawned on him.

Thor hands me my now full gun, and I spray Isaac straight in the chest, soaking his shirt.

He sprays back, and it devolves into our own water war on the back lawn. When I glance back at the hose, Thor is gone, probably retreating to try and get their flag again. Good. If I can keep Isaac distracted then their team is down two members.

We're running and shouting shit at each other. I'm laughing and it surprises me. This is the first time since Nino that I feel any of the weight I've been carrying around lift off my shoulders. Anora was right that a party was the right thing to do - it got me out of my head for a little bit. Isaac gets me out of my head too - it's why he's good for me to work with. He gets me thinking in the moment, reacting, instead of always retreating and defending.

Isaac takes my moment of realization to get close, entering my personal bubble and crowding me.

"Trying to distract me?" I ask.

"Is it working?" I sneer in response.

Our eyes lock and things get unexpectedly tense for a moment.

"Get away from her!" I jump back when I hear dad shouting from the back door, and turn to watch him and Gailen hurry from the door over to me and Isaac. He's holding papers in his hand, crushed in a tight grip.

Gailen grabs Isaac and yanks him away before grabbing one arm and twisting it up and back, holding it high enough that Isaac winces. My mouth drops open in shock and I look between the three of them. Dad is furious, Gailen looks smug, and to my surprise, Isaac looks resigned. Whatever this is, he already knows without being told.

I don't think I've ever seen dad this angry. He's radiating with anger, barely able to contain himself.

"What's going on?"

Dad whips around and points a finger at me. "I'll deal with you later."

It's like I've dropped into another dimension. None of this makes sense to me.

"I hired you to keep her safe, and this is what you do?" Dad holds up the papers that I can now see are pictures. He shoves them in Isaac's face. "You took advantage of her."

Isaac shakes his head. "No one could take advantage of her."

Without thinking, I dart forward and rip the papers from dad's hand. He growls and whirls on me, but it's too late. I've seen. Everything inside of me freezes as I take in the image in my hand. No. My entire body flinches at the images, my tight grip on privacy ripped from my hands.

It's from the parking garage. I'm bent over the car with Freelancer behind me, and my face is contorted in ecstasy. It looks like we're having sex, even though he was only using his fingers. The dead body of Dirk Andresson is also visible, bloody and slumped against the wall. My secrets are revealed: the killing, and the illicit affair with my stalker bodyguard.

Despite it's genius, my brain will not compute why this is a problem right this minute, and why dad is talking to Isaac like he's in trouble. I look up, glancing from dad to Isaac and back again, trying to accept the picture that's trying to force it's way in. "What?"

I focus on Isaac, but he's not looking at me. He's focused on dad.

"Not only did you not do the job, you seduced her - you really think that's keeping her safe? Did you do the job, Freelancer?"

"I kept her safe." Isaac's jaw flexes as something in the way he holds himself changes. I can see the very specific mannerisms he adopted as Isaac slip away, even when he's in Gailen's hold. Isaac holds himself straighter, his body more fluid, and I see it now.

Isaac is Freelancer.

"Safe is letting her leave the house at all hours, without anyone knowing? Letting her engage in obviously dangerous behavior, and then seducing her?"

"She was safe, I was with her. She needed to get out."

I'm still standing silent and stupid. Dad's still yelling. "It was a complete disregard for your orders, and you endangered her!"

"I would never do that - I love her. I know her and I love her and I kept her safe by doing what she needed."

The world stops. The whole entire planet stops moving, jerking to a quick and terrible stop with such force that it sends me flying off of it.

Freelancer is Isaac and he loves me.

I don't know what to do with that information. Silence surrounds our small group, no one sure what to say right now.

The yelling has drawn the rest of the party, and my eyes follow Anora, herding the civilians toward the food and acting as if nothing is wrong. She's good at that - at making people believe that everything is fine. They cast nervous looks in our direction, but she distracts them. Owen and the rest of our men come closer, blocking this scene from everyone else.

"That makes it worse," dad hisses at him. "You're fired. Get out. If I ever see your face again, I'll blow it off."

Gailen shoves Isaac away - Freelancer, I guess, since I doubt Isaac is even his real name - and he barely stumbles before regaining his balance. Watching him move, I marvel at how well he transformed himself. Isaac was a little stiff, smart, relaxed. As Freelancer, everything has always screamed predator and it all comes back as the mask is removed.

His real mask - the one that hid him from me in plain sight.

I don't know how to feel.

Freelancer stops and looks at me, our eyes meeting in a flare of heat and pain. He's waiting for me to do something, but until I process all of this I don't know what to do. I give him a small shake of my head and he grimaces before turning and walking away. The loping stride so different from the determined tread of his mask as Isaac.

Without a word to anyone, I walk into the house.

32

Freelancer

I want to turn around and kill them all, then drag Aster away with me. Where she belongs.

Love isn't something someone like me feels often, if ever. I never felt loved by my parents and I grew up avoiding my brother. While I think he felt some form of affection for me, and me for him, it wasn't love. It was something more like temporary loyalty before we went our separate ways.

It's both to my benefit and my annoyance that everyone is so caught off guard by what just happened they don't bother to have anyone follow me and make sure I leave the property. So I don't.

I hide my bike in the trees, and circle back around to watch the chaos and watch for Aster. She's not in the backyard anymore.

Gailen, Owen, and Don are talking together in a small group. Owen is trying to calm Don down - I do feel bad that he found about us this way. It was graphic and unnecessary and now the man who thinks well of everyone thinks terribly of me. Not exactly how I wanted my relationship with him to evolve.

Anora is still playing hostess, shutting down the party and making excuses as the rest of the team leaves. No one caught anyone's flag so the game is a draw. This one moment ruined everything. Aster was finally relaxing a little and having fun, and then it explodes in our faces.

The expression on hers when I looked back will haunt me until I hear from her.

It wasn't rejection, and she wasn't angry. She was stunned. Apparently I did a better job than I thought being Isaac. The persona of Isaac is as close to my real self as I've ever been on a job. We don't move or talk the same, but my history and the things I shared with her as Isaac were all true.

I abandoned my name a long time ago. If I could choose to be anyone, it would be the person I got to be with Aster. The one that got to work with her, laugh with her, support her at work and help her figure things out. The slightly uptight guy who hid his darker side, only letting it out to play at the right time.

The yard clears - the guests leave, and everyone else goes into the house.

I go back around to the front to keep an eye on Don's office.

What I watch through the window is worth the uncomfortable position crouching in the bushes. Aster and Don storm into the office, tailed by Gailen and Owen. I've never seen her this angry, and she throws her arm out and knocks everything off the desk.

Don moves around to stand behind the desk, taking that position of power and authority, and he's still the angriest I've ever seen. As they lean across toward each other, yelling in one another's faces, that's the moment they look like father and daughter. Alike in their fury, angry about the same thing for different reasons.

Aster is animated, waving her arms and gesturing, at one point she steps over to shove at Gailen and gets in his face. I'm amused when he pales and steps away from her, holding his hands up like he's surrendering. She's a wild animal right now, cornered and angry.

Don manages to keep a somewhat cooler head, pointing and gesturing with less vehemence. He holds his hands out, palms up as if in supplication, trying to get her to understand. Aster is rigid now with anger and annoyance.

Gailen tries to approach and I have to cover my mouth to smother a laugh when she punches him in the face and walks out of the office.

Owen steps forward and says something to Don, then follows Aster out.

I'll wait until dark and then find my way to my little monster, and remind her that we're good together in every way.

There's a rustle in the bushes behind me, and I still, waiting for it to pass. Instead, someone comes up next to me and before I can run, a small hand wraps around my arm. It's Aro.

"Hi," she whispers and smiles.

"Hi?"

"So you're the guy." She's full on grinning at me and it's very disconcerting. Not that I would ever hurt anyone Aster cares about, but Aro's immediate comfort with me is not my usual experience. "She told me about you."

"She did?"

"I told her to go for it - when she wasn't sure. I'm guessing that's what happened."

"Is this the part where you tell me you'll kill me if I hurt her?"

Aro snorts and then smothers her face in her hands as she laughs, and she's trying so hard to hold it back that tears fall down her cheeks. I watch in bemusement and she keeps trying to take a breath and then breaks down again. She waves at her face as if that's going to do anything, then finally takes a deep breath and wipes the tears away.

"Maybe you don't know her as well as I thought if you think I need to do that. Aster would destroy you with all the fire of heaven and hell if you ever hurt or betray her." Aro frowns. "Are you sure you can handle her?"

It's my turn to smirk. "Better than you can imagine."

"Gross. Anyway, I wanted to meet you as you, and tell you that me and Anora are on your side. Alina thinks you're evil but she'll come around when she sees what Aster has been like lately for herself."

"What do you mean?"

Aro stares off into the distance for so long that it starts to get awkward. I know she's the dreamiest of all of them, but it's kind of weird. I don't say that about many people.

"Aster has always made herself appear to be disaffected. Nothing can breach her calm. It's not who she really is, but it's who almost everyone sees. Once she told me about you, I noticed that it wasn't as true. She wasn't on the defensive all the time, burrowing herself away so that no one could see the good parts of her. I doubt she'll ever be like other people, which is good, but it's like a tie was cut and she moved more freely. It's the closest I've ever seen her to being happy that didn't involve murder." She frowns. "I mean, I guess it did involve murder, but I mean where she's happy outside those moments. Where that was her mood. It was weird, but I liked it."

Aro turns to look me directly in the eye. "Aster is my best friend, not that she knows it, and I would fight for her happiness. So yeah, fuck this up and I'll kill you, okay?"

"Okay. It was nice to meet you, officially. I'm Isaac." I hold out my hand and she takes it. We shake, and she gives me a nod before turning around and sneaking away from my hiding place. I don't hear anything as she goes, and wouldn't have even known she was there if I didn't see her sneaking across the lawn a few minutes later. Which means she made noise on purpose when she was coming to me, so I'd know.

Don Sorrelle's daughters really are a different breed of human.

I pull up Don's email and read the message that was sent with the pictures: *A life for a life. She will pay your debt with her blood.* It doesn't really work with the pictures, but perhaps the purpose is twofold. This is definitely personal, and it's more about Don than it is about Aster. She's the leverage they're using, except none of us are sure what they want. I'll have to stay as close as I can. It's the only way.

33

Aster

I'm so angry at everyone right now that I can't keep a lid on my emotions. I don't let go often but right now I can't hold on. When I get into the office, I scream at the normal and organized state of it, and then wipe everything off dad's desk. He stomps in after me and goes behind it - as if that's going to protect him from me. As if he needs protecting.

"Who I fuck is not up to you!" That's not a great place to start but it's the thing that's bothering me. Dad is more upset about Freelancer being with me than he is about the fact that I go into the city AND MURDER PEOPLE. I wonder how angry he would be if that was the only secret revealed by those photos.

"It is when you fuck an employee! For god's sake Aster, why would you keep doing this? Someone was after you and you traipse around the city in the dead of fucking night, when we have no idea you're out there, with only one man as backup? What could be so important that you would risk your life?"

"They hurt people."

"So do you!" He shouts.

My head snaps back and he immediately looks sorry. Gailen tries to step in and talk to me, but that's just making it worse.

"Aster…"

"No," I turn on him and get up in his face. "You have even less to say. You have no authority over me, and if you even fucking try right now I will cut off your balls and feed them to geese." He holds his hands up and steps back. I try to take deep breaths and regain control of myself.

"There's a thing inside me, dad, and you know it. I had to let it out. Freelancer helped me let it out."

"Did he coerce you for sexual favors to keep your secret, to help you?" Dad's voice is soft and it takes everything I have not to roll my eyes but I can't stop the amused laughter from breaking out.

"I'm not talking about that. I'm done talking about Freelancer. Since he's no longer your employee, it's none of your fucking business."

"It is our fucking business if he's-" Gailen tries to talk again and I'm done. With a deep inhale through my nostrils, I shift on my feet and punch him in the face. The way his head snaps back is immensely satisfying.

"I'll stop going out, but if I want to see Freelancer, I will." I don't look at any of them, I turn on my heel and leave the office.

I'm almost to my bedroom when I notice that I have a tail. My mind is running through scenarios, trying to figure out what feels right to do next. Trying to hear my instincts as my brain rushes to process all of the information that comes along with knowing Isaac and Freelancer are the same person. Who loves me.

No one loves me.

I try and slam the door in Owen's face, but he puts a hand out and despite his suave appearance the motherfucker is really strong. In a hand to hand fight, he'd kick my ass and break me in half, and we'd be about even with knives. It'd be 50-50 who would win because while I'm fast, he's a bulldozer.

"Can you and I talk like adults without too many emotions getting involved?" He closes my door and leans against it as I walk deeper into the room. I don't know what I'm doing, so I perch on the end of my bed. My face falls into a mask of serene sarcasm.

"Sure, Owen, let's give it a try."

"First, as your boss, please come up with a plan to accommodate the gap on your team."

I give him a salute that shifts into the finger. "Yes, sir." I stare at him. "You knew the whole time. About Isaac."

"Yes," he agrees, and then waits me out. Owen and I have similar communication styles. So similar in fact, that it will take us three times as long as other people to have this conversation. It will be a game of waiting to see which one of us breaks first.

"Why? Why did he need to be on the team?"

Owen looks away from me, jaw ticking as he considers what he's going to say.

"I don't know how to explain without it sounding patronizing."

I cock an eyebrow. "Because it probably is patronizing."

"Fair," he agrees. "I needed someone you wouldn't suspect to keep an eye on you. I figured you'd clock Freelancer in your off hours. That would either mean you'd fight them or you'd run harder. I needed to know that even at Designation you were safe, and what you were getting up to."

"So he gave you updates on me? Reported everything I did, what we talked about?"

"No," Owen sighs. "Only if your work was impacted by the outside threats, which it never was, or if you were using company resources on company time for Sorrelle family business. You did neither. Outside of the time you brought him to my office after the attack, he never had anything to report to me."

I'm somewhat mollified that things between Isaac and I stayed between us. We'd gotten close the last few weeks and I'd shared a lot with him. With Freelancer too. It's kind of nice in a way that they're the same person - there's less catching up to do about who I am.

Although I wonder if any of the things he told me as Isaac are real. Was it all part of some elaborate backstory, down to the details of the abuses that happened to him, the alienation from his family, the story of how he started messing around with code? He was a great programmer. I'll probably need two people to pick up the slack left behind by his absence.

"I'm sorry your privacy was invaded. Don will calm down - it's likely difficult to see any of his daughters in that kind of compromising position." Owen stands up straighter and puts his hands in his pockets. "I'm going to say something, and you're going to have questions, but I'm going to ask you not to ask them. To hear the words and leave the rest of it alone."

We stare each other down. That's a pretty big ask. Most of the time I'm nothing but questions, always searching for answers and solutions, finding ways to solve problems, and then asking new questions. I'm literally our family interrogator. For Owen to disclose something to me is a big deal though. He and I have always gotten along because we don't meddle with one another. Isaac on my team is the closest he's ever gotten to meddling. The thing is, my gut is telling me that whatever he's going to say is exactly what I need to hear right now. I always go with my gut.

"I'll leave it alone."

More staring, as Owen assesses if I'm telling the truth. He nods, coming to a decision.

"I know what it's like to find the right person at the wrong time, or in the wrong way. To feel like everything is against the two of you being together, and that every new challenge is insurmountable. He said that he loves you - do you love him?"

A long silence falls, and I crack. "I'm not telling you that."

A nod. "If you do, if both of you feel like being together is what you want, then nothing is insurmountable. When I look at the things that might stand in your way - they're nothing, Aster. If the person I love finally came to their senses and said come what may - nothing would stop us. Don't let this stop you."

I notice that he used love in the present tense, and those questions start floating around in my brain. The thing is, I don't want to know. Having someone mess around in your relationships and your feelings sucks, and I am not going to pry into something like that. Maybe I would have before, but not now. Whatever Owen is going through, if he wanted to talk about it, he would. So I'll send mental good vibes and leave it at that.

"Are you saying you're Team Freelaster?"

Owen groans and face palms. "Did you come up with that off the top of your head?"

"Yes."

"I'm not saying your portmanteau, but from what I know of Freelancer, yes. The two of you make sense together, and I don't think he did anything to compromise your safety. He was there for you and knew how to work *with* you instead of around you because he respects you. In every meeting, he's stood up for you when your dad, who did it because he loves you, wanted to keep you in a bubble."

Everything he's saying makes sense to me, and it's all in line with what I know of Freelancer. If I put aside that he's Isaac, I do know the truest version of him. The side that covered his face but showed that his soul was as warped and dark as mine. We worked well together, he trusted me and my skills, he didn't scoff at the reason for doing what I was doing, and he always talked things through with me. It was like having a partner, not a bodyguard.

I know that he kept his dual roles in my life from me because he was

210

contracted to do it. It was part of the requirements of the job that he was hired to do. In my bones I know that I haven't been a job to him in a long time. Still, hadn't we gotten to a point where he should have told me? What would have changed?

Okay, the dynamic at work would've been different, but would it have been so weird to be Aster and Isaac, and not only Aster and Freelancer? It also makes me feel like he'd be ashamed of me in front of them. These normal people with normal thoughts and feelings and hobbies, who despite our solid dynamic know that I'm outside the normal. They know, like a primal instinct, that I'm not like them. It's insecure and stupid to worry about it, and I never have before, but I do if it's a barrier for him.

Because if it is, then he's not worth it. If he doesn't want to be with me in the light, then he doesn't deserve me in the dark.

"How do I move past this? How do we talk about it?" It's a rare, vulnerable moment for me but Owen doesn't call me out. He wouldn't.

"If I knew, I'd fix my own shit," he sighs. "I think all you can do is talk and be honest, and see where it goes."

"Right. Thanks, Owen."

"I'll try and calm your dad down, and keep Gailen out of his ear."

"Yeah, what's Gailen's problem?"

Owen gives me a weird look, then shakes his head and turns to leave.

"Hey," I stop him, "I hope your person figures it out."

"Me too." Then he leaves.

I'm alone with my thoughts, sitting on my bed without moving for hours. It's like I'm so deep inside my own brain that I've disconnected from my body as I go around in circles. I know he'll come for me as soon as it gets dark. There's no putting off this conversation or giving either of us time to cool down. Someone is trying to kill me - until we figure out who, my minutes are precious.

34

Aster

I don't expect Freelancer to come in my window, and I'm a little bit impressed.

"They were guarding the doors. This was easier."

I know how high my window is from the ground, so I doubt it. It's weird to see him in Freelancer mode while he's wearing Isaac's face. The more I stare at him, the more I see the difference though. Isaac's expressions were always cautious and guarded. Freelancer isn't keeping a pinch of intensity out of his gaze. The way he's looking at me burns through my body, and I wonder how I never felt it even through his mask.

"Can we talk?"

"You are talking," I smile up at him, all teeth and falsity.

"Aster," he huffs, and kneels in front of me. He reaches for me and I jolt back. There's a flash of hurt as he puts his hands down on his thighs.

"I don't even know what to call you. Who are you?" My heart is still racing in my chest at his nearness, his realness, like it always did. It explains why I was drawn to Isaac too, even though my body never reacted this way to him. My brain did. My softer instincts did. I trusted Isaac, I obsessed over Freelancer. Where do they merge?

"My name actually is Isaac. I've never used my real name before and I think using it this time - there was a reason."

"If you start talking about fate, I'm going to punch you in the mouth."

"Go ahead." He throws his arms out and then lets them drop back to his sides. "Don't you feel it? The connection between us is something I've never known. I can sense you, I feel better when I'm next to you, I feel things I've never felt before, and I have no explanation except that we are meant to be together and I am fucking in love with you."

Following through on my threat, I punch him in the mouth.

Psychopath that he is, he laughs, and wipes the blood from his lip. My pussy clenches at the visual, and I'm tempted to lick the blood from his fingers and then taste the rest on his mouth. My libido is really getting in the way of this whole honest conversation thing that I'm trying to do.

"I feel it, too," I admit quietly. There's never been a time in my life when I didn't think I was living authentically, if cautiously. I've hid my violence from people I couldn't trust or who didn't deserve it, but I've never tried to be someone that I'm not. I've never tried to soften my edges to make other people more comfortable. Yet, being with him felt like something more real. As if there was a fog over me that I was unaware of until he made it dissipate.

The flavor of my life got better, at both Designation and my nocturnal activities. And when it comes to sex, I've never, ever let someone have my body the way I gave it over to him. Without question, hesitation, or fear. I hadn't even seen his face. I didn't need to because I knew. I knew on a different level I can't explain that he was something else. Someone like me.

"Why didn't you tell me?"

"If we'd been public, as Isaac and Aster, how do you think your dad would have reacted? He'd think I was doing it for the job and playing with your heart. If we told him we knew, we'd be where we are right now a hell of a lot sooner. I wanted more time with you without other people interfering. I'm sorry."

That explanation makes sense, but my fear makes me ask: "Are you embarrassed by me?"

Isaac stills completely, and then for the first time ever looks at me like I'm crazy. "What? Why would you ask me that?"

"You fit in, they saw you as normal. I'm not normal and not only can't I fake it, I don't want to. I would understand if you didn't want other people to know you were with me." I shrug. His eyes close like what I've said physically pains him.

"This is really hard to do when you won't let me touch you." He rubs his eyes with his first finger and thumb. "I have no idea why you would think that. Would I be worried about accusations of favoritism from the team, sure, but I was already getting those."

I stand up so fast he falls over. "WHAT?!"

"Not the point right now."

With a glower I sit back down, and he continues.

"You are my favorite person in the whole fucking world, Aster. If other people can't see you the way I do, that's their problem. I'm relieved that it's out there, and we don't have to hide anymore." He looks at me with hope, but I keep going through my mental checklist even if I do want to kiss him right now.

"What did you tell me that was real? We never talked about ourselves when you were Freelancer, but as Isaac…" I trail off, thinking about our lunches the last few weeks.

"It was all true. I never made up any details of who I am or my life because I knew that keeping it a secret was temporary, so I took every moment I could to share myself with you. The only thing about Isaac that wasn't me is the way I dressed."

"Who buttons their shirt sleeves?" I scoff.

214

"I know. I know!" As if sensing that I'm weakening, he moves closer, his chest pressing against my legs. When I don't shove him away, he runs his hands up the sides of my thighs until his strong hands are wrapped around my hips. "I love you, Aster Sorrelle. I am all yours, however you'll have me. Forgive me, punish me, but don't push me away."

I look into his eyes and let the versions of him that I know come together. Isaac is Freelancer, and both of them are this man on his knees before me. I take his face in my hands and run my thumb down his bloody lip. I want to taste all of him. When I lick the blood from my thumb, his eyes dilate, and I have to stop him before he goes too far.

"I forgive you," I start, and his eyes fall shut. "But I am going to punish you. Go away. Keep watching me, just don't talk to me. I need time and space. To process everything and to try and fix things with my dad. If we're going to be together, I don't want to be fighting him when we're already in too many battles as it is."

Isaac hangs his head for a moment. "Okay. I'll watch. If anything happens to you though, I'm not staying back." It's his turn to grab me, one hand around my nape and the other buried in my hair and roughly pulling at the strands. He pulls me close, our mouths and eyes lined up.

"I will kill anyone who tries to touch you. I will dance in their blood and celebrate their death because no one gets to hurt you except me. Got it?"

"Got it," I can barely nod and I'm so turned on that I am seriously regretting my decision not to fuck him right now. My nipples chafe against my shirt and I shift my hips, grinding myself into the mattress out of arousal. He smirks because he knows.

To make me wilder, he kisses me. It seals the deal between us - we belong to each other and I forgive him. Our tongues war with one

215

another, sliding and pushing, and the taste of him floods my senses. Everything about him overloads me in the best way - his flavor, his scent, the way his skin feels, and it's the only time I want to feel that way.

But I push him back and away, breaking the kiss. "I'll text you when I'm ready."

"Okay, little monster. I won't be far if you need me."

"I know." We lean against each other again and I dig my nails into the back of his neck, giving him a little something to remind him of me.

Isaac leaves out the window, sending me a smirk before he jumps to the ground. I run to the window and watch him roll on the lawn, then spring up immediately and run for the tree line. No one out there noticed a thing.

I can only hope my would-be assassins aren't as good at the job as he is.

I sit down on my bed again, drifting back into my thoughts, but one stands out: I didn't say that I loved him back, and he didn't care.

I don't know how long I'm doing the staring and processing thing before my door is opened without a knock. Anora and Aro, both in pajamas, stomp into the room. Aro locks the door behind her.

Instead of acknowledging them, I continue to stare at nothing. Then I hear the sound of FaceTime and look over to see Anora on her phone. Alina's face appears on the screen.

"I called for a sister convergence," Anora gracefully sinks to the floor with her legs crossed under her. Aro steals one of my pillows and then flops down on her stomach, shoving the pillow under her chin.

"What's going on?" Alina asks.

"Dad hired some guy named Freelancer to follow Aster because someone wants to kill her and then they started hooking up, but he's also this guy named Isaac that she worked with at Designation, and then someone took pictures of them fooling around in a parking garage and sent them to dad. So that all exploded today. Oh, and Aster is a vigilante in her free time and kept it a secret." Aro summarizes the situation, and as she does Anora gets paler and paler.

"How do you know all that?" I ask her, bewildered. She just smiles in response.

"Fucking Freelancer," Alina groans and I see her flop back on the couch in her space at Derick's house. "I was afraid of this."

"What?" I ask. "What do you mean?"

"He's got a reputation for being unhinged. When you mentioned him at the airport I was afraid that's who you were talking about - and don't think I missed your tone then, either. Is this serious? Is it real?" Says the woman who haphazardly entered into a marriage agreement and fell in love.

"Yeah. It's serious. He said he'd give up the job to be with me."

They all fall quiet. It's wild that he said that, especially since it was a lot longer ago in this complicated maneuver of being together but not together that we've been doing. The thing is, he's watched me. Investigated me. Invaded my privacy and knows everything about me. It makes sense that his attraction and certainty about his feelings happened faster for him than for me. It raises the question, too: why doesn't that bother me? Even a little bit? Would it, if it was anyone but him?

I don't want to be with anyone else. I want to feel the way I do when I'm with him. Is that love? Is being obsessed with another person the line between attraction and adoration?

"Owen told me that even if it's the right person at the wrong time, if we both want it - then no challenge is insurmountable."

Anora sits up straight. "Owen said that?"

"Yeah. He asked me if I loved Isaac and I didn't answer because the truth is - I don't know. How do I know if it's love or obsession or very,

217

very feral attraction?"

Aro grins at me. "Is this the time in the conversation where I can ask about the spicy time?"

"No!" Anora and Alina both shout.

I shake my head. "I'm serious." This is how I know something is wrong with me. Normal people must know their feelings better than this. I know that I love dad and my sisters, but it's a different kind of love. It's like a tether in my chest that tugs me into action when they need me. From what I've read and seen about love, it should be this obvious feeling inside me that I can't shut up about, or stop myself from saying to him. There are other things I want to tell him and other things I want to say, but "I love you" almost doesn't feel adequate. It's beyond that, and darker than that.

It's more like - you own me, and I own you. I don't want him to love me, I want him to devour me. I want to be consumed in the way we are together, the things we want and the things we can do, and to know without having to look that he's behind me or by my side. Isaac is my equal - mind, body, soul, and darkness.

"If you could save yourself, or save him, who would you choose?" Anora asks. I'm surprised the question comes from her but it's a good question.

"Him."

"Why?"

I want to choose my words carefully because I know I'll remember my answer to this forever. I know already that I'm going to be thinking about this answer over and over until I have a chance to tell Isaac how I feel, even if it's not using those three words. It's not me. I will not change myself for anyone, not even him, and I don't think he'd ask me to - if I never say it, I don't think it will matter to him. He'll know how I feel anyway.

"I don't know that I'd ever feel wholly myself again without him.

What he is to me is singular and unexpected and I don't think I'd ever find it again. I wouldn't even want to look for it. Isaac is the key to my lock." I shrug, hoping that makes sense to them the way that it does to me.

"I think that sounds like love," Alina says softly.

"Now you have to get dad to chill the eff out and come around." Aro rolls over onto her back. "My question is - who took the pictures? And what purpose did sending them to dad serve?"

"I think that's a great question," Alina agrees, "and I think dad's too worked up to consider it right now. Please, please be careful, Aster."

I give her a bland look because they should all know better than that. We say our goodbyes to Alina, and Anora excuses herself for the night. Aro climbs into the other side of my bed and curls herself under my blankets. Having her here with me tonight will be good. She always knows when I need her because I'll never be able to ask for comfort. Aro reads me, reads people in general, as if we were books. It's all laid out in front of her what we want and need without a word. The complete opposite of me, but maybe that's why it works.

"Goodnight, Aro."

"Goodnight, Aster. I'm glad you found your person. He's pretty cute too - are you sure we can't talk about the spicy stuff?"

"I don't think you can handle the spicy stuff."

Aro sighs. "You're probably right."

Five minutes later she's wheezing softly, deep asleep.

35

Freelancer

When Aster's light goes out, I go to my bike and to the hotel room that I've been renting long term but barely occupying. It's mostly empty. I don't have things. There's no roots, no home base for me, so I acquire what I need for the job when I need it, or it has to be able to travel with me with ease.

I get a few hours of sleep before getting up, making coffee, and setting up in front of my computer. They haven't shut me out of my access at Designation yet, and I feel like sending those photos was the beginning of a multi-front assault. Whoever is out to get Aster and Designation knew about me, figured out who I am, and made sure to separate me from her.

After seeing that everything looks secure, and hoping that Aster and the higher ups took my weird recommendations for some extra security measures, I start working my way into the networks of the buildings around the parking garage.

Neither Aster or I are easy people to catch unawares, even in the middle of an orgasm. We knew we were in public, with a dead body, our senses were on alert even if we were wrapped up in each other. Whoever took those pictures was very, very good, and the idea of that is terrifying. It's like a game of spy versus spy but breaking us before killing us is part of the plot.

The parking garage had cameras, but they weren't particularly helpful. People going in and out, no good view on their faces, and too many shapeless faceless bodies. The cameras focused more on the cars and a good angle on license plates. I made note of every plate that went in and out and set up a program to start running them in case any names that might be relevant pop up.

I was watching cameras from nearby businesses when a flicker of black caught my eye. It was a shoulder or an elbow, but it stood out. My fingers flew as I tried to track the source of it, to follow the movement back in all directions to see if the person was caught on camera anywhere. They were impossible - a few more flickers of black here and there, but they clearly clocked the cameras and knew to avoid them.

They were good. Not perfect, but good, and good enough to spy on us. It would have taken seconds - step in, see us, take a few photos, and walk away. This wasn't a full on stalking job. Just a few shots to separate me and Aster and make Don Sorrelle stop trusting me.

It made Aster vulnerable. Whoever was messing with the Sorrelles, Designation, and wanted Aster dead knew exactly where they were vulnerable. Don was protective but Aster was overconfident. Most of the time she was the most dangerous person in the room, but out in the world there were a lot of dangerous people. Some she could take, and some that she couldn't.

I'm pulled out of my digital tracking by the buzz of my phone. It's Clive.

"I have information for you - I heard something and thought you would want to know."

"I'm listening."

"It's gotten out that the hit on Aster has been canceled. Whatever is going down at Designation, they don't need her anymore."

Relief runs through me. We can fight to protect Designation, or we can rebuild whatever they break. There would be no replacing Aster. The fail safe measures in place would hopefully keep any hackers from getting what they wanted or destroying anything that was irreplaceable.

"There's a new hit. On Don."

"Fuck. Have you told him?"

"Of course. I called him first. You know I have a non-compete rule and the only reason I know is because they approached me first."

"Who was it?"

Clive sighs. "That I don't know. I'm sure you could find out with some digital digging, and even though you won't ask for it, I'm giving you permission to do it."

"Do you know who they did hire?"

"No I don't kid, sorry."

"Thanks, Clive."

Silence falls between us, and Clive clears his throat. "Things going okay with your girl?"

"We're getting there."

Clive chuckles slightly and we say our goodbyes. I don't hesitate to pull up everything I have that is owned or relates to Clive and start tracing. It was a program that I'd written years ago so all I have to do is plug in the information and let it run. It might take awhile since Clive has dozens of numbers and contact methods and he hasn't told me which avenue they'd contacted him through. No one likes a paper trail in our world but he lets enough crumbs stick around to cover his own ass as a backup plan.

My phone buzzes again and my heart leaps into my throat when I see that it's Aster.

"Hey."

"Isaac." Her voice sounds...wrong. A chill races through my body and before she can say anything else I'm grabbing my keys and moving to leave my apartment. The upset is detectable even over the phone.

"What happened? What do you need?"

"They crashed everything. They didn't steal it, they destroyed it."

"Keep going," I prompt her.

Aster explains, wavering between sadness and anger, about how the servers were hacked and instead of taking anything, which is harder, they destroyed it. All of the base codes, the programs, the projects being developed - gone. They left the client servers alone so anyone currently running Designation security programs is fine, but it's years of development work up in flames. The good news is, there was a plan in place if this happened. I'm just hoping they followed through on putting it in place.

"I failed." Ah. So that's what's really bothering her.

"No. Aster, did you make them implement the redundancies we talked about?"

"Yeah," she grumbles. "I don't care. It's not about that - and so much is still lost. I didn't think they'd do this. The focus had been on theft of information for so long that I didn't focus the way I should have. I let everyone down."

"Has anyone said that to you? Does anyone blame you?"

The silence is long and it's the only answer that I need.

"Has your dad talked to you today?"

"No. We haven't - we haven't spoken since yesterday."

"The hit on you was lifted. I think you need to go talk to your dad, now." Keeping information from her will only get me into trouble, but I think it's up to Don who knows about his hit so it's on him to tell Aster. "Please. Go talk to him."

"Fine. Will you - can we talk, later?"

"Text me. I'll be there."

"They don't need me anymore," her voice is quiet and contemplative, "this was what they wanted. So now what? What's the next move?"

I know, but I don't think it's my place to tell her. If Don doesn't when she talks to him though, I will. I'm not keeping anything from her ever again.

"I don't know, but I'll look into some things. I'm here, little monster."

"I know."

Aster hangs up on me, and I breathe slightly easier. Still, every sense is on alert that this is not the end of whatever has now been put into motion. I set up alerts to be sent to my phone when my programs start running or if any of my keywords or people are triggered. Then I get to the Sorrelle compound to watch and wait.

36

Aster

After a few fitful hours of sleep, I give up. It's a Sunday, but that doesn't stop me from stumbling over to my computer, remoting into the network, and working. There isn't a lot to do at the moment, but I'm checking security code over and over. My brain is itching that I missed something so I read, re-read, and write some of it out by hand, breaking it up into pieces to make sure it's doing exactly what I want it to be.

The screen starts to glitch, and chunks of code shift and disappear.

Panic shoots through my entire body, and I scramble to shut down the system connections.

I'm too late, and the attack is too strong when I'm doing this by myself.

Everything I'm looking at deletes and there's nothing that I can do to stop it. I open every file I can but they're empty, and then the files themselves disappear. I'm scrambling, completely useless, and then I'm staring at blank screens and I've been kicked off the network.

Alarms sound from my phone - the alerts a little too late. If I hadn't been on the system when it happened I would have tried to get in and everything would've been already fucked. Later, when we have a plan,

I can break down how the hack worked and figure out how to protect us from it ever happening again.

I run from my room and down the hall to Owen. My hand hurts from how hard I pound on his door. Part of me is tempted to open it, but I know better. I know Owen's boundaries even in a crisis.

He opens the door a crack, guarding the view inside with his body. He's shirtless in pajama pants, his blonde hair is a mess, and he looks pissed.

"Designation was hacked. Full meltdown."

Owen's eyes open wide. "I'll go in. Text me updates, tell me what we need. I'll send out the all hands on deck."

"What about me?"

"Stay here and do your job," his voice is cool and flinty. This is the Owen that's going to rule our world when dad is gone, and it's the one that I trust the most. He's practical and protective in equal measure. "You're still in danger. This family is still in danger. You can work from anywhere, and you'll be working from here. Get to it."

I can only nod, and then go back to my room. There's nothing for me to do but go into my personal, no ties to Designation, cloud account and pull up the for emergencies only redundancy procedure. Isaac and I had spent the slow times working on it. Thinking of weird and crafty ways to secure the most important parts of Designation's codes and programs where the hacker wouldn't find them.

From here, I send it to the printer in Owen's office, and then send him an email that he lets him know the restoration plan is waiting there. He can call me if he has any questions.

Even though I know things are going to be fine, the important things will be fixed, the squeezing turmoil in my gut won't go away. How could I not have seen this? Why wasn't I able to stop it? I should be better than this. I *am* better than this. This other hacker or collective or whoever they fuck they are have been running circles around me because I've been trying to follow the rules and play on the right side of the line when the line doesn't even exist for them.

I have no qualms about taking lives and punishing the people who hurt others, but there's a line I have to draw when I'm doing work for Designation. We can't draw scrutiny and expose any of our less than legal clients, and I don't want anyone to ever question the integrity of our legitimate work. It's too important, and doing something wrong would have a ripple effect that I could not control and would hurt people I care about.

It doesn't change that I've let them down. My team was created specifically to guard against something like this happening. I was supposed to lead them, protect Designation, and stop this from happening. This feels like the most crushing weight I've ever carried.

The burden of the lives I've taken is non-existent.

The burden of a hack destroying my family's work is crushing me. I'm in pieces.

There's only one person I want right now, so I call him.

Hearing his voice immediately relaxes my whole body, and I feel like I don't deserve it. I don't deserve it for him to reassure me or not blame me for not doing enough. Even though he reminds me of all the things I already know, which sound better coming from him, it only makes me feel slightly better.

Another weight lifts, one I hadn't realized I was carrying, when he tells me the hit on me has been canceled. It doesn't change all the death and damage that's happened as a result, but it means I'm off lockdown most likely. Whoever is after us got what they wanted by destroying Designation. They don't need me or to take me out anymore.

Isaac tells me to talk to dad - maybe clearing the air will make me feel better.

Before braving that conversation, I take a long, hot shower. The water feels like it's boiling and the punishment on my vulnerable flesh is cleansing on another level. In order to tackle this I need to beat myself up, clean myself off, and then get to fucking work.

It's quiet downstairs. I hope that dad is in his office and that Aro is not. That it's only him because this is going to be an awkward conversation and I don't need an audience. She also won't leave when I ask her because she's nosy.

When I turn the corner from the stairs, Gailen is leaving the office. He stills when he sees me, then finishes closing the door. Normally, we'd nod at one another and go about our business, but when I try and step toward the door he blocks me.

"We need to talk."

"About?"

"Freelancer. It's not safe, Aster. He is very good at what he does but he's not like other people - you entertain him now but what's going to happen to you when he gets bored?" Gailen reaches out like he's going to touch me and then drops his hand. "You deserve more than a nameless assassin."

The more he talks the faster the blood rushes through my body, my annoyance and frustration ratcheting up until he's lucky I don't punch him again.

"Gailen, if you keep talking we're going to have a problem. You don't even know him."

"I know his type."

I smirk. "You really don't. Why do you care? Why does it matter to you?"

He steps closer and I step back automatically, keeping the boundary that I always put up between me and other people. This time when he reaches for me, his fingers skim my cheek before I'm slapping his arm away.

"You're too good for him. He'll hurt you."

I shake my head. "Maybe I'll hurt him. This conversation is over."

With force, I shove past him so that he can't stop me again. Flustered, the door to the office slams shut behind me, and dad looks up with irritation.

His face softens when he sees that it's me, and something else uncoils in my body. The fear that the people I love will finally reject me never quite goes away. Knowing from that one look that he still loves me, and already forgives me to a certain extent, is a relief.

"I figured it would take you longer to want to talk."

"A lot's changed overnight." I shrug, and stay where I am by the door.

Dad shakes his head. "What happened at Designation is not your fault. If it wasn't for you, we wouldn't be able to recover anything. You saved us."

"Me and Isaac. The redundancy protocol was his idea. We built it together."

His reassuring expression falls into a deep frown. "Is that why you came to talk to me? About him?"

"Dad." I cover my face with my hands and try to think about how to make him understand. "Do you trust me?"

"Of course I trust you. It's him I don't trust."

"Those contradict each other - do you trust *my* judgment? Do you trust *me* to make the right choices for myself?"

Dad is silent for a long moment and he stares me down. "I do - I just don't want you to be hurt."

"That's part of life."

"It is," he frowns. "You know, people didn't understand what your mother saw in me either. She knew me better than anyone, and I knew her. I know you don't remember her but she would've understood you. I think your dark streak comes from her."

I've never heard dad talk about mom like this. It's not that he doesn't talk about her, but he usually talks about loving her, or let's my sisters talk about their memories. I think that anything before the incident after her death has been blocked for me. That was such a formative experience that it's like I was reborn. The sides of me flipped, the dark becoming more powerful because I had felt true power.

"Everyone always talks about her like she was an angel."

"True," Dad laughs, "but it was that she loved fiercely and it made her who she was. If she'd been alive for what happened with Roman - she would've killed him herself. Her love was unstoppable, it was a weapon and armor. You're like that too. I know you think you don't feel, but you do. You feel so much you're numb with it sometimes. I need to know that he sees you. All of you."

"I think he sees me better than I see myself, and I see him. Did mom make you feel whole? Like a side of yourself you didn't even know was missing suddenly came to life?"

The emotional sap that dad is, I see him tear up when I ask that. "I'm still pissed at him for crossing the line when he was an employee and we were the client, but I'll get over it. I expect him to do things the right way from now on. Dinner on Friday. The whole family."

I roll my eyes. "Fine."

"I love you peanut," dad says.

"Yeah, yeah," I wave that away, not in a place to embrace that emotion right now. Dad and I cleared the air, we're moving forward with Designation, and the path ahead is clearer for me to be with Isaac. Now I have to figure out what the next step is.

37

Freelancer

I have been temporarily re-hired at Designation. Monday morning, Aster went back in to the office and made a case to Don and Owen that replacing me now would be impossible, and she needs me more than ever, professionally.

Owen called me personally to let me know they'd appreciate it if I kept working remotely as a member of the team at Designation. I don't think Aster and I intended to build the redundancy protocol around our specific skills - which we've now identified as one of it's weaknesses - but it will go faster if I'm going through the plan with her.

It's kind of fun the rest of the week. We're on the phone with each other all day, sitting silently most of the time, but hearing her breathe on the other end of the line is enough for me. We talk through what we're doing and I try to imagine her in the team room, sitting in her corner in the dark, or curled up on her chair and working in a position that's going to make her achy later.

Other than keeping watch on the house, I haven't seen her. We haven't been together in person until this dinner tonight. Few things outside of centipedes and mimes unnerve me, but I am a bit anxious about this dinner. This is the first time I'm going to be with her family when they all know the truth of who I am, and as Aster's potential partner.

Calling myself her boyfriend feels first, inaccurate, and second, childish.

I ring the doorbell of a house I've walked into freely, or broken into, more times than I've kept count. The awkward feeling doesn't dissipate.

Anora opens the door, and I see Gailen standing guard and glaring at me over her shoulder.

"Hi Isaac, come on in." I hand her the bottle of whiskey I brought with me, and she smiles when she looks at the label. "One of dad's favorites - nice move." We walk through the house together and into the parlor next to the dining room.

Through the doorway, I can see that the table is set and some of the food is already out. In the parlor, everyone is sitting in an awkward tableau, as if posing for a painting. I'm not the only one feeling some anxiety about this, apparently. Don and Owen are in the chairs in front of the fire, Aro and Aster are at the bar, and Alonzo, Owen's guard, is standing just inside the door.

When Aster sees me, the corners of her lips tip up a little, and I see her body relax. Mine mirrors hers, feeling what she's feeling and letting that guide me. She walks close but doesn't touch me.

"You all know Isaac," she drawls, "can we eat now?"

"Sure," Don says as he stands up and leaves the room without more than a cursory glance at me. Everyone else follows his lead and leaves the room. Aster gives me a look, lifting one eyebrow, before she goes too.

The meal is mostly silent, and I can tell that this isn't surprising to anyone. Aro gives me an encouraging smile, and Anora and Owen are whispering to each other on their end of the table. The conversation seems tense. There's something going on there.

"How did you get into programming, Isaac?" Don finally asks.

"I spent a lot of time avoiding my house and hanging out at the library. They offered coding classes - mostly for adults but it clicked for me, and the man who taught the class worked with me. He got me started. I was doing things I probably shouldn't have been by the time I was 14."

Don smiles but it's a little forced. He's still being his pleasant self but there's an undercurrent of something else to the way he's interacting with me.

"Aster got up to similar trouble when she was 14. She was changing SAT scores in return for secrets."

I laugh. "Why didn't I think of that? I just changed grades." Aster shakes her head in embarrassment, whether it's at her dad's story or my statement. The silence falls again and everyone finishes their dinner.

Before we can start to figure out how to leave the table, Don clears his throat. "I have a surprise, since we didn't get to finish the party last week." Aster frowns at him, but he gives her a decidedly mischievous smile. There's some commotion and then the chef comes from the kitchen carrying a cake with lit candles.

Anora and Aster exchange a look as Aster's plate is cleared away and the cake set down in front of her.

"Since events transpired that disrupted Aster's birthday, I thought we could at least let you make a wish and have some cake."

Don looks over at me, and I realize he thinks this is going to make me feel bad or something. It doesn't, not even a little. I didn't choose to disrupt Aster's birthday - everything was going great and we were all having fun until the photos were received. Until someone intentionally put a damper on the day and broke the trust between all of us. I still don't understand how he can't see their intentions, and get past it. They see me as a threat, and that's all the more reason to keep me close to her.

"Make a wish," he prompts Aster.

"I never have before, why start now?" But she's staring at the cake and the candles, and then raises her eyes to meet mine across the table. A zing shoots through my entire body at the heat in them. Then she blows out the candles.

We eat cake, we make small talk, and I'm very purposely dismissed from the house. I've met the dinner obligation and am expected to leave without getting to spend any time with Aster. How little they know us both.

She walks me to the door. "See you upstairs?"

"If that's what you want."

"It is," she replies, and goes up on her toes to brush her lips quickly over mine. We go through the motions of saying goodbye, of me getting on my motorcycle and leaving. Then I do what I always do - hide it, and loop around to the back of the house on foot. I'll crawl in her window and I'll wait, like some swapped version of Rapunzel.

38

Aster

Before I can even set my foot on the bottom stair, dad is calling for me. I sigh and turn around, following him into the library. The lecture is coming. After our last conversation about Isaac, I'd thought things would be in a good place, but his little move with the cake tonight told me there's still some hard feelings there.

If he only knew that my wish had been to be with Isaac tonight he might've thought twice about it.

Dad leans against the desk and crosses his arms. It's hard to take him seriously when he's being like this because he's so cheerful 99% of the time. Despite some of the drama at Designation, I've heard the rumors that people have thanked my dad when he fired them. People like him. They're drawn to him because he's so comforting. The opposite of me. They don't know all of him though, and I can feel the grumpy in his stance and tone.

"I would appreciate that if you want to spend time with Freelancer, he comes to the house. Even if the hit has been called off, none of your Batgirl shit." He points a finger at me. "Not until we know what's really going on."

"His name is Isaac."

"Really?" Dad raises an eyebrow, and looks surprised when I nod. "Really."

"I'm fine spending time with him here, as long as you play nice." I point my finger back at him, and leave before he can say another word. My feet thump loudly as I race up the stairs, not even caring if anyone wonders about my hurry and my excitement.

Isaac is sitting on my bed when I walk in. I lock the door behind me. He's leaning back on his hands, his long torso on display and like an arrow straight to his crotch.

I am fucking starving for him. I need him to exhaust me again.

As I step further into the room, I strip out of my clothes. He watches, heat in his eyes. The first time we're going to be together in the light. The first time I'm going to be able to see his face while we pleasure each other. I know who he is now, completely, and I already know it's going to be different. More.

My shirt goes first. I'm not wearing a bra - the advantage of being tiny is having high, tight tits. My cutoff shorts slide down my legs and get caught on my feet a little bit. I wiggle my foot and they go flying away from me. It should break the tension but it doesn't at all.

The second I reach him I drop to my knees, undoing his belt and pants, then release his hot, hard cock into my eager hands. I stare up at him as I stroke it, watching his reaction when I change my grip and the pace, learning what he likes. When I slide my thumb along the underside of the head, his hips jerk.

Keeping eye contact, I lick his length from his balls to the tip. I do it over and over, driving him wild as he tries to hold back.

"Fuck, Aster. You keep teasing me like this and I'm going to punish you later. Suck my cock like you missed it, little monster." My pussy clenches at the harshness in his voice, so I stop teasing him. I wrap my lips around him and start blowing him in earnest - deep, slow, glides of my mouth up and down his delicious skin. I could come from doing

236

this. Barely a touch against my clit and I'd detonate, enjoying the taste of him and the power I have over him when we're like this.

When he's riled up, I stop and get to my feet. He wraps his big hands around the backs of my thighs and pulls me close. We look into each other's faces, and I slide my hands up into his silky hair, keeping him near me.

"I think you have a misplaced notion of who is playing with who," I whisper, dancing my mouth close to his and then away, teasing him. "I forgave you, now it's time to punish you."

"Anything you want." It's barely out of his mouth before I'm smashing our lips together and shoving my tongue inside to slide against his. It's a war - he won't let me dominate him easily, but we fall into a rhythm with our tongues and lips that makes me wet. I could slide on his cock so easily right now, and I'd come in seconds.

He's the one that taught me about edging. I think it's my turn to make sure he knows how it feels.

"Open your mouth," I tell him. He obeys. I lean over his face and let saliva drip from my mouth into his, returning the favor from our first time. "You like how I taste?"

"I love it."

"Then I want you to beg to taste me."

He looks confused, and I drop back to my knees and start sucking his cock again. I use my mouth and my hand, slicking the skin with my spit and going hard and fast. He's pumping into my mouth and I can feel when he's starting to get close.

I stop. Stop sucking and stop touching him. He lets out a pained breath, his chest heaving.

"Let me eat your pussy."

I smile at him and it's pure evil. "No."

His cock slides back into my mouth, and I go all the way down until he hits the back of my throat and I gag around him, the muscles spasming around his sensitive head. Isaac lifts off the bed completely, one hand landing on top of my head as he holds me there.

"Aster. Please. Sit on my fucking face until you suffocate me."

A trail of spit connects my lips to his dick when I slide off and look up at him again. "Not yet."

I get him close to the edge one more time, gently tugging his balls while bobbing my head up and down, sucking him quick and sloppy.

Isaac growls. "Sit on my face right fucking now or I will hold you down and come in that filthy little throat."

I smile at him serenely and rise up again. I take his shirt with me and he removes his pants the rest of the way. He lays back when I push on his chest and I do what he asked, although I take my time getting there. I kiss, lick, and bite his skin, tasting all of him that I can, before finally resting my knees on either side of his head.

"Don't even think about getting revenge," I warn him.

"Wouldn't dream of it, baby. I want your come all over my face." Then he wraps his arms and hands around me and yanks my pussy down to his mouth. I cry out immediately, having worked myself up in addition to him.

He does tease me a little, swirling his tongue in soft, taunting licks before sucking hard on my clit. I grind against him, chasing release and lean back and rest my hands on his torso so that I can watch him work. When he opens his eyes and they connect with mine, I'm gone.

The world goes white as I come. I can't even make a sound because I've lost all my breath as I ride his face and dig my nails into his abdomen. When I come back to my body, I glance behind me to see that I grabbed him so hard I broke the skin. The satisfaction and further arousal that gives me is delicious.

I slide bonelessly off him and onto my bed. Isaac doesn't let me take a break. He rolls over me and teases my folds and clit with his cock, the sound of my satisfaction wet and warm between us. I reach down and line him up with my entrance, lifting my hips slightly and letting the head of his cock slide in. It stretches me and I groan, rolling my hips and teasing him more. I watch the strain on his face and feel his muscles shake as he tries to hold still and hold back from plunging all the way into me.

I wrap my other hand around his throat, my thumb digging in to his chin, keeping him looking right at me.

"I want to watch you slide into me. I want to know how you look when you take my pussy."

Isaac leans down to kiss me, a wet slide of his tongue against mine. "Anything you want." He keeps his eyes on me, and I let go of his cock. Achingly slowly, so I feel it all, Isaac slides inside me. I'm stretched and aroused, working hard to keep myself still so I can enjoy this moment rather than losing all rationality and humping at him like the unhinged, horny woman I actually am. The expression on his face is heated, and the muscles in his jaw go slack as he gets deeper, relaxing in the pleasure of being inside me. I love seeing it.

When he's all the way inside, Isaac lowers himself so we're pressed close together. Then he moves inside me, his pace hard but slow, snapping his hips into me with force that pounds against my clit like a lightning strike. It won't take long for me. His eyes are locked on mine, satisfaction clear in his expression.

My arms wrap around him, and I reach down to grab his tight ass and enjoy the flexing of his muscles as he fucks me. I clench around him and he groans, speeding up a little.

"Did your pussy miss me, baby?" I can only nod, my brain beginning to buzz as I get closer and closer to the edge. "Show me. Come on my cock like the desperate slut you are." My back arches, changing the angle, and I'm coming all over him. The satisfaction as my pussy squeezes him over and over lasts for so long.

"We're not even close to done," he whispers, then leans his body up and away from mine. Isaac jerks my hips up so my ass rests on his thighs and he slides his cock back into me. At this angle he's hitting the front of my pussy, rubbing at a spot that borders on pain as it gives pleasure. My tits are bouncing and I pinch my own nipples and watch his body flex as he pounds into me.

Isaac slaps my pussy, hitting right over my clit, and I cry out and clench on him again.

"You liked that?" He slaps me again, and then pinches it, twisting slightly in a way that makes me go blind. "Dirty little monster. So pretty when you come all over me, your come dripping everywhere. Clean me up." Isaac slides out of me and stands next to the bed. I get up slow and crawl to the end of it, and suck my come off of him. It's a little sweet, a little sour, and beneath it is the taste of his cock, rich and musky. In this moment, it's the best fucking thing I've ever tasted. The nectar of the goddamn gods.

"Turn around." I do as he says. I'm not sure when I handed the control over to him, but I don't mind. Isaac teases me with the head of his cock, running it from my asshole, over my pussy, to my clit, then back again, all while he spanks the shit out of me. Each crack of his hand against my ass has me jolting forward and squeezing around nothing.

"I want to see you come," I command. "I want to make you come inside me."

"Fuck," Isaac grunts, and steps away from me. He lays down on the bed and I crawl over him, watching the ecstasy that takes over his expression as I slide down the length of him. When my ass is resting on him, he looks at the place where we're joined, and then back up at me. He cups my cheek in a tender move that's out of place with what we've been doing, but also feels right at the same time.

"I love you."

"You own me. All of me." I move his hand down so that it's resting over my heart, hoping that he understands. I'm still not there in terms of being able to say it in return, but he knows what I feel.

Isaac wraps his hands around my hips, fingers digging into my ass so deep I'll have bruises, and we grind and slide against one another until we find the pace and movement that drives us both to the brink.

"I can feel how close you are," Isaac groans as we move, desperate for friction and pleasure. "Make me come in that pussy, baby. Make me feel how bad you want it."

"Fuck!" I scream, his words making me feel so dirty and turned on that I start to come. Every muscle is tense and as I slam down and hold him tight inside me, he starts to come. Isaac groans and thrusts through the tight hold I have on him, extending my orgasm. I watch the way his eyes roll back in his head, and the way all his muscles flex as he loses himself. Everyone looks kind of ridiculous when they come but I can't help but enjoy being able to see him go over the edge. It's sexy as fuck to me.

I collapse on top of him. "Think you can handle this forever?"

"Even if it kills me." We both laugh, and I know that whatever happens, I'll never be lonely again.

39

Freelancer

I think I have answers, only I don't know what they mean.

I've had programs running, pulling together information and tracing funds, trying to figure out who Mr. Romeo is because that's a stupid name for a stupid man. Not only for going after the Sorrelles, but thinking that he could get Aster away from me.

I have a name, but it doesn't mean anything to me. I've never heard it before, but once things started breaking open for me it came up again and again. Benjamin Lassiter. He's on bank accounts and listed as the owner of record on companies and property. There's a number to call but the number leads to nowhere and nothing. If anyone dialed it, it would ring and ring with no answer. No answering machine, no one monitoring it or expecting a call. It's a dead end.

There's only one thing to do, because I can't find anything else out. Even Clive didn't know the name and he's got a full phone book of people in his mind. The name didn't stand out, but it meant something to whoever was setting all of this up.

Considering Don is still being a little cold to me, I call Owen. I need to inform the Sorrelles what I've found and maybe it will mean something to them.

"Carver," he answers, cold and annoyed.

"It's Isaac."

"This is inappropriate."

"It's not about work, and I didn't think Don would answer. I found something."

There's silence on the line, then, "Why didn't you tell Aster?"

"I'd rather tell all of you at once - I'm trying to be as open as I can be here."

I can hear Owen huff on the other end of the phone. "Fine. Come to the house tonight."

He hangs up before I can agree - I was going to the house tonight anyway, but now I'm formally invited. Part of me does want to go to Aster with what I have and see what she knows, but some instinctive buzz in my body tells me to keep it to myself. I'm worried that it might set her off and she'll take actions before there's a plan and put herself in danger.

Ever since Nino, she's been leaning slightly more toward her self-destructive side. The thing is, she knows. She knows that she's doing it and tries to catch herself. It's coming out anyway, in the fact that she's been running until she's so tired she almost falls on the treadmill. That she forgets to eat because she won't leave her computer and whatever idea she's working on at that moment. She'll go down to the gym and fight until the guys are worn out and tap out. I can feel it in the way she wants me to fuck her until she's too exhausted to feel the need to leave the house and hunt.

Her body is exhausted, but her mind keeps going and she doesn't know how to stop it.

I don't know how to help her do that, other than for moments at a time. When we fuck, she's focused on me and nothing else. It's intoxicating to be the full center of her attention, but I can't fuck her 24/7. Not that I'm unwilling to try.

Aster is better when we talk, she's getting sleep because I hold her and I make her, but she feels like she owes something and it's hurting her. Even her sisters and her dad see it, but none of us truly know how to stop her.

Maybe answers and a more concrete plan to move forward will help.

Dinner is slightly less awkward tonight, although everyone knows that we're filling time until the more intense conversation can begin. Aster barely touches her food. To my surprise, I share a look with Don, my concern mirrored in his eyes. He might be coming around on believing the depth of my feelings for Aster I just hate that it's under these circumstances.

Without saying anything, we all stand up and go to the library once the table is cleared. Even Aro and Anora follow, and they've been kept out of most things. I think they both know what's been going on, but they let Don have the illusion that he's protecting his children from the dangers of the world.

Everyone takes seats, and I sit in one of the two chairs across from Don's desk. Aster takes the seat next to me, and very deliberately reaches over to take my hand. She weaves her fingers through mine and let's it rest on the arm of the chair. Don frowns but then looks at me.

"Clive called me and told me that the hit on Aster had been lifted, and that there had been one taken out on you."

"WHAT?" Every head in the room turns toward the sharp, firm shout, and I think we're experiencing universal shock that such a sound came out of the usually soft spoken Anora. She's glaring at her father with an expression I didn't think she was capable of.

Aster turns back to Don first. "What she said. Why didn't you tell us?"

"I took precautions. If you haven't noticed, I haven't left the house.

I put myself in lockdown."

"Dad," Aro chimes in and sounds offended. "We should've been told."

"Yes," Aster grits, and frowns at me, "we should have. All of this is happening because of me - you can't keep things from me."

Don glowers. "I can do whatever I think will keep you safe."

"I'm not a child!" Aster is barely hanging on to her rage.

"You are MY child!" Don roars back at her, and then takes a deep breath to settle himself. Oddly, his outburst has settled Aster too. They stare at one another for a long time before she nods and leans back in her chair.

"What did you find?" she asks, voice soft and tired. It's devastating to see her so beaten down, especially when most of the beating is done by her to herself.

"The client reached out to Clive but he turned it down, since he was already working for Don. It gave me the first thread to pull to find out who was doing this, and a name kept coming up: Benjamin Lassiter."

Everyone else looks confused, frowning and trying to place the name. Don, on the other hand, turns fucking white and slumps back in his chair. He and Aster are sharing a look again, silent and heavy communication while everyone else in the room except me is oblivious.

"I don't know anyone named Lassiter," Anora responds, pacing on her side of the library. "And I know everybody."

"Who is Benjamin Lassiter, dad?" Aster asks. Her voice is quiet but it carries through the room, and everyone focuses back on Don. She already knows the answer. The question was for everyone else's benefit.

"He took his wife's name when he got married - she was from the better family," Don rasps. "We would know him as Benjamin Forrester."

"Fuck," Owen hisses and takes up Anora's pacing. Don doesn't react, but keeps his eyes on Aster. Waiting. When he doesn't get the reaction he wants, he keeps talking.

"He was a VP at Designation. After Arianna died, he tried to stage a corporate coup. Then he disappeared."

Pieces click together in my head - conversations with Don about the Forresters, the story he told me about Aster when she was young - and I understand it now.

"Why would someone be coming after you in the name of a dead man?" I ask.

"How do you know he's dead?" Aro frowns at me.

"Because I killed him," Aster's voice cracks and I reach over for her. She lets me take her hand, but it's limp in mine. I can almost read her mind for how clearly I know each thought racing through it right now. How she's already laying blame on herself, adding more bricks to the wall of guilt that she puts up between herself and everyone else in the world.

"What?" Aro's voice is filled with soft betrayal - it was a secret she didn't know.

"He tried to kidnap Aster - just after your mother," Don trails off. "She defended herself when that bastard was trying to take everything out from under me at the worst moment of my life."

"Who knows?" Owen asks.

"Other than the people in this room, Benjamin's wife. She was an old friend and I knew she was done with him - I paid the debt of the loss." Don looks at Aster, waiting until she meets his eyes. "He was not a good person, peanut. There was no one to miss him for all that he had done."

That doesn't seem to make Aster feel better, but it makes me even more proud of her.

"This is my fault," her voice is hollow. "I started all of this."

"No," Anora's voice is quiet but fills the whole room. She walks over to Aster and puts her hand on her shoulder. Anora knows that Aster doesn't like to be touched but sometimes what a moment needs is more than what a person wants. When Aster doesn't look at her, Anora kneels down in front of Aster and stares hard until Aster looks back.

"You were a child. You defended yourself." Anora lets out a huff, "Trust you to be a badass at 7. You did the right thing, and none of this is because of you. Whoever is doing this, it's about them. About the kind of slime they are. It is not because of you."

Aster nods, but there's no conviction in it. Aro moves over to sit on the arm of Aster's chair. She pats Aster's curls, both of her sisters trying to pull her in while respecting her boundaries.

"Look at me, Aster." Anora's voice is firm, every bit the oldest sibling I often forget she is. I think that I have greatly underestimated her, and I hope that I have the opportunity to correct my original assumptions. Aster turns her gaze on Anora again. "This is not on you. Say it."

"It's not on me."

"Again. I don't believe you." The harshness of Anora's tone versus the complete defeat in Aster's shouldn't work, but I know my girl. I know that this is what Aster has needed all along.

"It's not on me." There's a little more conviction in Aster's voice.

"We love you. We don't blame you. I would never let anything hurt you." Anora has dropped her voice even quieter, shutting out everyone except her, Aster, and Aro. "If they attack one of us, they attack all of us. This is not on you."

Aster's face relaxes slightly, really hearing Anora. "It's not on me."

Anora smiles at her. "Damn right." She stands up and moves back to where she was standing on the other side of the room, near Owen. The two share a look and I add that to my mental conspiracy board that they're fucking. Aster thinks I'm crazy, but I know what I see.

Aro stays a moment, until Aster nods to let her know she can step away. She curls back up in her green chair and stares off into space, listening but not quite with us as the conversation continues.

"Whoever is doing this," I move the conversation forward, "they know Benjamin extremely well. They know all of his vital information prior to his name change, and he worked pretty fucking hard to make Lassiter disappear. Is it the Forresters fucking with you?"

Don frowns. "It's too indirect and smart for the Forresters, and to be honest - he's not family to them. He married in and they wanted him out. We did them a favor, if anything."

"Fucking Forresters," Owen grumbles.

"They aren't all bad," Anora starts but then steps back when Owen raises a finger at her.

"If you start defending Elton Forrester right now, I swear I will go kill him." Yeah, definitely fucking.

Anora rolls her eyes and it's kind of entertaining to see her do something that isn't tightly dignified. I shoot my eyes to Aster and feel relief from the brief look of amusement on her face. She caught it too. It gives me a flare of hope that she's going to be alright.

"We still don't know enough," Don says quietly before sitting down, defeated and angry. "I'll reach out to Catherine and see what she knows. Maybe it's someone who wants us both to pay." He shakes his head. "Everyone be careful. We have a lead but that's all. We still don't know anything."

Everyone rumbles in agreement and the meeting breaks up, and everyone leaves the office except me and Aster.

"This isn't your fault," I say it even though it's useless.

"I know," her sigh is deep. "But I hate that I can't fix this - I've got nothing. You've done more than I have." Her hands curl into fists and she snarls, energy animating her quickly. "I don't understand!" Aster stands up and starts to pace the library. This is what was missing lately. The anger that fuels her to find the truth, or to find justice.

"We will figure this out."

"I have to know why this is happening. It will eat at me for the rest of my life." She turns toward me and the desperation on her face is plain to see. "I'll know why, and then I'll destroy them."

"Anything you want."

Aster comes toward me and I'm caught off guard when she smashes her face into my chest and wraps her arms around my waist.

"Are we hugging?"

"I will stab you."

I hold in my laugh and hold her like she needs. I swear I won't stop, won't sleep, until I find out what the fuck is going on.

40

Aster

For the next week, I try not to be lulled into a sense of normalcy. Life seeks patterns and routines and I get wrapped up in one.

We're rebuilding at Designation and I spend almost all day talking to Isaac as we work. Excuses were made to the team about why he's remote, and no one questioned it. If it wasn't for him, we'd be so behind.

After work, he comes to dinner and we hang out, playing video games or watching movies. He gets along with Aro and Anora, and even dad has started talking to him without anger in his voice. I know that he's there to be with me, but I also know that he's extra protection.

When he isn't working with me or babysitting me and my sisters, he's trying to find out more about Benjamin Lassiter, and more about his twisted branch of the Forrester family tree that he married into as well. It's not a lack of information in that case - it's that there's so fucking much because the Forresters are in everything, legally, illegally, and unethically. It's like sorting through a giant pile of needles looking for the most tarnished needle.

Every night he pretends to leave but climbs in my window. We still can't get enough of each other but weirdly, it's the million times a night that I wake up that are suddenly bearable when I can reach out and touch him. When I can roll over and kiss him, or devour him. I've never relied on another person for comfort other than Aro. It feels too good to be true.

Dad's getting paranoid. He forced all of the staff to take a vacation, and no one except Owen is allowed to leave right now. It's us and the guards. Something spooked him but he won't tell me what it is - as far as I can tell he won't tell any of us.

Finally, I crack and corner Gailen in the kitchen. He's got most of a muffin in his mouth when I sneak up on him, pretending like I wasn't.

"What's going on?" He flinches, nearly choking on the muffin. I keep going. "What do you know, Gailen? What's got dad so worried?"

Gailen's face gets red and he finally swallows the muffin. "If he wanted you to know, he'd tell you."

What a very politically neutral answer. I move closer, glaring at him, making it clear that I am a threat to him if it means getting answers. To my surprise, Gailen doesn't back down or back away. He leans into me, and over me, and for the first time I realize how tall he is. He's always been so unassuming around me that I didn't focus on him much. Alina said he could do the job and no one had a harsher opinion than her when it came to our safety.

"What are you going to do, Aster?" his voice is quiet. "I won't tell you. It's my job to protect you."

"It's all of our jobs to protect dad," I hiss back at him.

Gailen shakes his head and steps back from me, looking away. "You are one of a kind, Aster." He doesn't mean it as an insult, and I'm confused. "I've never seen anyone so motivated to self-destruct in the name of love." When Gailen looks back, I see the thing that I've been unaware of that explains all of his weird behavior toward me. He's looking at me with attraction, and I have been entirely oblivious to it. Shit.

That has me scrambling to back out of this conversation and his presence fast. I would never go there, and definitely never go there with him. It's not that I dislike Gailen - it's that we're like members of different species. I'm a viper, and he's a lion. My ethics and morals extend to keeping my family alive and making people who hurt other people pay. He, on the other hand, genuinely tried to have a conversation with me about the importance of democracy.

I mostly tuned it out, but he's an actual complete, unbroken human being. We aren't even on the same plane of existence. Even if I felt anything for him beyond confidence in his competence, it would never work. Gailen sees me with rose-colored glasses. He doesn't see *me*, and all the work it takes to be good.

I take another step back from him. "Gailen. No."

The soft look on his face hardens into a frown. "Because of Freelancer."

"No." I can't keep the pity out of my voice. "Because of you. That is not who we are meant to be to each other. Ever."

His face hardens further. "We could be. I could show you."

"No." I think this is the nicest I've ever been when rejecting someone. "I respect you, Gailen." Not that I've done a great job showing him that lately, what with the throwing a chair at him and the punching in the face, but that was more about him stepping into my bubble. I know that he keeps dad safe. I know that he was a good choice to take over for Alina because he wants to dig in here. He'll stay with us and try to protect us for the rest of his life. That kind of loyalty is pure fucking magic, and I don't want to do anything that breaks it.

"I respect you, but you and I...I'm not built for someone like you. You deserve better than me, and you'll find her. Please, Gailen," I am begging and it feels ugly and panicky in my chest.

He stares at me for a long time, and I watch as his face relaxes from annoyance into sadness. "Okay."

We nod at each other and then I turn and flee the kitchen. I didn't find out shit about what's making dad so paranoid, but wow did a lot of things from the last few weeks become clearer to me. I took our guys for granted to a certain extent that I missed something so damn obvious in front of my face. I'm betting Isaac - and probably dad - did not miss that.

Fuck, he's going to tease the shit out of me.

I spend the rest of the day hiding in my room, doing a deep dive on the Forresters and making a family tree. We cleared any of the existing Lassiters - the only ones left related to Benjamin were distant cousins that he never knew. It's like he lost his family and married into one, hoping to disappear completely.

Dad is clearly not a fan, despite what seems like a positive relation-ship with Catherine Forrester. She's the middle child of the main branch - her older brother Roger is a total dickbag who has crossed paths with Derick out in Seattle, and her younger brother Edward seems to have distanced himself from the family out in New York. Catherine has lived quietly in Chicago, not even getting involved in society, since her husband died. Her son Elton was in the same year as Owen, and seems to have spent his life as a finance bro.

Nothing connects them to the Sorrelles other than Benjamin working at Designation - a job which he only got because of the Forrester connection putting pressure on Roman to hire him. Fucking Roman. The source of so many problems. I'm sure Owen will love to hear that.

41

Aster

It's been almost two weeks and I'm going out of my mind in the house. We all are. None of us were prepared for true lockdown, and we still have no explanation from dad for his fear.

Aro hasn't showered in days, just sits in her chair and reads, lost to the world. Anora's voice is a constant down the halls as she carries out video meetings for all her society stuff, or talks on the phone for hours.

Isaac sneaks in to spend time with me when I ask for it, but I need to get out of here. The itch is going so deep and we have no answers. Since the meltdown at Designation, there have been zero attempts to get into any of our systems. It seems that chaos was the point, and it succeeded in throwing everything off balance. Even being back in the office would be preferable to this suffocating stillness. Dad's scared and I hate it.

I asked Isaac to give me some space this morning —not because anything is wrong but because I'm at the point in my cabin fever that when he's around I'm so horny I can't think. I throw open all the windows in my room, let in the early fall air, and try to put everything into fresh perspective.

Even though we still know so little about who is attacking Designation, we know they thought they needed to take me out in order to get their agenda completed. Was that just about Benjamin, or was it about my role at Designation? Maybe it was both. Honestly, I thought if anyone ever came after me it was definitely going to be about my vigilante tendencies or simply being a Sorrelle and not because I was a programmer. Who knew that would be my most dangerous trait?

The house is quiet today. Anora and Owen got permission to leave the house to make an appearance at a charity half marathon so the majority of the guards are with them. As far as I know, only Gailen, dad, and Aro are here with me. It means that I can put on my headphones, roll out my yoga mat, and stretch my body to its limit without being interrupted. Before leaving, everyone kept interrupting me while I was running this morning, so I didn't get quite the release from it that I wanted.

I move through my favorite sets and positions, trying to hold longer and go deeper. I'm covered in a sheen of sweat, trying to empty my mind of everything except my breathing and the movements that I need to make.

It's the moment when I'm done and open the floodgates that my intentions become clear to me. The first thoughts that return are the ones that I hold on to. They'll reveal to me what my conscious mind can't focus on.

I'm recovering in child's pose, then lay on my back and slide off my headphones.

Isaac is my first thought. I want to be with him, without supervision, limit, or interference. I want him with me all the time. I want him back at Designation with me. I need him if I'm going to protect us and improve the company. The two are intertwined, and it's going to be a long talk with dad and Owen to make them understand why he's necessary in the long term for business reasons, not only personal ones. I know that Isaac will work to regain their trust. Plus, he's leaving the contract life for me - he's going to need a job.

Before I can think much more, something sets off my instincts.

The hairs stand up on the back of my neck, and I don't know why. I grab a knife from the small table I keep by my door and open it slowly. My ears are straining to listen for whatever it was that set me off, but there's silence in the hallway. I step out quietly and walk down the stairs at the farthest edge, close to the wall so nothing squeaks.

When I get downstairs I feel a breeze. It's late in September and the heat is dissipating, so it's a cool whoosh of air. The front door is closed, which means it's coming from a window.

I turn toward the door to the office. Gailen isn't there, which is odd, and the door is open. The breeze is coming from there. I step up to the door and look inside, still staying as silent as I can. At first, I think the room is empty and I wonder where dad and Aro are.

Except from this angle I can see her green velvet chair, and behind it, a spill of dark hair on the floor. Panic flutters in my chest and I ruthlessly stomp on it. Not now. Not yet.

I step into the room and don't see anyone. The large window facing the front of the house is open, the curtains shoved aside and blowing in the breeze. Whoever was here appears to be gone - there's nowhere to hide in this room. That doesn't mean they aren't somewhere else in the house. I have to make sure the threat is gone or contained before taking any other action.

Where the hell is Gailen?

I run quietly across the room to where Aro lays on the floor. The first thing I register is that she's breathing - she's alive - but then I take in everything else. The darkening mark on her temple from being struck, and the pool of blood underneath her that isn't coming from the head wound. Carefully, I turn Aro's cheek and have to hold back a sound.

Whoever did this cut her face. A slash across her left cheek so deep that I can see her teeth. The bleeding has already slowed but there will be no saving her from the deep and brutal scar. It's clear she wasn't a target, but they wanted to mark her all the same. I'm a psycho but that's on another level.

They must've come for dad and she was simply here, in the library, like always. I look around and don't see my dad or any sign of him - the cold, rational snake inside me assumes that means they've taken him. Taken means alive, it means ransom, negotiations and the possibility of rescue. I step around his desk to look for anything left behind before I search the house and try to find Gailen.

My foot bumps into something as I move around the desk. It's a foot. It's dad's foot. They didn't take him. I follow his foot up to his leg, over the rest of his body, where he lays calmly on the floor.

He's on his back, his eyes open. My brain cannot comprehend what I'm seeing. We've been careful. Dad has been so damn careful. This is not a game we were supposed to lose.

"Dad?" His chest isn't moving. He's not breathing. I'm not breathing. I drop to my knees and slide to him to check his pulse, only to find the deep, dark cut through his throat. The dark pool of blood soaking through my workout leggings.

I'm crying. I'm crying for the first time since I was seven years old.

"Daddy?" I pound on his chest, as if I could wake him up, and I'm no longer capable of keeping myself quiet. The sobs rip out of me, shattering me in a way I didn't know I was capable of and I'm somewhere between screaming and roaring, both pain and anger warring for dominance inside me.

There's a sound behind me, and I fall back into the monster and let her take over. I turn and block the knife coming at me with my left arm. It digs into the flesh and hits the bone but I don't feel it. There's a man in a plain white mask standing over me - he hurt my sister and killed my father so I'm going to kill him. The exhaustion that's been ever present leaves me, but I know I'm starting from a weakened position on so many levels.

My right hand shifts and I slide further forward, bringing my knife up to slash across his chest. I cut his shirt but don't get his skin, but it gives me the moment I need to get back on my feet. This guy is big - probably a foot taller and at least a hundred pounds on me. He's also fast as fuck but this isn't personal for him - it is for me. I have justice on my side.

We're slashing at one another and I'm screaming nonsense at him as I do whatever I can to push him back and away, hoping that I'll get him to give up the fight and run because I'm not sure I can beat him or that I won't kill myself taking him down.

His knife slides into my side, getting under my defense. It's below my rib cage and it burns. I'm only going to get weaker now. I scream at him again, reminding him that he's messing with the scariest Sorrelle. That he violated our space, and there's only one response to that - death.

I manage to slash him down one forearm, the cut deep and bleeding freely which would be great, but it's his non-dominant hand. The two of us are sadly evenly matched, slashing and hitting our marks without making actual progress in terms of winning this battle. It's a circle of blood and pain and neither one of us is willing to back down. I don't know if he's trying to kill me or incapacitate me, but I can't take the chance.

When I dive under his guard and stab him in the stomach, he uses the proximity to stab me in the back. The knife dives in to my left shoulder and nerve pain shoots down my body. My left arm is practically useless, and numbly I wonder what he hit and if it'll ever heal. As my head gets light from the blood loss, I have the thought that I'd still be more deadly with one arm than most people are with two.

I stumble backward, and this time he goes for my throat, and I fall before he can slice me open. My knees hit the ground. It's wet and sticky with our blood already. So much fucking blood. I keep my knife at the ready in my hand, and make a move to slash at him even in my weakened position.

Someone calls my name. There's a sound of fury like I've never heard before. I crawl away from the killer, away from the sounds. Dad is dead but I need to protect Aro. I get to her, and there's sounds of shouting and crashing behind me, the muffled tumble of books falling off the shelves.

When I get to my sister, I wrap an arm around her and shield her from the fight. My knife is in my hand and ready for when I need it.

Then I watch. For the first time in awhile, I see Freelancer and not Isaac. I see him fight. My heart twinges a little that he's fighting for me.

I can't look away. I think watching him is the only thing keeping my conscious right now, and I am afraid to pass out because I might not wake back up. I can't even blink or I'll miss something. Even though I'm bleeding and things are getting fuzzy, his speed and power are magnetic. The masked man and Freelancer area frenetic, violent clashing of bodies, smashing each other into shelves, knocking over furniture, slashing and missing, slashing again, trying to get underneath each other's guard.

The assassin shifts his position in the room, and I can see the moment Isaac realizes that he's now between us - the assassin is on our side of the room, and we're vulnerable. I could maybe keep him off for a few seconds, but not enough to save either of our lives. Isaac rushes forward, and I scream because I'm so sure he's going to get hurt and I can't handle anymore hurt right now. The scream distracts the assassin - fucking amateur - and Isaac continues the fight.

Everything is hazy, but I'm still awake.

42

Freelancer

Stalker that I am, I'm giving Aster space while also sitting outside her house. There's still a hit on Don, they're all still in danger, so I'm not going far. Plus, I've been getting a lot more sleep lately when I'm lying beside her instead of watching her house and making sure she doesn't sneak out. Energy is thrumming through me and I'm on edge.

I know she's doing yoga because I can see it on her screen on my phone. I never shut down my mirror on her, and she's never asked me to. Deep down, she knows she's still in danger, and that she might need me. Plus, there's nothing to keep from me. No secrets between us that we haven't already shared. If she asked to have the same access to my phone, I'd give it to her. I'd give her anything.

So I watch, and I think, and I wait.

It takes me a minute to realize that anything is wrong, but I hear a sob. It's more like a raspy scream, but it's all I need to start moving toward the house. The front door is locked and I don't want to waste time picking it and setting off the alarm, so I move around to the side of the house.

A window is open.

The window to the office.

That's not right.

I hear grunting and shouting and I run, and almost drop to my knees as a masked man pulls Aster close and stabs her in the back. She's already covered in blood, as is the floor. From this view, I see Don on the ground behind his desk, and Aro deeper into the room behind her chair. Fuck. Neither of them is moving, and from this angle I can't tell if either of them is breathing.

I turn off my conscious thought and move into fight mode. I attack the intruder. He turns, not expecting me, and we square off. He's got a few inches on me in height, but I have more muscle. He's expecting a knife fight because mine is in my hand, but that's just a misdirect to make him comfortable.

Instead, I dive at his center and knock him over. He goes crashing into the bookshelves, books falling down around us and smashing us both in the face. It gives me the chance to grab and wrench his arm, the knife falling to the ground and out of either of our reach.

I go berserk then, now that the chance of injury has decreased. I pummel his stomach and face, making cuts across his clothes and skin, smashing the handle of the blade into his face to the point that the mask he's wearing cracks. I'm trying not to kill him so we can question him, and it makes me use my fists more. When I get him with a swift punch in the throat he bowls over, shoving me away and trying to swing at me. I feel no pain, have no thoughts, other than ending this man. He hurt Aster. He hurt the only person that's ever been mine.

Aster is watching and she's still in danger. Somehow this mother-fucker has maneuvered himself so he's between me and her - I have to go through him to get to her, or he could turn around and finish the job.

The purest rage I've ever felt in my life surges through me. I surge toward him, and Aster screams. It's the distraction I need - he turns slightly to look at her, and it's enough time for me to grab him and yank him away from her.

There are no rules in fighting for your life and revenge, so I don't hesitate to bring my knee straight up into his balls. When he falls forward, I slam my elbow on the back of his head. He goes down, and I punch him a few more times for good measure and to make sure he's unconscious. When I think he's out, I remove my belt and tie his arms behind his back.

Then I run for Aster.

She's barely sitting up, leaning heavily against Aro's chair, holding her knife in the air and ready to slash at the enemy approaching. Her body is blocking Aro's, using all that's left of her energy to protect her sister. What a fierce little monster she is.

"Aster," I hold up my hands and approach her. "It's me."

"Is it safe?"

"Safe enough. I need to see Aro. We need to call for help."

Before I can take a step closer, I freeze when I hear the front door open. My knife is back in my hand, ready to hurt, and I move to the door of the library and brace for an attack.

Gailen walks into the room. I swing before I can stop myself but he dodges back.

"What the fuck?" He's taking in everything way too fucking slowly.

"Where the hell were you?" I shout at him. I get up in his face and before he can stop me, I take a move from Aster's book and punch him in the face. "Where were you?"

Gailen drops what's in his hands and I see that it's the goddamn mail and a food order since everything had been called in lately due to Don's paranoia about leaving or having the staff around. The assassin probably danced to himself when he saw the lone fucking guard walk out the door and down the long drive to the gate.

"Call an ambulance. Call a doctor." I shove him away from me and move back to Aster and Aro.

"What - " Gailen trails off when he walks deeper into the room. I feel no sympathy for him when he sees his boss dead on the floor. The biggest fucking failure of a bodyguard. Gailen swallows but raises his phone to his ear, calling emergency services. I whisper random nonsense to Aster to keep her awake and aware as he gives them information and directions.

We'll have to cover this up somehow, but for now, they need help and they need it fast. They aren't actual criminals, there's no corrupt doctor on standby to come stitch up their wounds and make things disappear. It's going to be hefty donations and payoffs and hoping that the media doesn't get wind of any of the truth.

I stand up to check on my captive - except there's no one there. Gailen didn't even notice the guy and had his back turned away from him, and I was wrapped up in making sure the women lived through this. Smart guy not to attack when we were vulnerable, which speaks to it not being personal for him. He saw his gap, he ran.

I look out the window and see nothing. Defeat buries itself inside me as I walk back to Aster and hold her until an EMT takes her out of my arms.

43

Freelancer

The wait for Aster to wake up is endless and painful, even if she's going to be okay. None of the hits were fatal although one of her kidneys is still touch and go. There's a chance she might lose it and it's a waiting game now that they've done everything they can.

Aro is asleep in the other bed in the room, her face stitched up by the best plastic surgeon in the state, although he wasn't very hopeful. She also had a bad concussion from the blow to her head and some intercranial bleeding, so they're keeping her sedated and monitored for now. She's going to wake up to a different world.

I've been getting updates from Owen, who we were all surprised to learn, was each sister's medical power of attorney. Even if Don was alive right now, he'd be the one to make the call for each of them when they could not for themselves. It was Owen who decided that they wait on Aster's kidney, and who tracked down the doctor for Aro's face. It was Owen who signed off on Anora being admitted to the hospital for a psychiatric evaluation after her breakdown.

I haven't lost many people I cared about in my life, so this feeling I have about losing Don is new. I will never get the chance to show him how much I love Aster, to be a part of his family, or be accepted by him. I'll never hear him laugh again as he tells stories about his girls, or be able to admire him for what a good parent he is. If I'm feeling this way, I cannot even begin to imagine what it's going to be like for Aster and her sisters.

They're orphans now.

It doesn't matter that they're all adults - there's something different about being in the world without parents to guide you or fall back on. For all intents and purposes I've been one since the day I turned 18 and there had been hundreds of times I'd wished for advice, support, or guidance. I got all of that when I found Clive, but it still stings sometimes that my parents weren't there. That we couldn't mean anything to each other for fear of my brother, who didn't give a shit about any of us.

Aster squeezes my hand, and her eyes are open when I look up.

"Is Aro okay?"

"She will be," I look over my shoulder and she follows my gaze, some tension leaving her body when she sees her sister.

"Her face..."

"I know."

"Did you kill him?"

I look down, shame flooding me. "No. He got away. I'm so sorry, Aster."

She shakes her head and then winces. "We'll get him. We'll make him tell us who hired him and then I will make him wish he'd never been born."

My eyes lock with hers. "I promise you, I will make that happen or die trying."

"No!" She looks a little frantic, and I'm shocked when her eyes glisten with tears. "You cannot leave me."

Even though I know it will hurt, I stand and pull her into my arms.

266

She can't raise her left arm to hold me back - it'll heal in time - but her right arm clings to me and she buries her face in my chest. This is a storm that I can weather with her. I will do everything I can to make sure she heals, that she gets well, and then gets even better, before we exact revenge for what's been done to her family.

"Where's Anora?"

"Uh…" I swallow. "Let's call Owen." I send him a text and he replies that he's in the hospital. He walks in a few minutes later.

"What's going on?" Aster demands, coming back to herself more with every moment. She's trying to kill him with a look and Owen is entirely unaffected by it.

"Anora did not take things well," Owen says diplomatically. "She's been sedated, and is likely in shock."

"Fuck," Aster swears and shakes her head. "Alina?"

"I thought it would be better coming from you. We've kept things quiet and it's only been a few hours."

Aster nods and swallows. "I'll call her." She looks down at her hands, and Owen and I both wait, knowing there's more. "What happens now?"

"We'll talk about everything when you're well enough to be home. There's nothing that needs to happen except you healing so we can do what we do best - take out the enemy."

Aster looks at Owen and something passes between them. I almost feel jealous, but it's something more like affection and understanding. Owen has kept his distance from the sisters, but I get the feeling that he cares about all of them very deeply. He'd be hard-pressed to admit that they are his family, but I think the events of the last few months, and the ones that are ahead, are going to provide some clarity on that fact. He's not as distanced from them as he thinks he is.

"Get some rest. I'll have your phone and some clothes brought, and until then I'll keep Isaac updated. Let me know if you need anything."

They nod at each other, and Owen leaves. Aster takes a few deep breaths to steel herself. "I need to borrow your phone."

I hold Aster in my arms as she calls Alina, and I keep her strong as she comforts her sister. Everything changes now. Aster is silent as her sister cries, but I can see how hard she's working to keep herself from reacting. Alina breaks against her, and I let her break against me.

When she hangs up the phone, Aster lays back on the pillow with an exhausted huff. "She'll be here as soon as she can." She looks up at me, something indecipherable on her face. "I need some time."

"I'll give it to you." I kiss her hand above where her IV is going in and step out of the room. Owen is in the hallway leaning against the wall when I step out. He's always a still, withdrawn person but it's as if all of his energy left him. I've never seen anyone look so severe and defeated at the same time.

"Now what?" I ask him.

He frowns down at the tiled floor, pain in every line of his expression.

"I'm getting the idea that you plan on sticking around?" Owen finally looks up at me.

"I'm never leaving her."

"Good. We'll need you. It can't get out what really happened - it will be hard for the girls to live with the lie, and this isn't over. They shook Designation and shattered the Sorrelles, but my gut says this is the beginning."

"I agree. Clive is keeping an ear out, and even though he knows I'm out, he'll let me know if he hears anything."

"Good. Thank you." He starts to step away. "I need to be with Anora, but keep me updated. You're one of us now, Isaac."

I nod, feeling oddly choked up. This is where I want to belong, and with that calm, solid sentence from Owen, now the head of the family, I am accepted. Even in the midst of heartbreak, I've found home.

44

Aster

It's raining on the day we inter my father with my mother.

It feels appropriate. The sky is crying for me because I can't do it for myself. After that day when I found him, I haven't been able to shed another tear. Alina's mostly held it together and her arrival brought Anora back from the brink of madness. Aro is currently scaring the shit out of me.

She's barely spoken since waking up in the hospital. The doctor gave her a handheld mirror, she looked for a second, looked away, and then it was like something descended over her that I don't know how to penetrate. Words come out of her mouth but they're not her. We've had nothing but time and she hasn't touched a book.

We don't go in the library anymore.

I'd be losing my mind without the men in my life, and that's a complete fucking shocker to me. Isaac listens to me when I tell him what I need. Owen is making decisions and talking about what needs to happen, and he's kept Designation steady through everything. If I didn't have work I'd really be unhinged. Then there's Derick, who maneuvered all of the secret keeping that needed to happen to keep us safe. It's more of a benefit than I realized to have an in-law who knows the underworld so intimately. I might even like him now.

The media said it was a tragic car crash. It killed dad, and wounded Aro. A plausible story and we stick by it. It doesn't hurt as much as I thought it would to stand by the lie, but I think it's because the truth is so much worse. The truth that we weren't careful enough. I don't think I could have saved dad. I don't think Aro could have either. But I still wonder if there was something more that could have happened that day that would've stopped the assassin from getting there in the first place.

I'm standing with Anora and Alina as dad is carried in to rest beside mom. Isaac, Owen, and Derick on the one side, Alonzo, Gailen, and one of our newer guards, Gio, on the other. It's so simple but so final to carry someone to their last rest. I don't believe in an afterlife, but I am oddly comforted at the idea that my parents are together again. They were never complete without each other anyway.

Aro stayed in the car. She's still got a huge bandage over her face, there's media here, and she doesn't want people looking at her. Staring, speculating, splashing her face all over the news when we've all worked very hard to keep ourselves under the radar. When she looks at us, she doesn't make eye contact. She's faking it well, looking at our eyebrows or foreheads, but I have yet to have Aro meet my eyes since she woke up in the hospital.

I know what's happening inside her head. It doesn't matter what we say - she thinks it's her fault and she's the one that will have to sort that out.

The priest drones on making a last statement. The doors of the mausoleum are closed. It's very final, and I feel the harsh snap of the sound of those doors in my chest. I will never see my dad again. The family standing here with me, and hiding in the car, are all that I have left, and we are all that will keep us whole and together.

We walk across the wet grass of the cemetery, breaking up into our respecting vehicles. Isaac is driving me. We've relaxed security somewhat - whoever was out to hurt us got what they wanted. The Tahoe turns the other direction from everyone else, driving into the city rather than back to the house.

"Where are we going?"

Isaac gives me a small smile, one that doesn't quite reach his eyes. "You need a break."

"I do."

"And I got in touch with Dinah."

My stomach flutters. "Oh, really?"

"We've got a hunt tonight. I thought you could use it."

I stare at him for a long time. So long, and so silent that Isaac pulls over to look at me.

"Are you okay?"

No. I'm nowhere near okay. My family is in upheaval and my sense of safety in my home has been rocked. But I'm also sitting with a man who sees and knows me in a way I never believed possible. I didn't even know how alone I felt until he was at my side. I'm not okay because my fundamental understanding of the flow of my life was diverted off course when I met him - by the circumstances as well as by who he is, and who he is to me. Isaac isn't my other half - we weren't missing something without each other. It's beyond that. He's the accelerant to my flame - I am more because of him, and I hope that he feels the same.

"I love you."

Isaac blinks. "Seriously, are you okay?"

I frown at him. "I don't know how to answer that question right now, but I needed to tell you. I won't say it a lot, but I need you to hear it. I love you, and there will never be anyone else for me. I will never let you go."

With a slightly cocky smirk, Isaac leans over the console and kisses me. "I'm with you until it kills me."

45

Epilogue - Freelancer

Three Months Later

It's 2am when Aster's phone buzzing wakes us up. She grumbles and reaches around for it on the table next to our bed. When she sits up quickly, it pulls me up to being awake and alert.

"Dinah?"

I hold in a groan. Just what we need tonight.

"Yeah, we can come get her. Just…keep her in the back room. I'm sorry. Owen says he has a plan - I…" Aster listens. "Thank you."

"Let me get some pants on," I tell her as I roll out of my bed. My discarded jeans are on the floor and I pull them on. Aster slides into some leggings and a hoodie before throwing her hair up and out of the way. The house is quiet as we walk through the darkness, and I think about waking up Owen and making him deal with the shit show, but I know Aster wants to handle this.

We grab our coats and step out into the fucking freezing December night. Aster resets the code on the front door and a guard darts forward to check on us and we let him know where we're going. We take the Range Rover because it has four wheel drive in case the roads are icy.

The first snow fell a couple of days ago, a heavy 6 inches, and even though things are mostly clear we're not taking any chances.

We don't talk as we drive into the city. Mostly because we're both exhausted, but also because we don't know how to talk about this. It's hard not to feel sympathy alongside the well of disappointment and concern that gets deeper with every one of these calls.

Luckily, I find street parking not too far from the entrance to the alley behind the club. We walk through it and around to the back door. I can't even enjoy the memory of Aster sucking my dick in this alley because there's no time for a repeat. We've come back and done all sorts of kinky shit here, but now is not the time.

Aster pounds on the door and Dinah's right hand, Patrick, opens the door. He looks so stereotypically Irish mob that you almost wouldn't believe it - tall, pale, red hair, freckles, and green eyes that are cold as a snake. He does Dinah's dirty work. She's the sole heir to the Riley family and all their accompanying millions, and lately that dirty work includes cleaning up after the Sorrelles. I don't think Dinah would do it if it wasn't for her history with Aster.

I try not to be jealous.

We follow Patrick down the hall and he unlocks the office door.

Aro is sitting on the couch inside, sloppy and drunk as fuck. The scar on her cheek is red and livid because drinking makes it worse. She's glaring at Dinah, who is working on her computer as if Aro isn't even in the room.

Dinah gives us both a look full of pain and pity. "She tried to kiss a bartender."

"Which one?" Aster asks.

"Grady."

"Good choice."

"I know, right? But he wasn't into it and she would regret it, so that's when I called you." Dinah stands up and walks with us as we pick up a silent, glaring Aro and drag her down the hall.

She holds the back door open for us. "I know it won't be the last time I call you at bar close. Things will get better with time." Dinah sounds more like she hopes that, rather than believes it. I don't blame her.

We pour Aro into the backseat. It's already got a bucket, sparkling water, a towel, and a few candy bars. It's stocked to deal with her at this point. She lays down and mumbles angrily, words slurred and untranslatable. Aster chews her thumbnail as we drive back to the Sorrelle house. It's a new habit since Aro started drinking.

The house is lit up when we get back. That's unusual.

Aro has sobered up slightly from drinking two cans of water, and eating one candy bar. She leans between the seats. "What the hell is going on?" A waft of alcohol breath assaults us, but we don't say anything.

We park the car and drag Aro into the house. Before, we'd turn right and go into the library, but no one goes in there anymore. The books were put away and the furniture removed, and then the windows and doors were locked and no one went in again. Not even to clean. Maybe someday the Sorrelle women will feel like they can make this space their own again. That they can reclaim it from the ghosts that now occupy it.

Now, we turn into the front parlor. Almost all the guards are there, as well as Owen and Anora. The room is tense but it's with an active anxiety, not passive dread. Something happened while we were gone, and it's big.

"What's going on?" Aster asks.

"We identified the assassin," Owen speaks. "A connection of mine put out some inquiries and we got an answer. Sphinx can helps us catch the assassin - but he wants something in return." Anora and Owen exchange a look, and he rubs his forehead before continuing.

"He wants Aro."

Playlist

Taste of You - Rezz, Dove Cameron

I Get Off - Halestorm

Gravedigger - MXMS

I Wanna Be Your Slave - Maneskin

Feral Love - Chelsea Wolfe

Nothing Can Kill Us - K. Flay

Warm Me Up - the Audition

Bad Romance - Halestorm

Smooth - Santana feat. Rob Thomas

Rest Your Love - the Vamps

Sex on Fire - Cannons

I'm Gonna Show You Crazy - Bebe Rexha

Acknowledgments

My husband, for listening to me explain the plot to him and enduring spoilers because I want his opinion. For being so much more proud of me than I will ever be of myself. He is all the best book boyfriends and I get to keep him.

Jenn! I added 3 whole chapters because of you. Your feedback and thoughts are essential to me continuing to follow this path and tell this story and I am so grateful to the Tiktok gods that we found each other.

Vik, even though you were a little slow on this one, your excitement and willingness means so much. I promise to let you borrow the dog for a weekend as a thank you.

Annie, for always reading everything first, always being honest with me, and being generally supportive of whatever weird thing I text you about. BFFL.

Cati, for sticking around since undergrad and putting our shared degree to work for me.

All the people willing to read ARCs for me and give me feedback, or catch what I missed.

Rachel McEwan, my excellent cover designer, who took my request for a more "threatening" mouth and found something that passed the vibe check. I can't wait to see what you find me next.

My family got really excited about the first book and the support I received from everyone, the enthusiasm even while slightly shocked about the content, has been fun, terrifying, and uplifting.

Everyone who read Alina and Derick's book, I am so grateful for every review and for you taking the time to read it. I'm also sorry in advance for making you wait until book 4 for Anora and Owen. If the messages I've gotten are any indication, they've already got a fan base and *you don't even know* what's coming for them.

To all of the authors that I've met and connected with the last few years who shared their excitement with me, I cannot tell you how much it means to be validated by you. Taking time to either read the book or congratulate me meant a lot.

Sophie Lark, a true goddess, for sharing your wisdom and telling it like it is. You're the absolute bomb.

Molly Doyle for writing the Masked Men because despite having read many, many masked hero books, it wasn't until you that it clicked in my head this might be a thing for me. It then inspired this story, which was the thread that started the entire series. Thank you. Give me more of them, immediately.

Lastly, while Aster has wild and eclectic music taste, I wrote most of this book listening to ASMR videos on YouTube. Thanks to ASMR Doctor Who, ASMR Jas, Tena ASMR, and Ozley ASMR for all the brain tingles.

Also by Ashley Mack

The Senses

The Sight of You (Alina and Derick)

The Taste of You (Aster and Freelancer)

The Sound of You (December 2022)

The Feel of You (February 2023)

The Scent of You (Spring 2023)

Companion Novellas

Look at Me (Kade and Cara)

Savor Me (November 2022)

Standalones

Nevertheless (November 2022)

About the Author

Ash lives in the Midwest with her husband, two girls, a dog, and a cat. She reads during every spare moment. She hopes that her characters go in new directions with terrifying, strong women who go feral for their men, and that sometimes the men are the damsels in distress who need saving. Connect on Instagram and Tiktok at @totalsassreads

You can connect with me on:

🌐 http://www.ashleymackauthor.com

Subscribe to my newsletter:

✉ http://www.ashleymackauthor.com/contact

www.ingramcontent.com/pod-product-compliance
Lightning Source LLC
Chambersburg PA
CBHW050713180626
46814CB00002B/409